MISSING
CLARISSA

MISSING CLARISSA

A Novel

RIPLEY JONES

WEDNESDAY
BOOKS
NEW YORK

Published in the United States by Wednesday Books, an imprint of St. Martin's Publishing Group

MISSING CLARISSA. Copyright © 2023 by 3BD Holdings, Inc. All rights reserved. Printed in the United States of America. For information, address St. Martin's Publishing Group, 120 Broadway, New York, NY 10271.

Excerpt from *The Other Lola* © 2024 by 3BD Holdings, Inc.

www.wednesdaybooks.com

Designed by Kelly S. Too

The Library of Congress has cataloged the hardcover edition as follows:

Names: Jones, Ripley, author.
Title: Missing Clarissa : a novel / Ripley Jones.
Description: First edition. | New York : Wednesday Books, 2023. |
Identifiers: LCCN 2022035454 | ISBN 9781250801968 (hardcover) |
  ISBN 9781250801975 (ebook)
Subjects: CYAC: Podcasts—Fiction. | Cold cases (Criminal investigation)—
  Fiction. | LGBTQ+ people—Fiction. | Mystery and detective stories. |
  LCGFT: Thrillers (Fiction) | Detective and mystery fiction. | Novels.
Classification: LCC PZ7.1.J73 Mi 2023 | DDC [Fic]—dc23
LC record available at https://lccn.loc.gov/2022035454

ISBN 978-1-250-32338-5 (trade paperback)

Our books may be purchased in bulk for promotional, educational, or business use. Please contact your local bookseller or the Macmillan Corporate and Premium Sales Department at 1-800-221-7945, extension 5442, or by email at MacmillanSpecialMarkets@macmillan.com.

First Wednesday Books Trade Paperback Edition: 2024

10 9 8 7 6 5 4 3 2 1

for Sara G., with love

The death of a beautiful woman is unquestionably the most poetical topic in the world.

—Edgar Allan Poe

MISSING
CLARISSA

IMAGINE this: A fairy-tale summer, blue and wild. Skinny-dipping in the Salish Sea with a trail of phosphorescence in your wake, sunburnt shoulders, salt-sticky hair drying in the twilight as the stars come out. The kind of summer you hold in your heart for the rest of your life: the last best summer, a summer summoned in vivid Technicolor decades later with a flash of a song that soundtracked your late-night drives, the briny smell of the ocean wafting through hot concrete streets on your way to a job you never imagined yourself having, your own daughters slinking home after curfew with their weed-reddened eyes and wine-cooler breath.

That summer for us in Oreville was the summer of 1999. Thorny branches so heavy with blackberries they brushed the ground. The air so warm the Sound was balmy enough to swim. Old-timers worried the heat wave heralded the end of the world. The rest of us greased our bodies with Coppertone and lay out on our lawns to bronze.

Our summer was the most epic party summer of anyone who ever lived. We knew no other summer would ever match. We felt sorry for everyone who came after us, who would never know our glory. The football players driving their pickup trucks shirtless to the woods out behind town at sunset, their cabs stuffed with cases of Rainier and their truck beds with cheerleaders. The grunge kids in their dads' flannel shirts, the theater kids belting lines from *Oklahoma!*, the valedictorian looking over her shoulder as if her college acceptance letters would catch her with a jury-rigged bong built out of empty five-gallon milk containers. The stoners showing up late as always, their pockets bulging with plastic baggies.

That summer, our summer. The last free summer before adulthood closed in.

And then Clarissa Campbell disappeared.

Oreville's a small town. Everybody knew Clarissa. We all knew Brad Bennett too.

The head cheerleader and the captain of the football team: a story you already know. Clarissa was gorgeous, a limber executor of flawless pikes. Brad had a strong arm and a chiseled face. They moved through the world together in a cloud of their own beauty. We expected great things of them. Reality television, maybe. A career in Hollywood. Brad would go on to play for a team. Which team? We didn't think about it too hard.

We didn't think about much of anything that summer, except how to find the next party.

Until the night Clarissa vanished from the forest. After that, all we thought about was Clarissa. The whole country thought about Clarissa. You remember the headlines.

A COMMUNITY MOURNS IN MYSTERY.

UNEXPLAINED DISAPPEARANCE OF SMALL-TOWN GIRL
CAPTURES THE HEART OF A NATION.

CHEERLEADER'S BOYFRIEND QUESTIONED IN
WASHINGTON STATE DISAPPEARANCE.

STILL NO ANSWERS FOR BEAUTY QUEEN'S FAMILY.

WHERE IS CLARISSA CAMPBELL?

Clarissa's perfect face plastered across newspapers from Washington to West Virginia. Clarissa on the evening news. Clarissa's white teeth and blue eyes. Clarissa's long blond hair. Endless speculations on Clarissa's lost future, what she might have become. (All of them futures none of us could remember her wanting when she was real.) No body ever found, the mystery never solved. Even without blood and violence, without answers, her name stayed in circulation. After the headlines came the late-night TV specials. The dramatic reenactments with B-list actors. The straight-to-video feature starring a round-cheeked actress who later overdosed in the bathtub of a much-more-famous married actor. (Yes, we watched them all.)

Despite all this, the details are blurry for those of us who were there. The darkness is heavy out in those woods. We had a bonfire, but its glow didn't stretch far, and the forest goes on for miles. Most of us were pretty drunk.

Here's what we told the police we knew: Clarissa Campbell was crying. Clarissa Campbell was so wasted even the freshmen noticed. (That part didn't make *People*.) Clarissa and Brad weren't speaking. (One of us was pretty sure she saw Brad with his tongue down Reenie Muñoz's throat at some point that night, but she kept that to herself. *Reenie? She's not even that pretty. Did he lose his mind?*)

The king and queen were over. Clarissa had never ugly-cried in public before. Clarissa's mascara was smeared. Clarissa would have been mortified, if she'd known.

We looked away out of respect. We could give her that much. We could pretend we didn't notice. We weren't happy to see her fall. We liked her. She was nice.

Most of the time.

None of us saw Clarissa leave the party.

And none of us saw her again.

And, in our hearts, we know no one will. Because that's one

thing we're sure of, though we'll never say it out loud: Clarissa Campbell, wherever she went that night, is dead. And the last person who saw her is the person who killed her.

We don't know who. Not for sure.

But we have a few ideas. And we know this much:

Everybody loves a dead girl.

THE
BEGINNING

"EVERYBODY loves a dead girl!"

"Not *everybody*, Cameron."

"Almost everybody loves a dead pretty white girl."

Blair shuts her locker door, turns to face her best friend. "So we what, cash in on the obsession of gross people?"

Cam huffs in exasperation at Blair's unwillingness to see the light. "Not only gross people. Like, all people. Plus, everyone loves podcasts. Millions of people listen to podcasts."

"You don't love podcasts. Have you ever listened to a podcast?"

"I'm not everyone. The point is to develop something with broad appeal. Think how good it will look on our college applications if we break an unsolved case."

"Like you need to worry about college applications," Blair says. Cam's transcript already reads like a completed checklist from a handbook for the precocious overachiever, and they're only juniors.

"Think how good it will look on *your* college application, then. Are you in?" Cam pushes her chin-length black hair out of her eyes, the same impatient gesture Blair's seen her make since the sixth grade, when Ms. Rubin partnered Cam and Blair on their end-of-year science project. They were as unlikely a pair then as they are now. Blair wanted to get her first A. Cam wanted to make a scale model of an exploding volcano. Cam almost blew up the classroom, Blair got an A+ for managing the chaos, and they've been best friends ever since.

Blair learned long ago that when Cam gets a Bright Idea, it's easiest to say yes and deal with the consequences later. And, as far as Cam's brainchildren go, Blair has to admit this could be a good one: turn their shared semester-long Journalism project into a podcast on the eternal local mystery that is the disappearance of Clarissa Campbell.

Everyone from Oreville knows the story of Clarissa. Her living ghost haunts the long rain-dark winters alongside the looming specters of Washington's grim army of infamous serial killers and litany of missing girls. Clarissa Campbell: the prettiest, most popular cheerleader to spring from the soil of Oreville, who disappeared one flawless August night twenty years ago from a party in the middle of the woods outside of town. Clarissa Campbell, who vanished so completely that no one has found a trace of her—not the full investigative force of the Oreville police department, not legions of armchair sleuths and online obsessives, not television news crews or magazine reporters or Clarissa's friends and family.

No one.

The odds of Blair Johnson and Cameron Muñoz, Teen Podcasters, succeeding where hundreds have failed are slim to none, Blair thinks. But *No* is not a command the vast machine of Cam's brain is capable of processing.

"Look at all this," Cam's saying, thumbing through open

windows on her phone. *People* magazine, CNN.com, conspiracy threads, true-crime forums, a missing persons database. Dozens of pictures of Clarissa's face; Clarissa's long, tan legs; Clarissa in her cheer uniform; Clarissa accepting an award. A candid shot of Clarissa looking melancholy, as if she can sense her own future as a legendary lost girl.

"People are obsessed. This one guy has a whole website saying Clarissa was abducted by a Sasquatch. He updates it monthly with new evidence. I bet we get famous."

"I kind of doubt that," Blair says.

"Seriously. Here"—Cam tabs to a page with two shiny-haired brunettes grinning like maniacs and holding stage-bloody daggers—"these chicks have a podcast where they just, like, get drunk and read the Wikipedia pages for crimes that are *already solved* and they make like a hundred thousand dollars a *month*."

"I don't think Mr. Park will like it if we get drunk," Blair says.

"I'm not saying we have to get drunk," Cam says. "I'm saying podcasting is easy."

"We have to ask Mr. Park first," Blair says. "He could say no."

"He won't say no. We are the best thing that has happened and will happen to Mr. Park in his entire career."

Silently, Blair blesses Cam for that *we*. The likelihood that Mr. Park will remember Blair alone after graduation is small.

"Come on, say yes. It'll be fun. She's probably still alive. That would be amazing, right? We'll find her drinking martinis next to a pool in Los Angeles or something. Maybe she'll get us parts in the movie about her."

"You have no idea how to make a podcast."

"How hard can it be to record ourselves talking?"

"Cam," Blair says, laughing, "I think it takes more than that."

"Say yes."

"Fine. Yes," Blair says. She checks her reflection in her phone camera, the same self-conscious impulse Cam's been trying to get her to give up since they both turned thirteen and Blair discovered boys.

"You look great," Cam says. "You always do."

"I do not."

"Oh, shut up, B. Come on, I'm going to be late for Calc."

But then Cam sniffs, wrinkling her nose at the all-too-familiar smell of rich jock that permanently precedes Blair's boyfriend's entrance. He sweeps up behind Blair, a vision of muscle and artful five-o'clock shadow and cheekbones: James Howard, the handsomest boy in all the school.

Cam would happily knife him.

He covers Blair's eyes with his hands. She giggles, a sound she only makes around James. A sound Cam loathes.

"Guess who," he says.

"Look, B, it's your knight in shining armor," Cam says.

Cam is not a subtle person, and the only reason James is unaware of the full extent to which she hates him is that it is unfathomable to James that any girl, even one as weird as Cam, could be wholly unmoved by his charms. Nevertheless, he avoids her as much as he is able, a tacit agreement that suits them both.

"Mmm, you smell good," Blair says as he dips her into a dramatic kiss.

"Mom got you a new bottle of Axe?" Cam suggests.

James sets Blair back on her feet. "Ralph Lauren," he says.

"*Cam,*" says Blair.

"Classy," Cam says. "See you in Journo, B? I gotta run."

"We're going the same direction—" Blair begins, but Cam's already darting away through the crowded hall, waving a hand behind her like a retinue-dismissing queen.

"She's such a freak," James says, not for the first time. "I don't know what you see in her."

She doesn't know what I see in you, Blair thinks, rueful. Her bestie's enmity toward her boyfriend remains the sole bone of contention between them. Why can't Cam see how lucky Blair is? James is a senior, gorgeous, adored by teachers and students alike, all-state basketball star, rich parents, those *eyes*.

Plus, James is going places: Duke on a basketball scholarship, to be precise, the first Oreville High sports star to head so far in so long he made the front page of the *Oreville Examiner*.

And of all the girls James could have—which is any of them— he's picked, for whatever reason, Blair Johnson. Their first date, she kept pinching herself. Their first month, she was sure he'd ghost. James and *her*?

But here they are, two years later, all in love.

"She's like that with everyone," Blair lies, not for the first time either.

James beams down at her, ruffling her carefully curled hair. She'll have to spend five minutes in the bathroom later fixing the damage, but it's worth it for the look in his eyes when he looks at her.

"I have to go to class," Blair says.

"Meet me after practice?"

"I'm working on this Journalism project with Cam."

"What project?"

"We're making a podcast." She opens her mouth to tell him about Clarissa. She doesn't have Cam's enthusiasm, but she knows it's a good idea. James will get it.

"A podcast?" he says. "That's so cute."

"It's not cute. It's serious," she says, and ruins the effect with another giggle.

"Sure, babe," he says. "But it's only the second week of school and you spend all your time with her already."

"I don't," she says. She doesn't. Cam has the same complaint about James.

The problem is, there's only so much of Blair to go around.

"Have it your way. See you later."

"Love you," she says in a small voice, but he's already walking away.

Blair hurries off in the same direction Cam headed, torn as usual between the person who knows her best and the person who—she swears—loves her most.

CAM'S TAKEN JOURNALISM every semester since freshman year. Not so much because she wants a future as a girl reporter—truth is, Cam's not much of a writer—but because Mr. Park is one of the two things in Cam's life that make high school bearable. Mr. Park, the only teacher who gets it—who gets anything—and Blair. This year Cam convinced Blair to sign up with her, which makes Journalism the only place at school Cam feels at home.

There are so many things Cam knows about Blair that Blair refuses to know about herself: that she's beautiful, that she makes jumping hurdles in track look like ballet, that she's generous and wise and funny, that she has an intuitive understanding of the thing you do with liquid eyeliner to draw matching flicks at the outside corner of each eye. (Cam tried once; it went badly.) Blair is patient and tolerant, supports Cam's good ideas and checks her worst ones, sees through Cam's prickle and bluster to the best of her. Cam's strung together out of barbed wire and broken glass, a person too sharp for the world, every part of her trying to go in fourteen thousand different directions at once. It's Blair who keeps her electrons in orbit around a fixed center, roots her in the real world, knocks her head back to level and her heart back into her chest.

Blair's the most generous person Cam knows, and sometimes Cam wants to shake her, shout *Stop giving other people everything that you are!* But that's Blair's superpower. She can care and care and keep going with her own heart intact, a phenomenon that's as incomprehensible to Cam as spooky action at a distance.

How a girl as good as Blair can't see her own worth is a mystery far greater than whatever happened to Clarissa Campbell.

Cam crashes into Journo with her usual chaos energy. Mr. Park doesn't bother to glance up at Cam's commotion. Journalism's an elective, and not a popular one: The whole class this year is six students. Blair, Cam, a couple of white freshman boys whose names Cam will be unable to retain until at least winter break, a white sophomore girl, and Sophie Jenkins, who's Pinay. Sophie is a senior and a total vamp who crosses and uncrosses her legs in front of Mr. Park a lot, which is crazy, because Mr. Park is seven hundred years old. Like, at least forty.

Blair's already at her desk, notebook out and pen at the ready. Cam collapses into the seat next to her, panting. Pens explode from her bag. Papers fly. A book falls on the floor with a bang. Where did that come from? Oops.

"Good of you to join us today, Ms. Muñoz," Mr. Park says, as he always does when Cam is late, which is always. *How* is she always late? She really, truly does not mean to be always, always late. "As you're all aware, today we'll be discussing our semester reporting projects with each other. I'm excited to hear what you've come up with."

The assignment was open-ended: Pick a topic, pick a medium. Pick a partner, or not, as they chose. But Cam knows that doesn't mean Mr. Park will go easy on them. He gives his classes a lot of free rein, but his standards are high. It's one of the things Cam likes best about him: He treats his students like adults.

Mr. Park is Korean American. He looks like he was airlifted in out of some teen show about a librarian who helps teenage girls battle vampires. His hair is a mess, his sweater a rumpled mass of moss-colored wool. Cam knows without looking that he's sporting the same shapeless brown corduroy pants he wears every Tuesday.

And behind his funny old-fashioned glasses, his dark eyes are ruthless as mirrors.

Plenty of students have made the mistake of falling for Mr. Park's space-cadet act, but not Cam. Mr. Park is the smartest person she's ever met. Mr. Park is maybe, just maybe, smarter than her. If the undead do come for the students of Oreville (unlikely; even creatures of the night would find her hometown a waste of effort), Mr. Park could handle it.

Cam's so ready to show off their podcast she's almost hopping out of her chair. Mr. Park shoots her an amused glance and then points to the freshmen. Mike and Mark? Mick and Marty? How can anyone remember these things? Martlemicky are two pimply white boys who play video games. Who can tell such entities apart?

"Matt and Miles, you've decided to work together, correct? Let's start with you and go around the room."

Matt? Miles? whispers something into his notebook. "We're making a documentary about Area 51," the other one says, louder.

Cam catches a flicker of Mr. Park's grin. "How exciting," he says. "I'll be sure to keep a lookout for government agents. Jenna?"

The sophomore sits up straight and pushes her glasses up her nose. "I'm researching a reported piece on the immediate effects of climate change on the Pacific Northwest coastal environment," she says.

"We should have thought of that," Blair whispers.

"I *did*," Cam says under her breath.

"Excellent, Jenna," Mr. Park says. "I'm looking forward to seeing where your research goes. Let me know if you'd like some examples of long-form environmental journalism to take a look at. Sophie?"

Today Sophie's wearing fire-engine red lipstick and an actual pencil skirt. Cam wonders what dopey angle she'll come out with. Best Blushes for Fall? Ten Tips for Sexy Selfies? Somebody as pretty as Sophie is surely a dim bulb.

Sophie flips her glossy ponytail over one tastefully cardiganed shoulder and smiles brightly. "I'm doing an oral history of how local Native communities maintain their cultural traditions and indigenous knowledge across generations while navigating settler encroachments on their sovereignty," she says.

One of Mr. Park's eyebrows goes up, something that happens only when he's impressed. "Excellent, Sophie. Where are you starting?"

"I have some relatives by marriage in the S'Klallam Tribe, so I'm talking to them first," Sophie says. "As an outsider, I want to be careful about how I approach the interview process. I don't want to replicate colonial intrusions."

Mr. Park's other eyebrow goes up—an unheard-of accolade. Cam's heart sinks. Are they going to be bested by *Sophie Jenkins*? Cam has to admit Sophie's idea is good. And Sophie is a lot smarter than Cam thought.

Next to her, Blair grins at Cam's visible distress. Cam will not stand for being upstaged.

"We're going to find Clarissa Campbell and make a podcast about it!" Cam blurts, steamrolling Sophie's moment of glory. Sophie turns and gives Cam an amused look, which for some reason makes Cam blush. Jenna's face is blank. Mattmiles looks ready to hide under a desk, but they look like that every day.

Mr. Park leans back in his chair, silent for a long moment. His eyebrows stay lowered.

"Interesting," he says, his tone giving nothing away. "Do you have a new angle on the case?"

"Not yet," Cam says. "It's only the second week of the semester."

"Fair enough. Do either of you have experience making podcasts?"

Why's he grilling them? Why isn't he excited? Cam doesn't get it. Blair kicks her under her desk, but she barges ahead. "Do we need it? All we have to do is hit Record and put it online."

Mr. Park's face is impossible to read. "Keep in mind that's a sensitive issue for a lot of people here. Tread carefully. And you might want to do a bit of research into podcasting before you 'hit Record and put it online.'"

"Yes, Mr. Park," Blair says before Cam can argue. Cam slumps back in her seat, the air around her crackling with fury and hurt.

Tread carefully? thinks Cam. *What's that supposed to mean? What's wrong with Mr. Park?*

Tread carefully? thinks Blair. *What does Mr. Park know that we don't?*

———

BLAIR'S BETTER AT track than she is at school, but the way she sees it, she's still only herself: nobody you'd notice. She's made it to State, but she'll never place. She's not James, with college recruiters lining up to offer her the future.

Still, she's fast, consistent, logs mile after mile after mile. She likes the feeling of freedom, knowing that her legs can carry her as far as she wants to go. She likes the time alone to think.

Most of the time it's the only time alone she gets.

Today practice is tempo, hills, tempo, cooldown. She dances through it, showers fast, sprints to meet Cam at her car for fun. Like most of the once-valuable objects in her life—bicycle, computer, bedroom TV—it's a hand-me-down that's already passed through all her brothers. Blair tries not to feel like an afterthought in her own house.

Cam's raided the school library while Blair sweated through her paces. She has a pile of books with titles like *American Predator* and *In Cold Blood*.

"I'm not reading those," Blair says, unlocking the driver's side. Cam chucks the stack in the back seat and climbs in front.

"You don't have to," Cam says. "I'm looking at narrative arcs."

Right, Blair thinks. Because first and foremost, what they're doing is telling a story. A story about a girl who disappeared.

Her phone chimes with an incoming text, chimes again. She doesn't have to check to know who it is, but she looks anyway.

> See u soon?
> Baby?

With Cam remember? she types.

> I thought we had plans

Did they? They couldn't have. She would remember. No. They didn't. She told him by her locker she was meeting Cam after practice. He's being jealous. Of Cam, which is crazy. But maybe he's right. He's her boyfriend! Cam will be around forever, but boyfriends need tending.

Still, she promised. And anyway, here's Cam. In her car. With half the library.

Sorry baby, she types. Gotta work on this project. Tomorrow?

She waits, but gets only silence. Cam gives her phone a foul look, but to Blair's relief she doesn't say anything.

"Your house?" Blair asks.

"Onward," Cam says. "To fame and fortune."

"I'll settle for an A," Blair says.

Cam smiles. "Please," she says. "The A is already guaranteed."

Cam's room is extremely Cam. Books everywhere, piles of papers, several plants in varying states of distress, a poster of the periodic table that's hung crooked on one wall for as long as Blair's known her. Cam's cat, Kitten, snores peacefully on her unmade bed. Cam named him when she was ten and he was, in fact, a kitten. Six years later he's an immense pitch-black tyrant who weighs at least twenty pounds.

Unlike Blair, Cam's an only child. It's just Cam; her mom, Irene; and Kitten. When she was younger, Blair thought Cam must get lonely. Now, she envies Cam her peace.

Cam's laptop is the only pristine thing in her room. It has a special place on her desk, occupying the sole point of order in a maelstrom of chaos. Blair knows Irene saved for months to buy it, and Cam treats it like it's on loan from a museum of fine art.

"We can get started now," Cam says. "I'll record us on my phone and edit it later. I downloaded this free sound editing program a lot of people use."

Blair settles herself cross-legged on Cam's floor. "Started with what, though? Talking?"

"Isn't that what a podcast is? People talking?"

"What should we say?"

Cam looks at her phone as if it will give her an answer. "First we could talk about the mystery," she says. "And then our theories of what happened."

"We don't have any theories of what happened."

Cam frowns. "Not yet. But we will. Just talk until it sounds good."

Blair doesn't think this is much of a plan. But Cam always gets to where she wants to go, even if the route is a mystery to everyone but her.

"Sure," Blair says. Cam pushes a stack of chemistry quizzes aside and sits on the floor in front of Blair, their foreheads almost touching, Cam's phone on the floor between them.

"Here we go," Cam says, and taps Record.

CAM

Uh, I think it's on. Yeah, it's on. Well, this is a podcast about, um, about this girl who was . . . Well, she grew up in our town, and then she disappeared.

BLAIR

We should maybe say who we are, Cam.

CAM

Uh, right. I'm Cam.

[A long pause.]

BLAIR

Did you want to—should we, like, say more about ourselves?

CAM

Like what else?

BLAIR

Um, I'm Blair. We're in Mr. Park's Journalism class. This is our project. In high school. I mean, for high school Journalism class. Our project is Clarissa.

CAM

Clarissa Campbell.

BLAIR

Right. Clarissa Campbell.

CAM

Which is the most famous unsolved mystery in Oreville.

BLAIR

Is it?

CAM

Are there any other ones?

BLAIR

The Mystery of the Puget Sound Golf Course Senior Prank Day Vandal last year.

CAM

They never figured out who peed on Officer Em's patrol car during drug awareness week in seventh grade.

BLAIR

Not a lot happens in Oreville.

CAM

[Laughing] Nope.

BLAIR

We have to do interviews, though. I mean, this can't only be us talking the whole time.

CAM

Yeah, we'll interview people.

BLAIR

Who?

CAM

Clarissa's friends. Uh, her parents. You know. People who knew her.

BLAIR

Just, like, call them? Out of the blue?

CAM

Why not?

BLAIR

Mr. Park says we have to have a research component too.

CAM

We *are* doing research. I *did* research. I mean, this is just the introduction. *[Pause.]* Mr. Park is our Journalism teacher.

BLAIR

I think I already said that. Wait, what is our podcast called?

[Silence.]

CAM

Uh, *Into the Woods*?

BLAIR

Isn't that a musical? Technically Clarissa went out of the woods. We think.

[Silence.]

CAM

We could start with the facts. *[Sound of papers rustling.]*

CAM

[Muffled.] Oops. *[More clearly.]* The facts are, um, that in August 1999—the second weekend of August—

BLAIR

The nineteenth, right?

CAM

The fourteenth. On Saturday, the fourteenth of August, 1999, the, uh, the seniors from Oreville that had just graduated threw a party in the woods. And—

BLAIR

We should tell them about the woods.

CAM

What about the woods?

BLAIR

Like, where they are. And what they look like and stuff. I think podcasts usually start with atmosphere.

CAM

This totally—

Cam leans forward and taps Pause—"sucks," she finishes. "We sound like nitwits."

"Maybe it's not as bad as you think," Blair says hopefully.

Cam replays the recording and they listen to themselves talk in excruciating silence.

"Maybe we need a script," Blair says.

"A script!" Cam says. "That's a good idea."

"Do I really say 'like' that much?"

"That one was practice," Cam says, and swipes to delete.

"To get the bugs out."

"It never happened."

"We do need a name first, right? *The Girl in the Woods*?"

Cam googles. "Already a mystery novel. *The Dead Girl*?"

"Don't we want her not to be dead?"

Cam googles again. "It's the name of a movie anyway. And like fifteen books."

"*Escape from Oreville?*"

Cam laughs. "*What Happened to Clarissa Campbell?*"

"Kind of literal," Blair says.

They sit in companionable silence for a moment, thinking.

"*Clarissa Is Missing*?" Blair suggests. They look at each other and say at the same time, "*Missing Clarissa*."

"Yes!" Cam says with satisfaction. "That's it. You did it, B."

"You think so?"

"Podcast names always have this double entendre thing," Cam says authoritatively.

"Why?"

"I don't know why. They just do. Let's start over."

"We decided on a script."

Cam arranges her notes in front of her. "I can read from this. The first episode is the introduction. For the next one we can interview someone who knew her."

"Let me write some stuff down first."

Cam flips through *The Big Book of Serial Killers* while Blair scratches away in her notebook, crosses things out, mutters to herself. She sits back and nods.

"Ready?" Cam asks.

"Ready."

CAM

Uh, hi, everybody. I'm Cameron Muñoz.

BLAIR

And I'm Blair Johnson. We're juniors at Oreville High School.

CAM

And this is Episode One of *Missing Clarissa*. So, even if you're not from Oreville, Washington—even if you've never heard of Oreville, Washington, which is pretty likely, given that it's a dump of a town with twenty thousand inhabitants, and that's including the whole county—you've probably heard of Clarissa Campbell. Her story was national news in 1999 and has spawned a, uh, whole wave of conspiracy theories and investigations. No one knows what happened to her. No one has heard from her since she disappeared—or, if they have, they're not telling. But a Google search of Clarissa's name still yields thousands of results twenty years later—everything from wingnuts who think she was abducted by forest monsters to people who think she wanted to start over somewhere else.

BLAIR

So, um, anyway, the disappearance of Clarissa Campbell is the most exciting thing that's happened in our town. It's sort of like an urban legend. A story you know without remembering how you heard it first.

CAM

But when she disappeared, it was big news. For a while, the whole country was obsessed with Clarissa. A young, beautiful white girl with a promising future, disappearing into thin air? It was a narrative made for late-night true-crime specials and—

BLAIR

Cam, we were going to stick to the facts of the case for now.

CAM

That *is* a fact. *[Clears throat.]* Anyway, we think . . . Well, we don't think anything yet. We don't have a theory of what happened. We think she might still be alive, and it would be pretty cool if we can find her.

BLAIR

She can give us tips for getting out of Oreville. So, Clarissa disappeared from a party in the woods west of here. If you've never been to Oreville, you're not alone. It's a small town on the Olympic Peninsula, way out near the edge of the world where the continent drops off into the Pacific Ocean. The summers here are sweet and golden, sandwiched between long, wet gray winters where the sky comes down to meet the treetops. And everywhere out here is forest. The woods where Clarissa disappeared are beautiful, but they're not what I would call friendly. They're green and dark even in the middle of the day and so big you feel like you can drown in them. And at night . . .

Blair trails off, embarrassed. Cam's staring at her. "What?" she mumbles, hitting Pause.

"Where did *that* come from?"

"Sorry," Blair mumbles, crumpling the paper she's reading from.

"No, I mean it was good," Cam says. "Total atmosphere."

"It was dumb. Let's cut it."

"It wasn't dumb," Cam says. Blair's eyes are welling with tears. "Are you okay? What's going on?"

"Nothing!" Blair says. "I'm fine! It's stupid, that's all."

"Okay, okay," Cam says. "It's cool. We can cut it if you want. I can go to the library after school tomorrow. Not that I don't think Sasquatch Man did his homework, but Mr. Park says we should use primary sources for our project."

"As long as we redo the first one," Blair says.

But before Cam can argue, Irene pokes her head around the doorframe.

Her skin's a few shades darker than Cam's—Irene's Mexican American, Cam's dad was white—but otherwise they look unnervingly alike: same high cheekbones, same sharp dark eyes. Except where Cam's black hair is a cowlicky mess chopped short at her chin, Irene's falls to the middle of her back in a smooth wave on the rare occasions when she takes it out of its tidy bun. And while Cam dresses like she ran through a Goodwill men's department grabbing things at random, Blair's only seen Irene in some version of stretchy jeans, tank top, and zip-up sweatshirt in all the years she's known her.

"Hi, Blair," Irene says.

"Hi, Irene," says Blair. Cam's mom hasn't been Ms. Muñoz to her in years. Sometimes she slips up and calls Irene Mom too.

Irene registers Cam's phone and open laptop. "What are you up to?"

"Making a podcast," Cam says. "For Journalism."

Cam's impatient with her mom the same way she is with all adults, which Irene endures with bemused tolerance. Blair has told Cam more than once how lucky she is: Irene isn't just cool. She lets Cam run free, doesn't ask Cam to be anything she isn't. But Cam's too headstrong to recognize her own fortune.

"What's the podcast about?" Irene asks.

"That cheerleader who disappeared in the nineties," Cam says. She sits up, alert. "Wait, did you know her?"

"Clarissa? Sure, I knew who she was. She was a year behind me."

Irene's from Oreville too, although she got out for a while before Cam was born, to New York City of all places. Irene's early adulthood has the haze of legend: squatting in abandoned warehouses in Williamsburg, running feral from dive bar to dive bar in the East Village, playing drums in an all-girl, all-Latinx punk band called the Young Lourdes.

Irene met Cam's dad, Oliver, at the February 15 anti–Iraq War protest in 2003. Irene was a black bloc street medic, Oliver a leftist professor of economics at NYU. The police kettled them, along with a hundred other protestors, outside the Cooper Station post office; nightsticks descended. (Cam asked once if Irene had thought Oliver was handsome when they first saw each other. "I had no idea," Irene said matter-of-factly. "He was covered in blood.")

Irene treated Oliver's head wound and they spent the night in jail together. ("And every night thereafter," Irene said, the one time she told Cam the whole story.) Less than a year later, Irene was pregnant. And four years after that, Oliver died of a fast-moving, late-diagnosed cancer. Irene came back to Oreville so her parents could help her out, but now that Cam's grandparents are dead too, she has no idea why Irene insists on remaining imprisoned here.

Cam holds her phone out, thumb poised over Record. "Want to tell us about it? We have to interview people who knew her."

"I didn't know her personally," Irene says. "I don't feel like cooking—want pizza?"

"But you must have heard the story," Cam persists.

Irene gives Cam a look.

"Pizza sounds great," Blair says hastily.

Irene winks. "Don't tell your parents I won't cook for you, Blair. They already think I'm a reprobate."

It's a long-running joke between them, how diligently wholesome Blair's family is, how Cam's mom is more like a teenager herself. But Blair knows Irene knows that this house is the one where she can breathe.

"Give us half an hour to practice some more?" Cam asks.

"Deal," Irene says, and leaves them to it.

Later, after Blair goes home, Cam listens to what they've done. Their voices are burbly, as if they recorded underwater. But the part where Blair talks about the woods sends a thrilling chill down Cam's back. It's too good to cut! It's magnificent! Blair is brilliant! She will just have to come around.

Cam transfers the audio file to her laptop, cuts in a few seconds of synth-y pop music at the beginning, adds a segment of herself recapping what they've gone over so far and telling their imaginary audience to check out the next episode. The sound is truly abysmal. They'll have to figure something out. But for a first try, she thinks, it's not half bad.

She finds a hosting site. It only takes a few minutes to make an account. She debates what to call the first episode, settles on "The Beginning." Clicks Upload. Blair is going to kill her, but she can't help herself.

She creates a burner account, FindClarissa1999, in the biggest Clarissa forum.

Hey, check out this podcast from Clarissa's hometown, she types, and adds the link.

Satisfied at last, she goes to bed.

EPISODE II

THE
MOTHERS

THE next morning, *Missing Clarissa* "The Beginning" has not blown up. In fact, it currently has a total audience of two people. Cam scowls. A total audience of two is not the plan. Something will have to be done about this.

Irene's in the kitchen, smoking the one daily cigarette she allows herself with her morning cup of coffee.

"Gross," Cam says peaceably, as she always does.

"Leave your poor mother alone," responds Irene, as she always does. It's their ritual. Cam opens the fridge, roots around. Kitten waddles into the kitchen and howls.

"I already fed the cat," Irene says.

"Tell him that," Cam says, emerging with a carton of orange juice and the butter. "Can I drink the rest of this coffee?"

"Stunts your growth," Irene says. Cam's five foot ten. Irene barely comes up to her chin; she assumes her father was a skyscraper. She pours the last of the pot in a mug, begins to assemble toast.

"So, you're making a podcast about Clarissa?" Irene's voice is casual, but Cam's Spidey-sense sounds an alarm. Irene will yell about politics until she's blue in the face, go on about books until Cam's ready to throw her out a window, and patiently field Cam's endless complaints about Blair's wretched boyfriend, but she's never asked Cam about her homework before.

"It's an interesting story," Cam says. "Local legend and all."

"I can't imagine anyone outside Oreville caring about it anymore."

"Are you serious? There are still forums."

"People with nothing better to do," says Irene.

"I care," Cam says. "Don't you want to know what happened to her?"

"It's not that I don't care," Irene says. She is wearing her I'm-a-superior-and-more-enlightened-than-you-adult face, which never fails to drive Cam nuts.

"Do you think someone killed her?" Cam asks.

"Why would anyone kill her?"

"If nobody killed her, what happened to her? Alien abduction?"

"I have no idea," Irene says calmly. "But her family was devastated after she went missing. I don't see how dragging all this out into the open again is going to be good for anyone."

"It already is out in the open," Cam says. "Did you know her family? How did you know they were devastated?"

"How do you think, Cameron? Their daughter disappeared. How would you feel?"

"Is there something you're not telling me?" Cam transports buttered toast, coffee mug, and the orange juice to the kitchen table. She crams an entire piece of toast in her mouth, chases it down with a slug of juice from the carton, and looks at Irene expectantly.

Irene covers her eyes. "Dear god," she says.

"Sorry," says Cam, who isn't.

"Want a ride to school? I have to leave for work in a few minutes."

"You didn't answer my question."

"Come on," Irene says. "We're going to be late if we don't get moving."

———

AFTER SCHOOL CAM walks to the public library. The *Oreville Examiner* has only recently entered the twenty-first century, and nothing printed before 2013 is online. With the help of a friendly—and bored—librarian, she's soon ensconced in front of an ancient microfiche machine, flipping through the paper's archives from when Clarissa Campbell disappeared.

She finds a high-school graduation special issue from June 8, 1999. Cam scans its profiles of Oreville High's finest: Heidi Wells plans to work in her dad's pharmacy and save up for vet school. Rosalin Pham is majoring in pre-med in Seattle. Jason Martner wants to get married and raise his kids in Oreville.

"Cruel," Cam mutters.

And there she is: Clarissa. *Parents: Joe and Marian Campbell. GPA: 3.86. Favorite subject: Art. Most influential teacher and why: Mr. Friley, who taught me to see the world differently.* (*Friley*, Cam writes in her notebook.) *What I do for fun: Learn new cheer stunts, go to movies and concerts. Future plans: Move in with my amazing boyfriend!!!!!*

Cam snaps a picture of the screen with her phone, although there's not much there. This Clarissa doesn't sound like the kind of girl who'd up and run from her life, but if she wanted to escape something—or someone—it's not like she'd tell the *Oreville Examiner*.

Cam flips ahead to July. EndFest tickets went on sale July 15, offering attendees the opportunity to see Blink-182 and Eve 6, with Moby headlining the Electronic Pavilion. A new branch of the Oreville Community Bank opened on July 20. Driver Travis Schmidt, 22, and four passengers, all minors, were killed on July 27 when Schmidt ran off Highway 3 into a tree; alcohol was involved in the incident. On August 8 the state ferries implemented a new bicycle-loading system. On August 12 Mabel Frey, 82, complained bitterly about the new bicycle-loading system in the Letters to the Editor.

And on August 15, Clarissa Campbell was reported missing by her parents.

Cam peers closer.

DETECTIVES NEED HELP TO FIND MISSING 17-YEAR-OLD OREVILLE GIRL

TUESDAY, AUGUST 17, OREVILLE, Wash. [*Examiner* Staff]

Detectives are asking for the public's help to find a 17-year-old girl who was reported missing on Sunday by her parents, says the Hoquiam County Sheriff's Office.

The parents of recent Oreville High graduate Clarissa Campbell became concerned when she did not return home after attending a party in a wooded area outside city limits. Investigators said that Campbell was last seen at the party around 2 a.m. on the morning of August 15th.

"Detectives are continuing to speak to subjects who were in attendance at the party in question at this time," said Officer Aaron Liechty this morning. The Sheriff's Office plans to use tracking dogs to aid the investigation.

Police are asking anyone with information about Campbell's whereabouts to contact Hoquiam County Central Dispatch at 646-307-5055.

Liechty, Cam writes.

She pulls out her phone, searches Clarissa's name. The story didn't hit the big leagues for another week or so. National newspapers picked it up on August 20. *People* magazine did a full spread in September, complete with an airbrushed glamour shot of Clarissa, eyes soft and hair shining, and a candid snap of her weeping parents clutching each other and gazing beseechingly into the camera.

More pictures: Clarissa in her graduation cap, in which she improbably manages to appear both wholesome and sultry. Clarissa in a cheer uniform, catapulting through the air. Clarissa in the arms of a beefy white guy in a letterman jacket with sharp cheekbones and sleepy-sexy eyes. The caption reads *Clarissa and boyfriend Brad Bennett.*

Brad Bennett, Cam writes. A few lines from the grieving swain: "Clarissa was the most amazing person," "Clarissa never would have run away," et al. Clarissa's story resurfaces in *People* a week later; this time Brad himself is the suspect in her disappearance, the photos of him unflattering. He hulks, menacing, on the football field, looming over some hapless lesser player. Clarissa's reported best friend, Jenny Alexander, denies the possibility of Brad's involvement. "He adored Clarissa," she declares. "He worshiped the ground she walked on."

Brad is never arrested; there's no evidence to suggest his involvement, and no body to prove Clarissa's dead.

But Clarissa's story doesn't fade. It snowballs. Every other month or so a major magazine runs a feature, dredging a seemingly infinite well of Clarissa pictures. Clarissa as a baby. Preteen Clarissa, chubby-cheeked and in braces, but already with that uncanny beauty, a siren song of innocent blue eyes and a full, quirking smile that hints at something else.

Everyone does *love a dead girl,* Cam thinks.

Clarissa's serene blue stare from her phone screen is faintly mocking.

Cam returns to the microfiche on the off chance the humble *Oreville Examiner* reported something the bigger outlets did not.

"Cameron?" someone says behind her. She jumps, turning around so fast she nearly upsets the hard plastic chair, flooded with a strange embarrassment. As if she's doing something perverse, looking at all these sexy online photos of a maybe dead girl she never knew.

It's Sophie. She's wearing white jeans—*white* jeans!!! how does she keep them *clean*!!!—and a creamy-pink scoop-neck shirt that Cam is pretty sure falls into the category of *blouse*. A slender gold chain glimmers at her throat. Her lipstick is, as usual, siren red and perfectly applied.

Cam feels suddenly frumpy and awkward in her shapeless old T-shirt and age-faded jeans.

"What are you doing here?" she asks rudely.

"Research," Sophie says. "Isn't that what you're doing here?"

"No," Cam says, flustered. "I mean, yes." Why is Sophie always wearing lipstick? Does she think people in Oreville will care? Is Cam supposed to care? *Does* Cam care?

"Is something wrong?"

"Yes!" Cam yelps. "No! I'm fine!"

The librarian looks up from his desk, shoots her an irritated glare.

"I'm *fine*," Cam hisses.

"It was nice to see you," Sophie says, backing away. But then she registers the screen over Cam's shoulder. "Whoa, you're going through microfiche? Old-school. Is that the *Examiner*?"

Cam catches a whiff of Sophie's subtle perfume, which smells like things Cam's formidable vocabulary cannot capture. *Paris,* Cam, who has never set foot outside of Washington State, thinks. *Sophie smells like Paris.*

". . . byline?" Sophie's asking.

"What?"

"I said, did you check out the byline on this article?"

Paris-stinky Sophie's pointing over Cam's shoulder at the screen.

"Byline?" Cam echoes stupidly.

Sophie leans in and taps the screen with a manicured fingernail. And then Cam sees what Sophie means.

The article's a short piece on the continuing search for Clarissa, nothing Cam hasn't already seen covered in *People* magazine with a sidebar on search-dog training methods to boot.

It's not the article that matters. It's who wrote it.

Thomas Park.

"Mr. Park wrote for the *Examiner*?" Cam asks. "Did you know?"

Sophie shakes her head, her auburn-glinting ponytail bobbing prettily. "No idea. He's never said anything about it."

"Why wouldn't he tell us that?"

"I don't know," Sophie says, "but it's strange."

She leans farther over Cam's shoulder as Cam pages through old stories. Cam holds her breath. She will not be sent to Paris! She has work to do!

"He must have been the main reporter on the case," Sophie says. "He wrote almost every article about it."

Together they go through August, September, October. Mr. Park wrote articles about Clarissa, the school board, a water usage controversy, the October Pumpkin Festival, drunk driving, and a new hire at the police department.

And then, at the end of October, Mr. Park's name disappears. Cam pages forward, looking for more Clarissa articles. In November, a follow-up surfaces, this one by a Mona Simpkins. The next article about Clarissa is credited to the *Examiner* staff. Then Mona Simpkins again.

Nothing further from Mr. Park. Not about Clarissa, and not about anything else.

"Check the masthead," Sophie suggests.

In October, Thomas Park is listed as a staff reporter. In November, his name is gone.

"He must have quit," Sophie says.

"Or gotten fired," Cam says.

"Why would they fire him?"

Cam flips backward in time to before Clarissa disappeared. Mr. Park's byline is all over the paper.

Then he covers Clarissa.

Then, like Clarissa, he disappears.

Cam searches her phone for Oreville High's homepage, looks up Mr. Park.

"He left the paper in 1999. And then he started teaching at Oreville High in 2002," Sophie says, still reading over Cam's shoulder.

"God, he must be ancient," Cam says.

"He's not *that* old," Sophie says.

Cam thinks of Sophie crossing her legs in class, is inexplicably awash in fury. "Well, you would know," she says.

Sophie looks at her in astonishment. "What's that supposed to mean?"

"Nothing," Cam mumbles, mortified as swiftly as she was enraged. What on earth is wrong with her? Maybe she is allergic to Sophie's perfume. Whatever is happening to her, she wants out. Now.

"I have to go," Cam says, standing up so fast her skull almost hits Sophie's chin. "I have to do homework." Her phone sails from her hand, clunks to the floor. Somehow her notebook and pen follow it. She scrabbles after them, bumping into Sophie, who's trying to help.

"This is homework," Sophie says, bewildered. She holds out Cam's phone. Cam snatches it without thanks, stuffing it into her bag. Her heart is galloping as hard as if she's launched herself into a marathon. Does she need the bathroom? Is she going to barf?

"Cam? Is something wrong?"

Sophie's calling after her, sounding almost hurt, as Cam speeds for the exit. She doesn't stop. She has better things to do than look at ancient newspapers with dopey lipsticky Sophie Jenkins.

Now she has to remember what those better things are.

———

"I THINK WE should talk to Clarissa's parents first," says Cam, sprawled across her bedroom floor. Kitten snores thunderously at her side.

"Are they still in Oreville?" Blair asks.

"Dunno. Marian and"—Cam squints at her notebook—"Joe."

"What if they don't want to talk to us?"

"Only one way to find out," Cam says sensibly. She opens her laptop, searches for the Campbells. "This brings up a million old articles about Clarissa."

"Maybe Irene knows where they lived."

"Irene's being weird. Wait, I have an idea." Cam hops up, disappears out the door. Blair hears several crashing noises. Kitten twitches in his sleep. Something shatters. Cam reappears, her hair in disarray, clutching an enormous yellow-and-white paperback book.

"Did you break something?"

"What? No. Just a plate that was in the closet. Irene never throws anything out. Look!" Cam hefts her burden.

"What *is* that?"

"Phone book," Cam says triumphantly. "From . . ." She consults the cover. "2002. This thing is older than we are."

She sits down with a thump, dropping the book. Kitten snorts and lurches to his feet, lumbering away sulkily. Cam flips through the phone book, running one finger down tiny columns of black type.

"Here they are. Joe and Marian Campbell. 2133 Rhododendron Lane. I think that's over by the golf course."

"Fancy," Blair says. "They must be rich."

Cam looks up. "Like, ransom money rich, you think?"

"I'm sure it would have been in the news if someone asked them for ransom money."

But Cam's on a roll. "Maybe something went wrong!" she says eagerly. "Like, they were going to kidnap Clarissa and ask for money, but then she fought back or something and they killed her by accident and had to cover it up!"

"In *Oreville*?"

Cam frowns. "You never know. We should remain open to all the possibilities," she says. "Should we call her parents?"

"Do you think they still live here?"

"Normally parents of missing kids don't go anywhere," Cam says. "That's what it says in all the books. In case the kid comes home."

"That's sad," Blair says.

"I didn't think about that," Cam says, getting out her phone.

"You're calling them now? What are you going to say?" Blair asks.

Cam's already dialing. "Hello? Is this Marian Campbell?" She gives Blair a thumbs-up. "My name is Cameron and I'm a student at Oreville High—"

I'm so sorry to bother you, Blair mouths.

Cam rolls her eyes. "Um, I'm so sorry to bother you, but my friend and I are working on a journalism project about the—uh—about Clarissa's disappearance and we were hoping we could—" Cam stops, listens. "You can? That would be— My friend has track practice but after that would be— Rhododendron Lane? We'll see you then."

Cam hangs up. "Whoa," she says. "That was creepy."

"What did she say?"

"We can go see her tomorrow after your practice."

"Tomorrow? At their house?"

"She sounded excited about it."

"She wasn't mad?"

"No," Cam says. "It was weird. It was like she was waiting by the phone for someone to call about Clarissa."

"But Clarissa disappeared twenty years ago."

"I know that, Blair," Cam says. "That's what made it creepy."

———

THE CAMPBELLS' HOUSE sits at the end of a cul-de-sac in a subdivision that was probably new around the time Clarissa disappeared. The streets are named after what they paved over: Meadow Avenue, Forest Drive, Rhododendron Lane. The houses are large and identical, each with its own exact rectangular stamp of Ortho-green lawn. There is nothing to distinguish the Campbells' house from its neighbors except for a wooden pot of geraniums on the front stoop with a jaunty ceramic cat washing its paw stuck in the soil.

The front door opens seconds after Blair rings the bell. Mrs. Campbell is small and immaculate, her silver-blond hair arranged in a neat mom bob.

"Please come in," she says.

Blair and Cam follow her through the house, which is as well-groomed as she is. All the furniture matches. Side tables sport tasteful arrangements of themed objects—a grouping of seashells that look like they've never seen a beach, a series of family photos in identical silver frames. Blair can see the lines the vacuum cleaner's made across the spotless carpets. The house is warm and stuffy and smells strongly of potpourri.

"Have a seat, girls," Mrs. Campbell says. "Would you like something to drink? Tea? Lemonade?" She points them to a sofa that faces a bookshelf filled with pictures of Clarissa. Clarissa as a rosy-cheeked toddler, Clarissa as a preteen with a much younger-looking Mrs. Campbell and a handsome man who must be her father, Clarissa in her graduation cap and gown. Cam recognizes most of them from the magazine articles about her disappearance.

There are, she notes, no pictures of Clarissa and Brad.

"No, thank you," Cam says to the offer of drinks. Mrs. Campbell sits carefully in an armchair, as if she's afraid she'll leave a dent in the overstuffed cushion.

"Thank you so much for having us, Mrs. Campbell—" Blair begins as Cam takes out her notebook and pen.

"Marian, please, dear."

"—Marian," Blair corrects. "We're making a podcast about Clarissa's—about Clarissa. We were hoping we could ask you a few questions."

Marian crosses her legs daintily and folds her hands in her lap. "It's so wonderful people are still interested," she murmurs. "We want Clarissa to know we're still thinking about her. Each new story could be the one that brings her home."

Cam has no idea how to respond to this. Does Marian think Clarissa is out there googling her own name for some sign that it's time to return to Oreville? There is something so disturbing about this silent, sterile house, Mrs. Campbell's uncanny-valley calm. Cam takes out her phone.

"Is it all right if we record you?" she asks.

Marian flutters her eyelashes coquettishly. "Certainly. How exciting," she says. "I haven't been on the radio in ages."

Cam blinks. What is going on with this woman?

Blair clears her throat. "Mrs. Campbell—Marian—is there anything in particular you want us to know about Clarissa? Maybe you could help our—uh, our audience—picture her."

Marian tilts her head and looks thoughtful, as if she's never been asked this question before. "Clarissa is simply a wonderful girl," she says. "We've never had a moment of trouble with her." *Clarissa no trouble,* Cam writes in her notebook, wondering if this is true and how they can find out if it isn't. "She's an only child," Marian continues. "We hoped for more, but God didn't bless us in that way. Clarissa's our angel. And so beautiful too. We're very lucky."

Clarissa was, Cam thinks. *Not Clarissa* is. "Is there—was there—anything different about her that summer?" she asks. "Something that might have made her want to—" Blair kicks her ankle, and Cam changes the question. "To, uh, spend time alone?"

Marian looks at her blankly. The silence stretches.

"What about her friends?" Blair asks, desperate to end it.

Marian smiles. "Allen was such a help to us," she says. "Such a wonderful young man."

"Allen?" Cam echoes, pen at the ready.

"Allen Dawson. A dear friend of Clarissa's. He was simply a godsend during—that time. He was the one who helped us talk to all the reporters. There were so many of them! Everyone wanted to ask us about Clarissa. Allen said some of them didn't have our best interests at heart." She shakes her head in disgust. "Can you imagine that? A family in need, and people trying to take advantage of us?"

"That must have been awful," Blair says.

"I'm used to it now," Marian says. "But at the time, it was so overwhelming. I don't know what we would've done without Allen. He started the ribbon campaign, you know."

"That was him?" Cam asks. "I read about that." In the weeks after Clarissa disappeared, her friends were supposed to wear orange ribbons as a symbol of hope. Orange had been Clarissa's favorite color. Allen's name hasn't shown up in any of the stories she's read, but maybe he wanted to stay out of the spotlight. Who was he? Was Clarissa cheating on Brad with him? Would that have given Brad a reason to kill her?

"Does Allen live in Oreville?" Cam asks.

"He moved away for college. He's quite successful now, I believe. I'm afraid we lost touch over the years, but his mother still lives here. Kathleen."

Mother, Cam writes. *Kathleen Dawson.*

"What about her other friends?" Cam asks. "Jenny Alexander's name was in some of the articles about her."

Marian's mouth twitches. "I haven't spoken to Jenny in some time," she says.

"But she was Clarissa's best friend?" Cam prompts.

"We've lost touch," Marian says. "You know, Clarissa always wanted to see the Louvre. She's a wonderful painter."

"You think she's in France?" Cam asks. If she's trying to keep the astonishment out of her voice, she isn't succeeding.

"She does have an adventurous spirit," Marian says. "I imagine she'd want to visit all the most artistic museums. There's a famous one in Amsterdam she talks about. I can't think of the name. One of those funny Dutch words."

Dutch museum, Cam writes in her notebook. She feels like she's been thrown into dark water with no idea where the bottom lies. Next to her, Blair is equally at a loss. Is Marian nuts? Does she seriously think Clarissa is on a twenty-year tour of European cultural institutions?

"Would you like to see her room?" Marian asks.

"Yes," Cam blurts, relieved to have something to do. Anything other than sitting across from this shell of a woman. Blair follows them reluctantly up the carpeted stairs. *She doesn't want to be in this house anymore,* Cam thinks.

Neither does Cam, but she doesn't want to end the interview. There's something fascinating about Clarissa's mother. Like watching a horror movie: the dark thrill of seeing someone else's blood and knowing you can't get hurt yourself.

All the doors on the second-floor landing are closed. Marian opens the nearest one, revealing a bedroom much larger than Cam's. The walls are painted a pale seashell pink. The double bed is neatly made, the bedspread sprigged with pink rosebuds that match the walls. There's a white desk with a pretty, old-fashioned glass lamp and a frilly-cushioned chair and a dresser with a mirrored tray holding several bottles of perfume.

A framed poster of a voluptuous platinum-blond woman in a black satin dress lying sideways on a bed and looking dreamily out into space is centered on one wall. Across from it a shelf displays Clarissa's cheerleading trophies and more pictures of Clarissa with friends. Here, Cam spots Brad among the smiling faces.

The room, like everywhere else in the house, is clean and still and suffocating.

"We're keeping it the way she likes for her," Marian says, as though Clarissa has popped out for a brief holiday and will be back shortly to spritz her wrists with Sunflowers and listen to the CDs tidily stacked next to the stereo.

"'Truth or Dare'?" Cam asks, reading the words on the poster. "What does that mean?"

"Clarissa's a huge Madonna fan," Marian says. "Thank goodness she's not into that awful rap music. Don't you girls still listen to Madonna?"

"No," Cam says.

"That's the only thing we changed," Marian says, pointing to a painting that hangs in a corner of the room hidden by the door. "The school gave it to us after—" She pauses for a heartbeat, corrects herself. "The school gave it to us. She had just finished it."

Cam steps closer. The painting looks vaguely familiar. After a minute, she realizes it's an echo of a famous one she's seen prints of: a woman lying in the prairie grass, reaching toward an old farmhouse. In Clarissa's version, the woman's face is hers, turned toward the viewer. She looks haunted and wild.

"Is that the high school?" Blair asks, looking over Cam's shoulder at the building where the farmhouse would be in the original.

"It's a perfect resemblance, isn't it?" Marian says. "Clarissa's so talented."

Which doesn't explain why she's hidden the painting away in Clarissa's room, or why it never showed up in any of the coverage of her disappearance. Cam doesn't know much about art, but even she can tell the painting is almost supernaturally good. But there's something frightening about it.

She can't face it, Blair thinks. *Clarissa's mom can't throw this out. But she can't look at it either.*

"It's spooky," Cam says. "Almost unhappy."

"Clarissa is never unhappy," Marian snaps.

Bet you she was, Blair thinks, looking at the painting. Who did Clarissa paint this for? What was she trying to say? That she hated high school, or that something bad was happening there?

"Can I take a picture?" Cam asks, leaning in to snap a photo without waiting for Marian's nod. "What about Clarissa's art teacher? Mr. Friley, right? She said he was her favorite teacher."

Marian brightens. "Dan Friley, yes. He's been such a mentor to Clarissa," she says. "He's a *real* artist, you know. From *New York.* Can you believe that? And there he was, in little old Oreville! Dan told Clarissa she has a real gift. I'm sure he doesn't say that to just anyone."

"Did she take a lot of art classes?" Blair asks.

"She took her first painting class as a freshman. Dan thought she was so talented he did an independent tutorial with her each semester after that," Marian says. "Her father and I know how special Clarissa is, but we're always so proud of her when other people see it too."

"He's not at Oreville anymore," Blair says. "The art teacher now is Ms. Clark."

"Dan's a fantastic teacher, but he's not much of one for bureaucracy," Marian says. "What with his artistic temperament. He runs the Silverwater now."

"The Silverwater?" Cam asks, writing busily.

"Out on the Peninsula. It's a beautiful place. An artists' retreat of sorts. I'm sure there'll be a place for Clarissa there when she comes back. She'll be so well suited to something like that. She can teach and paint. I'm sure the other artists will adore her. Everyone loves Clarissa. It will be so wonderful to have her home again."

Neither Cam nor Blair can imagine a response to this. Another long, painful silence stretches and thickens. Blair steps away from the painting, pretending to examine Clarissa's trophies.

Get us out of here, she telepaths at Cam. *Please get us out of here.*

There's a noise from downstairs. Garage door opening, car door slamming, key in a lock.

"And the night she disappeared?" Cam asks, getting down to business. "Did she tell you she was going to the party?"

Marian's eyes flick to the shelf of photos, her gaze landing on one of Brad before jittering away. "Clarissa doesn't go to parties," she says.

"What about Brad?" Cam asks.

Mrs. Campbell is silent again. Cam wonders if she's drugged with some kind of mom pill. Xanax? Valium?

And then—there is no other way Cam can describe it—her face cracks open, the eerie, placid mask splitting to reveal sheer, unadulterated hatred.

"You ask him," she snarls. "You ask him where she is. Mark my words, *he knows where our Clarissa is! He knows!*" The last words come out as a shriek.

Quick footsteps on the stairs and a man's voice, calling out in concern. "Marian? Marian?"

Mrs. Campbell is sobbing. Cam's face is a study in horror. Blair's pretty sure she looks equally scared. Clarissa's bedroom door opens all the way with a bang and a silver-haired man runs into the room, gathering up a hysterical Marian.

"What's going on here?" he barks. "Who the hell are you? What have you done to my wife?"

Cam's mouth is literally hanging open. Blair manages to rally. "Mr. Campbell? I'm so sorry, we were just talking—we're doing a school project on Clarissa and—"

At the sound of his daughter's name, Mr. Campbell stops short. "Wait here," he says curtly, ushering his still-weeping wife from the room. Blair and Cam exchange wide-eyed glances. Should they run?

They hear a door open and close, muffled voices. After a few minutes Mr. Campbell returns. He looks exhausted in a way Cam's never seen in an adult before, as if he's weathered decades of sleepless nights.

"She invited you here, didn't she?" he asks.

"Yes," Blair says, looking at Cam again. Mr. Campbell runs a hand through his short silver hair. He's recognizable as the man in the pictures downstairs, but he looks as though he's aged a hundred years instead of twenty.

"I'm sorry," he says. "My wife isn't well. I apologize for the confusion, but I'm going to have to ask you to leave now."

"Can we talk to you about—" Cam begins, but the expression on his face is enough to silence even her.

"No," he says. "You can't. Please don't come here again."

AFTER THE CLOSED-UP, artificially sweetened air of the Campbells' house, the familiar brotherly stink of Blair's car is a relief. Blair drives to the edge of the Campbells' development, pulls over.

"Your hands are shaking," Cam says. Cam's paler than normal and her forehead is sheened with nervous sweat, but Blair decides not to point that out.

"Cam, that was messed up," Blair says. "Did you see her face? When she started screaming?"

"Like a horror movie," Cam says. "She didn't ask us a single question about what we're doing, did you notice? It's like that's her whole life. Sitting around that house waiting for people to come talk to her about Clarissa."

"She thinks Clarissa's coming back," Blair says.

"Maybe she is."

"Not like that," Blair says with a shudder. "She's in her thirties now. She's not going to move back into that bedroom."

"Present tense," Cam says. "You're doing it too." Cam stares out the window at the golf course, where an old white man is yelling at someone driving a little cart.

"Cam?" Blair asks.

"Yeah?"

"Should we be doing this?"

"Doing what?"

"This." Blair waves a hand vaguely, encompassing the Campbells, the past, all of Oreville. "The podcast."

"We might find her," Cam says. "We could give them closure."

"Or a nervous breakdown. What do you think will happen

to Marian if she finds out Clarissa's dead? What if"—Blair's not sure how to say it—"somebody did something, like, bad? What if somebody—you know—hurt her?"

"She might be alive," Cam says. "We owe it to her parents to find out the truth."

"What do you mean, we owe it to her parents? I thought this was for our college applications."

Cam won't look at her.

Whatever. She's in this with Cam now whether she likes it or not. Whatever this is.

"She thinks Brad knows where Clarissa is," Cam says.

"Should we go talk to him next?"

Cam meets Blair's eyes at that *we,* gratitude flashing across her face.

She thought I was going to bail on her, Blair thinks. The truth is, Blair's tempted. She never wants to see anything like Mrs. Campbell's horrifying breakdown again.

But Cam's fever is catching. And what if she's right? What if they do find Clarissa, when nobody else could?

"I think we should talk to Mr. Park before we do anything else," Cam says. "I want to know why he didn't tell us he was the reporter following Clarissa's story. Maybe he knows something that didn't make it into the news."

Blair starts the car again. "When? I have track."

"Tomorrow," Cam says. "I'll talk to him after class myself."

———

CAM LINGERS AFTER class as everyone else packs up their bags and shuffles out the door. Blair gives her a wave and a thumbs-up, mouths *See you after practice.* Sophie takes a long time to leave, as if she wants to say something, but Cam resolutely ignores her until she walks out of the room trailing a faint whiff of the Eiffel Tower.

Mr. Park, shuffling papers at his desk, looks up.

"Can I help you, Cameron?" he asks dryly.

Technically, Cam is aware, this is an ambush. But she is not above guerrilla warfare in service of a higher cause.

"I was hoping to interview you for our podcast," she says in a voice sweet as Starburst. "Since you know *so much* about the case."

Mr. Park gives her A Look, but Cam can do Who, Me? with the best of them. He sighs, settles in his chair, takes off his glasses, polishes them on his sweater, examines them for smudges, sighs again, puts them back on, squints at Cam.

"Let's hear what you've got so far first," he says.

"Why?"

"Humor an old man."

Mr. Park is silent as the first episode of *Missing Clarissa* plays. Cam scrutinizes his face. When the podcast ends, he looks at her over his glasses.

"Did you record this in a bathroom?"

"What? No," Cam says. "Why didn't you tell us you were the reporter covering the case?"

"You might want to do some research on recording quality. Catchy name, though."

"Is that a yes or a no?"

"Yes what, Cameron?"

"'Yes, Cameron, I will talk to you for your podcast, a project which I myself assigned, and upon which your final grade for your most beloved class depends.'"

"You chose the project," Mr. Park says mildly.

"You assigned it."

"I assigned *a* project. I did not assign *this* one."

Cam waits, phone in hand. Mr. Park sighs a third time in an ostentatious way, but Cam can see the spark in his eyes.

"Yes," he says.

"Great," says Cam, turning on her phone's recorder. "Tell me everything."

"Cameron."

"What?"

"Have you looked up obtaining consent for a recorded interview? Have you listened to nothing I have said in class for the last three years?"

Now it's Cam's turn to sigh dramatically. "I will be recording our conversation," she says. "Do I have your consent?"

Mr. Park *tut-tut*s at her. "And?"

"For the record, can you confirm your name and that you consent to this recording?"

Mr. Park nods.

"Let the record show that Mr. Park is nodding," Cam says, grinning at him. "Can you confirm verbally, for the record? Like, out loud? Can I ask you a real question now?"

"Thomas Park, for the record, confirming consent," Mr. Park says, grinning back. "Ask away."

"You were the *Oreville Examiner* reporter covering Clarissa Campbell's disappearance in 1999," Cam says.

"Is that a question?"

"Well, you were."

"Yes," says Mr. Park. "I was."

"Can you tell me what happened the night she went missing?"

"I wasn't there," Mr. Park says.

"Can you describe the reported version?" Cam asks. He's going to make her work for it. She doesn't mind. It makes her feel like he's taking her seriously.

Mr. Park steeples his fingers and settles his chin on his knuckles. "On the night of August fourteenth, 1999," he says, sounding like he's reading from a book, "seventeen-year-old Clarissa Campbell disappeared from a party in rural Hoquiam County outside of Oreville, Washington. Campbell had just graduated and, according to her friends and her boyfriend, Brad Bennett, was planning on moving to Seattle with said boyfriend in the fall. Around a hundred people were in the woods that night—mostly high school students, but a few people in their early twenties as well. A concrete timeline was difficult to establish. Most of the attendees were intoxicated, and the location was outdoors and remote. The last person who confirmed seeing Clarissa was a sophomore from Oreville High who thought she saw Clarissa crying in the woods around one or two a.m."

"Crying?" Cam asks. That wasn't in *People*.

"If anyone knew what she was upset about, they didn't admit to it. The sophomore wasn't sure that Clarissa was crying, only that it was her."

"Was there evidence of foul play at the scene?"

Mr. Park squints at her. "Have you been watching television?"

"Irene likes that one show with the forensic anthropologist who solves murders," Cam says.

"Mm," says Mr. Park. "Not as such, if you mean something like a telltale bloodied garment. For all intents and purposes, Clarissa vanished into thin air. As you may have surmised, there were three possible explanations for her disappearance. First, that she ran away of her own volition. Second, that she had hurt herself or gotten lost and was incapable of reaching help. And third, that someone killed or abducted her. Her parents called the police at three thirty p.m. on the Sunday after the party, saying that their daughter had not come home—"

"Why so late?" Cam interrupts. "Why not that morning?"

"Clarissa often told her parents that she was spending the night at a friend's on Fridays and Saturdays. They were accustomed to her coming home later in the morning the next day."

"Was she?"

"That depends on how you define 'friend,'" Mr. Park says. "Although she did often stay over at her best friend's house."

"Jenny Alexander?"

"Yes."

Cam looks at her notes. "So the Campbells called the police on Sunday. Then what?"

"The police told the Campbells not to worry."

"They did?"

"She was almost eighteen. It was the middle of the summer. They said she must be with friends or had gone off somewhere on her own. The Campbells protested, but to no avail. It took them until Tuesday to convince the police to take the disappearance seriously."

"Three days?" Cam says in disbelief. "The cops ignored her disappearance for three days?"

"It turned out to be rather embarrassing for them, in the end," Mr. Park agrees. "Oreville is a small town. No one would say anything to me directly, but I got the impression that Clarissa had a bit of a reputation. The police knew who she was already. She'd never been charged with anything, but she liked to get into trouble. Pranks, minor vandalism, that kind of thing."

Cam thinks of the endless soft-focus media coverage of Clarissa, her pink bedroom, her robot mother.

"What happened after the police got involved?"

"The police worked with the community to organize search parties. There was a lot of interest, even before the story went national."

"Clarissa was beautiful."

"Yes, she was," Mr. Park says. "Anyway, high schoolers regularly partied on the site where she went missing, which was more or less in the middle of hundreds of acres of managed timberland out in the county. From what I understand"—he gives Cam a sharp look—"they still do."

"I am the last person you want to ask about keg parties in the county," Cam says with distaste.

Mr. Park concedes this point with a nod. "By Wednesday evening, the search parties had covered an area of several square miles without finding any sign of Clarissa. At that time, the police were ready to rule out the possibility that she had been hurt or gotten lost."

"Why? She could have gone more than a mile if she was lost. Or maybe she was lying in a ravine somewhere."

"It's possible, but it wasn't that likely. The searchers were using dogs. We're talking about a teenager wandering around in heavily logged woods, not some backpacker off-trail in old-growth wilderness."

"That's when they started thinking she had been murdered?"

"I'm sure they thought that was a significant possibility as soon as they took the disappearance seriously. But they began looking pretty hard at Brad. The odds of a stranger being involved were virtually nonexistent. Someone would've had to drive down four miles of private logging roads in the middle of the night on a Saturday to find that party. Again, not impossible, but it's a stretch."

"Why Brad?"

"It's usually the boyfriend or the husband," Mr. Park says.

"It is?" Cam asks.

"Statistically, yes. And several witnesses saw Brad and Clarissa arguing at the party, although the police could never pin down what time the fight happened or how much time elapsed between the fight and when Brad went home. Clarissa was popular, beloved by her friends, her parents, her teachers—you name it. Nobody had a reason to hurt her. Her fight with Brad was the only thing the police came up with."

"What was the fight about?"

"He insisted he was too drunk at the time to remember."

"The police believed him?"

"No, but he stuck to that story."

"Why didn't he get arrested?"

"No body," Mr. Park says succinctly. "No body, no murder. And the police couldn't establish anything longer than a forty-five-minute or so interval where Brad was completely unaccounted for."

"Forty-five minutes is plenty of time to kill someone."

"Sure," Mr. Park says. "But that leaves him in the middle of a crowded party with a body. He hardly had time to bury her. There was no possible way he could have carried her outside the search radius, hidden her body somewhere, and gotten back to the party in under an hour. And if he did somehow manage to do all that, it's hard to imagine he could pull it off with no one seeing him."

"He could've driven her somewhere."

"His truck was blocked in by other cars until the time he left the party."

"He could've planned it in advance. What if he borrowed someone else's car?"

"Aha!" Mr. Park's eyes glitter. *He's enjoying this,* Cam thinks. "An excellent point. He could have. But if he'd planned her murder in advance, why get in a fight with Clarissa at the party? If the fight had been serious enough to lead to her death, he couldn't have hidden her body. If he'd planned the murder, he'd have to be a fool to fight with her in front of other people the night he killed her. And there was no history of abuse, nothing to suggest he would hurt Clarissa. By all accounts, he adored her."

"He could have had a secret dark side," Cam argues. "People are always going on about killers having secret dark sides."

"Ah, yes, the Dr. Jekyll theory of investigative reporting," Mr. Park says.

"Well, that's what they say," Cam says. "You can never tell. It's always the nice quiet guy."

"I'm not sure anyone would've described Brad as either nice or quiet."

"I thought you said he was nice to Clarissa."

"I said people said he adored her."

"Do you think he killed her?"

"I thought the police gave up pretty quickly."

"What do you mean?" Cam asks. "Clarissa was all over the news."

"Clarissa was, yes," says Mr. Park. "That doesn't mean the police were doing their jobs."

"How do you remember all this stuff so well?" Cam asks.

"Because I got fired for reporting it."

"You got *fired*? For writing about Clarissa?"

"I was a bit of a firebrand," Mr. Park says placidly. "Wrote an editorial about the extent to which I thought the police had bungled the case. I wasn't subtle. But the *Examiner* is a small-town paper. I was the only reporter on staff who wasn't white, and at the time I was the only openly gay employee of the paper in its entire history. Then I had to go and antagonize the police department? They told me they were downsizing, but I knew why they were firing me."

"Couldn't you sue them or something?" Cam is outraged on Mr. Park's behalf.

"In 1999? In rural Washington? Not a chance. Luckily, the high school had an opening for a journalism teacher."

"Why didn't you leave Oreville? I mean, go work at a paper in a real city or something?"

"My husband—he wasn't my husband then; it wasn't legal for us to get married until 2012—has his family and his business in town. I love this area. It's quiet, and it's next door to some of the most beautiful forests in the world. We're on the Salish Sea. I can walk outside and look at the water. I'm not a big-city person, and I don't have the temperament of a big-city reporter. And I find that I like teaching high school. One meets the most intriguing young people."

Cam digests this extraordinary series of revelations. "What about a serial killer? Do you think a serial killer murdered her?"

"What on earth gave you that idea?"

"Someone on the internet thinks it's that one guy. Ted Bundy."

Mr. Park laughs through his nose. "Ted Bundy was executed when Clarissa was in middle school."

"Serial killers on TV always have a diabolical master plan and disciples to carry out their depraved wishes after they're captured," Cam says, to see what Mr. Park will do. He doesn't fall for the bait.

"No, Cameron, I do not think a serial killer's depraved apprentice murdered Clarissa. Whatever you see on television, most serial killers aren't very intelligent, including Ted Bundy. They just pick victims other people see as disposable."

"People like stories about serial killers," Cam says, thinking of *The Big Book of Serial Killers*.

"Do *you* think a serial killer murdered Clarissa?" Mr. Park asks.

"I guess it would make our podcast more popular if one did. It's like the most interesting thing a girl can do is die in a gross way."

"Would you prefer a popular podcast or the truth?"

"The truth!" Cam says indignantly. "But I want to make something people care about. Why does anybody make anything? You didn't write newspaper articles hoping nobody would read them, right? But I guess . . ." Cam trails off. "It would be cool if we found her somewhere. Like if she was happy and laughing at us."

"Do you think Clarissa is alive?"

"We went to interview her mom yesterday after school," Cam says, dodging the question.

"How did that go?"

"It was awful. Her mom is so messed up. And her dad was

so angry with us, but he seemed so sad too. Clarissa would have to be sort of a horrible person to let her family suffer like that."

"So it's better if she isn't alive after all?"

"No!" Cam says, frustrated. "Maybe there's no good ending for this story."

Mr. Park leans back in his chair. "Some questions don't have pretty answers, Cameron. Clarissa might be a funny story to you, but real people cared about her, and real people had their lives torn apart by her disappearance. Don't forget that."

"She's not a funny story to us," Cam says. Mr. Park gives her a sharp look. "Anymore," Cam says. "Do you think the case would have gotten so big if she had been somebody else? Somebody less pretty?"

"Honestly?"

"Honestly."

"No," Mr. Park says. "I don't."

"Would you have cared?"

"Would *you* have, Cameron?"

"Yes," Cam says. Mr. Park looks at her. "Maybe not," she admits.

"I wouldn't have gotten paid to write about her if she wasn't a pretty white girl, let's put it that way," Mr. Park says.

"You want to know where she is too."

"I do."

"What do you think happened to her?"

"I have no idea. I stopped asking questions after I got fired from the paper," Mr. Park says. "But something interesting happened the year after she disappeared. Aaron Liechty, the detective in charge of the case, ran for sheriff against the incumbent. It was a tight race, but his campaign was well funded and he won by the skin of his teeth. He's been the sheriff ever since."

"Well funded by who?" Cam asks.

Mr. Park yawns and checks his watch. "Whom. I believe it's time for me to go home."

"Mr. Park! Well funded by *whom*?"

"You're the intrepid reporter, Cameron Muñoz," Mr. Park says. "Do some intrepid reporting."

———

JAMES DOESN'T USUALLY wait around for Blair if they don't have plans, which is why she's surprised to see him leaning against her car scrolling through videos on his phone after track.

Even after two years, she prefers he see only her made-up self, polished and carefully presented. She's self-conscious about her just-washed hair up in a ponytail, her bare face, her faded old sweats. She doesn't like him to come to her track and cross-country meets. Not that he often does. Which is the right order of things. Track is her own meaningless hobby, and James's basketball stardom is hers to cheer from the sidelines, the way a good girlfriend should.

"Au naturel," James says, giving her a perfunctory kiss. "Looks different."

Blair runs her hands down her thighs, nervous. "I didn't think I was going to see you."

"Why not? Too busy with Cam?"

His tone is familiar, casual and cutting, a tenor that stiffens Blair's spine and spikes her heartbeat with anxiety. He's in a bad mood. He doesn't like to be kept waiting, even when she doesn't know she's late.

"I thought you had practice."

"Out early. What's wrong? Don't I get to see my girl?"

He's wearing a hangdog face that doesn't fool her for a second. She's a master diviner of his moods, can read the sulk beneath the veneer of injury. He's feeling neglected. It's her fault, she knows. All this time with Cam.

"I'm so sorry, I know I've been busy—" she begins, but she's interrupted by a familiar shout from across the parking lot. She flinches. Cam's timing is always—well, it's always Cam. Which, today, is bad.

James sees Cam at the same time she does, hurtling toward them with her phone held aloft.

"Sorry, I didn't know you had better things to do," James says. "I thought we could get pizza and watch a movie, but I guess not."

"It's not—" Blair tries again, helpless, but here's Cam, crashing between them like a demented meteor.

"Sorry, James!" Cam elbows him aside. "I need her."

"Cam, I have to—"

James cuts Blair off. "Don't let me get between you," he says. "I'm sure you have better things to do than spend time with your boyfriend, Blair. I'll call you later."

He walks off, over her protest. Cam babbles excitedly, waving her phone in Blair's face. Between the two of them, Blair thinks ruefully, she'll never finish a sentence in her life.

Why do they both have to be impossible? Why can't she love two people slightly better suited to harmony?

"You aren't listening to me," Cam says.

"What?"

"I *said*, we have to figure out who bankrolled his *campaign*."

"Whose campaign?" Blair's still befuddled by the fracas, trying to think of a way to patch things up with James before this turns into a real fight. Which she'll lose.

"The sheriff!" Cam shouts. "Because the police didn't ask enough questions and maybe somebody influenced them and then Mr. Park got fired! What planet are you on right now? Have you noticed how Sophie Jenkins smells?"

"*What?*"

"I think there's something wrong with her perfume."

Blair buries her face in her hands, not sure whether to laugh or cry. She thinks of Coach Bell's recommendation for stressful situations: Inhale on a five count, exhale on a five count, repeat.

When she looks up again Cam is silent.

"What," Blair says.

"Also I have to tell you something. But you have to promise not to get mad."

Blair reviews the possibilities. Cam poisoned James's Gatorade. Cam slashed James's tires. Cam is building a spaceship in her backyard with which to launch James into the sun. "No promises," she says.

Cam won't quite meet her eyes. "I put the podcast online," she says.

"You did *what?*"

"It's good!" Cam protests. "Mr. Park said so. I played it for him, because he—"

And now, at last, Blair is furious. Cam with her bad timing, her exhausting anti-James campaign, her funny and understanding mother she doesn't appreciate, her rocket-scientist brain she takes for granted: All of this, Blair can manage. But Cameron Muñoz, Relentless Trespasser of Boundaries, is too much. Not today.

"I told you not to! You promised!"

"But it's good, B!"

"No, it's not!" Blair shouts. "And that doesn't matter!" Whether Cam deserves it or not—okay, she deserves it—it feels so good to yell, Blair does it again. "What the *hell*, Cameron! You can't go around doing whatever you want without thinking about anybody else!"

"But I was thinking about you!"

"You promised me!" Across the parking lot, a pack of dirtbag sophomores passing around a single contraband cigarette is watching the fight with their mouths open. "I told you not to post it!"

"You told me to cut your part out."

"It's the same thing!"

"No, it isn't! Anyway, you're wrong!"

"You think you're always right!" Blair shouts.

"Because I *am* always right!" Cam bellows.

This is so patently absurd that under any other circumstances Blair would laugh. But she is tired, and angry, and now James is mad at her, and it's Cam's fault, and she's horrified by the thought of anyone listening to her babble on about forests and Clarissa, and why can't Cam back down for once anyway?

"Why do you always have to do things your way?" Blair fumbles for her car keys. "Give me a break, Cam! I told you I didn't want that stuff online!"

"But it's good, B," Cam says in a normal tone of voice. "I swear. It's good."

"No, it's not!" To her utter mortification, Blair bursts into tears. She yanks open the driver's side door, hurls herself into the car, starts the engine.

"B—" Cam begins. Blair slams the door on the rest of the sentence and drives off as violently as is possible in a 2012 baby blue Ford Focus.

Cam rubs her forehead with one hand. First Sophie at the library, now this. She's a one-person master class in how to lose friends and alienate people. Probably she should've asked Blair before she uploaded the podcast, but Blair would have told her no. And then what? There would be no podcast.

What else was she supposed to do?

She trudges back toward the school, her heart heavy. Maybe Irene and Mr. Park are right. This wretched podcast is already more trouble than it's worth.

MOMENTS AFTER HER dramatic exit, Blair's vision is so blurry with tears that she pulls up to a McDonald's, drops her head on the steering wheel, and lets herself sob it out, hoping no one in the drive-through line is someone she knows.

Teen Podcasting Failure Caught Crying Like Baby in Area Fast-Food Franchise Parking Lot, she thinks. What is wrong with her? Cam is infuriating, sure, but that's nothing new. James is moody and jealous of Cam, but she's used to that too. And they're both more than worth the trouble when things are good.

So why is she so upset?

She already knows the answer, deep in her secret heart, though she'd never admit it to either one of her best-beloveds. She can barely admit it to herself.

She's terrified. Terrified of her own voice, terrified of how stupid she must sound, terrified that someone will *listen* to Cam's heinous brainchild and realize what an absolute, categorical dimwit Blair Johnson is, Blair Johnson who has never done or said or been anything interesting in all the sixteen years of her life.

Blair Johnson the Boring. Blair Johnson the Dull. Blair Johnson, the delusional fool who—more than she wants James to love her unconditionally, more than she wants Cam to calm down, more than she wants her parents to say something supportive and not vaguely patronizing for once, more than she wants good grades and a fancy college, more than she wants anything else in the entire vast map of the charted universe—

—wants to be a writer.

Blair Johnson wants to be a writer.

Blair Johnson wants to be a *good* writer.

A great writer.

She scrubs her teary eyes with her knuckles, laughing at herself.

Right. Blair Johnson, secret creative genius. As if. More like Blair Johnson, unsecret cretin. She knows what she is: nobody special. Nobody with anything to say worth reading, that's for sure.

And she knows what will happen if she confesses the biggest secret of her tiny life. She'll get laughed out of town. By her parents, by her boyfriend, and no doubt by her best friend, who, although unfailingly supportive, has never been put to the real test of facing Blair's darkest, most precious dream.

And she'll deserve their mockery.

Blair Johnson knows what good writing reads like, and she knows it's nothing like what she does. Nothing she'll ever be capable of, not in a thousand million lifetimes of writing a thousand million words. She's below average at best, and that's giving herself the benefit of the doubt.

No matter how many nights she's spent scribbling in her journal, no matter how many crappy short stories she's tapped out in secret on her dad's old laptop and then deleted in a rush of shame, she'll never be good. She's never had the guts to take a writing class. Letting Cam badger her into Journo this year was the bravest thing she's done. And if she had any promise whatsoever, surely Mr. Park would have told her. Surely *someone* would have said *something*.

(The fact that Blair has never shown anyone else a single word she's written escapes her here.)

How dare Cam upload what doesn't even count as a first draft? How dare she lie and tell Blair it was good? Cam doesn't mean to be cruel. She has no idea what kind of terrible hope lives in Blair's heart. She'd never guess.

No one would. That's the point. The idea of Blair as a writer is more ridiculous than an astronaut Blair or a rock-star Blair or Blair as President of the United States.

Blair cycles through her breathing exercise until her tears dry and she can manage a steady count to ten. It's not Cam's fault Blair's an idiot, she decides. The stuff with James is Cam's fault, sure, but Cam can't help herself. She has no idea how belligerent she is, or how impossible normal people—well, mostly boring small-town people, but also James—find her. Even if she did, it wouldn't occur to her to care.

Blair finds her phone, checks for messages. Nothing from James, but seventeen from Cam: variations on Are you okay? What did I say? and, incredibly enough, Whatever I did I'm really sorry!!!!!!!!!!!!!!

Cam must've poisoned her own Gatorade. Blair has never known her to apologize.

Cam picks up on the first ring.

"Hi."

"Hi," says Blair.

There is a silence.

"Want to come over?" Cam asks.

This is another thing Blair loves about Cam: She is capable of dismissing all conflict in the space of a sentence, letting whole mountains of the unsaid slide past.

"Sure," Blair says. She should be chasing after James, she knows. Cam will always be there. James, maybe not so much.

But today she's surprising herself. James can dangle for a bit. Maybe James shouldn't be so sure of her all the time.

"Cool," Cam says. "See you in a few?"

"Yeah. Cam?"

"Yeah?"

"Did you mean it?"

"Did I mean what?"

"About the podcast? About what I wrote being—good?"

"Yeah, dummy," Cam says, affronted anyone would question her judgment.

"Okay," says Blair. "See you soon." When she hangs up, she's smiling.

"All right, Clarissa," she says to the rearview mirror. "Here we come."

She starts the car and heads for Cam's.

MARIAN

Clarissa never gave us a moment of trouble as a baby. What other parent can say such a thing? I used to wake late in the morning—she slept through the night, every night, I don't think we had any idea how lucky we were—and go in to look at her in her crib, the miracle of her, her wee rump in the air and her head against the crib bumper, fast asleep—this perfect girl, ours. The answer to all our prayers.

We wanted more children. Truth be told, I wanted a whole passel of them! I'd had this idea since I was a young girl, that God would bless me with a whole family. Two boys and two girls, maybe twins—I'm not ashamed to admit I'd dress them in matching outfits their whole lives, and take such pride in the fact that only their father and I could know which one of ours was which. I'm not from here, you know. I grew up in heartland country, and I had a whole army of brothers and sisters myself. The most wonderful upbringing. I wanted that so badly for her, to know she was part of something bigger than she was, a real family. Big turkey at Thanksgiving and a tree for Christmas with all the trimmings. I wanted her to have a sense of tradition. Our family, going back all the way to the Mayflower, celebrating the same things in the same way.

Well, my grandparents didn't come over on the Mayflower. They came through Ellis Island. But you know what I mean. Tradition. What my own mother wanted for me.

But the Lord works in His own ways, and He only gave us Clarissa. And what a blessing she was. She obeyed us, everything we said, she never spoke back—well, as a child. I suppose it's normal enough for girls to find their own minds when the change comes, and she did talk back a bit then. When she was thirteen, fourteen—oh, that was a hard time, I can't speak a falsehood. But she was still so beautiful. Our Clarissa.

Everybody loved her as much as we did. Everywhere she went. No one could say no to her. The cashier at the grocery store used to hold her favorite candy behind the register—she could have picked it off the shelf, but she loved their routine. We'd go through the checkout, and he'd say, "Anything else, Mrs. Campbell?" And she'd say, "Don't you have something special for me?" Oh, how we laughed! She was about seven then. Our perfect angel. You would've had to look all over the entire world to find a girl as beautiful as Clarissa.

She was such a wonderful baby. So perfect and so good. We adored her. Of course we adored her. With a little girl like that, how could you do anything else?

THE
FRIENDS

CAM has gotten nowhere with her campaign finance research. She explains her undertaking to Blair as she clicks through website after website.

"He wouldn't tell you himself?" Blair asks.

Cam makes an outraged noise. "These county websites are in, like, Geocities. No, he wouldn't tell me who it was. And he wouldn't tell me how he found out. Do you have to go around town and ask people personally if they made a political donation in the county sheriff election twenty years ago?"

Blair is not sure if this question is meant to be rhetorical. "That's supposed to be public information, right? Aren't the donation records online?"

"They're not online that far back for Hoquiam County," Cam says. She types something rapidly into a form. "If we lived in a real city I bet they would be. I'm gonna try emailing County Records."

"You could torture Mr. Park for more information," Blair says.

Cam looks thoughtful, as if she is seriously considering this. "That's not a bad idea. I bet he can hold out against a lot, though."

Which leaves them for now with Brad Bennett, Jenny Alexander, and Allen Dawson, Parts Unknown.

"I think we should hold off on talking to Brad, since he was the main suspect," Blair says.

"For dramatic pacing?"

"So we don't blow the interview," Blair says. "Right now, we don't know what to ask him."

"Fine," Cam mutters.

An internet search turns up hundreds of Jenny Alexanders, and she's not in Irene's phone book. "She could've gotten married and changed her name," Blair points out. "We don't know if we're searching for the right person."

"Kathleen Dawson's in the phone book," Cam says. "We could ask her where Allen is."

"She's not going to give us her son's phone number," Blair says.

"She will if you talk to her," Cam says, already dialing. "You're good at talking to little old ladies."

"Why, thank you, Cam," Blair says.

"You're welcome," Cam says seriously.

Someone picks up Kathleen Dawson's phone almost immediately, but the voice is a man's. "Hello?"

"Could I speak with Mrs. Dawson?"

"I'm afraid she can't come to the phone at the moment. May I take a message?"

"I'm trying to reach her son, Allen. I was hoping she could tell me how to get in touch with him."

"What is this regarding?"

"My friend and I are students at Oreville High. We're working on a project for school and wanted to ask him a few questions. It's nothing urgent."

Cam shakes her head violently, mouthing *It is urgent!* Blair smiles.

"What is the school project?"

"We're making a podcast about Clarissa Campbell, the cheerleader who disappeared in 1999, for our journalism class. We've spoken to her mother already, and she mentioned that Clarissa was good friends with Allen. Do you know how we can reach him?"

"You interviewed Marian?"

"She said Allen could tell us more about what Clarissa was like."

A long pause. Then: "Actually, this is Allen. I suppose I can answer some questions over the phone."

Cam shakes her head again. *NO,* she mouths.

"Would it be at all possible to talk to you in person, Mr. Dawson?" Blair asks sweetly, rolling her eyes at Cam. *I know,* she mouths back. *Calm down.*

"I'm not sure how I can help you."

"We're trying to get a sense of Clarissa as a person. Talking to her friends and that sort of thing," Blair explains.

"I suppose I could make some time for an in-person appointment," he says cautiously. His phone manner is oddly formal. Blair imagines a pinched little man with an office job. An accountant, maybe. Someone who would wear a button-down shirt to work even if he didn't have to.

As it turns out, she's not far off. The white man who answers the door at Kathleen Dawson's house is not as diminutive as she imagined, but he's pinched-looking and spindly. He's wearing round glasses with silver frames, and his graying hair is carefully combed over a thinning spot on his head. He is, Blair notes triumphantly, wearing a drab button-down, although it's tucked into faded jeans.

"Good afternoon, girls," he says. His voice is as thin as he is. "Please do come in." Cam's already craning her neck, trying to see around him.

The house reminds Blair of her grandmother's. The decor is cozy and dated, like the set from a 1980s sitcom. Lots of fussy decorative plates in china cabinets and crocheted sofa accoutrements. A giant Pegasus-shaped porcelain lamp sits on an end table. Allen catches Blair's surprised look and smiles. "My mother's," he says, as if that were unclear.

Cam and Blair introduce themselves, and Allen offers them a seat on an overstuffed sofa emblazoned with lurid roses. They sit.

"I didn't know you still lived in Oreville," Cam says.

"I don't," Allen replies. "Well, I didn't. I moved back when my mother's MS progressed to where she needed help."

"Do we have guests, dear?" A bright-eyed, white-haired white woman wheels herself in using a wheelchair. Her lined features are a match for Allen's, but unlike her son, she seems to favor bright colors. She's wearing a purple sweater and turquoise leggings that match a heavy turquoise pendant around her neck. Her sneakers are pink, and her socks are a festive yellow.

"These girls are here to ask some questions about Clarissa for a school project," Allen says.

"Clarissa Campbell? That poor girl." Mrs. Dawson makes a tutting noise and shakes her head. "Why would two nice young ladies like you want to go around asking questions about that? My poor father would roll over in his grave if I did such a thing, may he rest in peace."

"They let us out of the house now," Cam says.

Mrs. Dawson laughs. "Aren't you cheeky."

"The girls are making a podcast about Clarissa's disappearance," Allen says. "Like a radio show, Mother."

"Radio!" exclaims Mrs. Dawson. "Imagine that! Young people still listening to the radio!"

"It's not like—" Cam begins. Blair steps on her foot, and she shuts up.

"Do you think you can find out what happened to her? After all this time?" Allen asks.

"We don't know," Blair says. "But we can try."

"Like Nancy Drew," Mrs. Dawson says.

"We are not anything like—" Cam starts, looks down at Blair's twitching foot, and stops.

"Like Nancy Drew," Blair says.

"I don't think I'll be much help," Allen says. "It was such a long time ago. I told the police everything I knew, and I wasn't much help to begin with."

"Mrs. Campbell said you were close."

"Clarissa was friendly with everyone. It was her way. She was a wonderful person. So kind and so beautiful. I suppose she was close with a lot of people. But she was popular, and I— Let's say we traveled in different circles."

"Allen didn't travel in any circles," Mrs. Dawson says. Allen looks at her with resignation.

"That's right," he says. Blair can imagine the shy, nerdy teenager Allen must have been. She wonders if he had any real friends at all, and feels sorry for him.

"A late bloomer," Mrs. Dawson says.

"Mrs. Campbell said you were helpful after Clarissa disappeared," Blair says.

Allen smiles. "Did she? That was sweet of her. I pitched in where I could, but lots of other people did too. The whole town came together to support the Campbells. We were all devastated by Clarissa's disappearance."

"Clarissa must have been special to you."

"Clarissa was special to everyone," Allen says.

"Do you remember the night she disappeared?" Cam asks.

"You mean the party?" He shakes his head. "I wasn't there. I don't think I heard she was missing until . . ." He pauses, thinking. "I guess it must have been a few days later, when they were putting the search parties together."

"Allen didn't go to parties," Mrs. Dawson offers. "He was always studious."

Blair remembers Marian Campbell telling them the same thing. *Clarissa doesn't go to parties.* In Allen's case, though, she can imagine it's the truth.

Allen gives Mrs. Dawson a wry smile. "Thanks, Mother," he says.

"Straight As in high school *and* college," Mrs. Dawson adds.

"Not quite," Allen counters.

"An A-minus in Calculus is still an A." They have clearly been over this before.

"I got an A-plus in Calculus," Cam says, unable to help herself.

"You girls are seniors?" Allen asks.

"I took it as a freshman," Cam says.

"Goodness," Allen says.

"My son is a very intelligent young man," Mrs. Dawson says accusingly.

"What did you think of Brad?" Blair asks quickly.

Allen frowns. "Brad and I weren't friends."

"But what was your impression of him?" Cam asks.

"I shouldn't say anything," Allen says. "Not after all this time."

"Tell them what you told the police," Mrs. Dawson says.

"It was years ago, Mother. We were just kids."

"Brad didn't treat Clarissa well," Mrs. Dawson says to Cam.

"Like, he was abusive?" Blair asks, startled. Nothing in the coverage of Clarissa's disappearance had suggested there was evidence Brad had hurt Clarissa before the night she vanished.

"I don't have any proof," Allen says. "Not of that. But he was a bully, honestly. I never knew what Clarissa saw in him. A girl like her, and he was . . . boorish. He always seemed so angry, like he was keeping something dark bottled up inside. There were rumors he'd beaten up a boy in junior high, put him in the hospital. Because the boy was . . . you know."

"I don't know," Cam says.

Allen looks out the window. "Homosexual," he says, as if there's one standing in the yard.

"Brad Bennett was homophobic?" Blair asks.

"It was just a rumor," Allen says.

"Did he hurt anyone else? Other girls?"

"I wouldn't be surprised," Mrs. Dawson says. "A boy with a temper like that. He was probably upset that Clarissa was"—she lowers her voice to a stagey whisper—"promiscuous."

"Mother," Allen says sharply. "She wasn't."

Mrs. Dawson settles back in her wheelchair. "Allen never could see past a pretty face," she says. "But that girl wasn't the saint everybody made her out to be, you mark my words. They never are."

"My mother watches a lot of television," Allen says.

"Documentaries," Mrs. Dawson corrects.

"True crime," Allen says.

"Who besides Brad might have wanted to hurt Clarissa?" Cam asks.

"No one," Allen says.

"What did you do when you found out she was missing?" Blair asks.

"I was heartbroken," Allen says. "I know it's stupid, but I kept thinking about that party. If I'd been there, maybe I could have . . ."

"Could have what?" Blair prompts.

Allen's face crumples with grief. For a moment, Blair is terrified he'll start crying, which is more middle-aged-man emotion than she knows how to deal with. "I used to imagine I could fight off whoever hurt her," he says. "Whoever took her away from us. God, that was an awful time."

He rallies a bit as he tells them about the reporters descending like a cloud of locusts, the search parties, the posters of Clarissa wallpapering Oreville's downtown. "It was an accident that I ended up helping out the Campbells," he says. "I went over one day to say how sorry I was that she was missing, how we were all so hopeful she'd come back."

"The orange ribbons," Cam says. "Marian said that was you."

"I wanted to find a way to show how much we all cared. Marian sort of latched on to me. Not in a bad way," he adds. "I mean that she needed someone to be around, and I happened to be there. I couldn't abandon them."

Blair can easily imagine him helping out the Campbells of his own volition. He's the kind of person who volunteered to monitor his grade-school class when the teacher had to leave the room for a minute. Not a snitch. Someone who wants to believe in the healing power of order.

"In the end, they stopped talking to the press," Allen continues. "Marian thought it was helping, but Joe hated the attention. After a few months, he won out. Marian was a nice woman. Really nice. The whole thing tore her apart."

"Yeah," Blair says quietly.

"How was she?" Allen asks. "When you talked to her?"

"She still misses Clarissa a lot," Blair says neutrally.

"That poor woman," Mrs. Dawson says with relish.

"And who else are you talking to?" Allen asks.

"We haven't decided yet," Cam says.

"Do you have a theory of what happened?"

"Not yet," Blair says. "Do you?"

Allen shakes his head. "I can't imagine. Do you think you'll uncover something new?"

"I hope so," Cam says.

"I'd love to hear how you progress," Allen says. "We all want so badly to know what happened to her."

"You'll have to listen to the podcast," Cam says.

"Yes," Allen says. "I suppose I will."

"He doesn't get out much," Mrs. Dawson says. "Never did."

"*Mother*," Allen says. "I think it's time for your nap. Excuse me for a moment. I'll get her settled, and then we can say goodbye."

Cam turns off her phone recorder, recognizing that the interview is over. Allen wheels his mother out of the room over her feeble protests.

Cam gnaws meditatively on the end of her pen. "Maybe Brad did kill her," she says. "We have to talk to him. But you're right. I think we should wait until we have more proof."

"Any proof," Blair says.

"More than a rumor," Cam agrees. "At least we have more background for the podcast. What the town was like after Clarissa went missing."

"We can't say anything about Brad yet," Blair says. "We can't confirm that he beat up that kid."

"How can we prove that? Old school records? We don't know the kid's name."

"Maybe someone else who went to high school with Clarissa."

Brad violent??? Cam writes. *Find kid. Find proof.* If Brad Bennett did go around beating people up, the police must've found out. But maybe people were scared enough to protect his secret. If he was hurting Clarissa, someone had to have known. Even if they've kept their mouth shut this whole time.

Allen is gone a long time. Cam riffles through the end table drawers until Blair hisses at her to stop. "It's just old bills and rubber bands anyway," Cam says, wounded.

"Sorry about that," Allen says when he returns at last. "She can be a bit feisty."

"How long have you been back?" Blair asks.

"A few months. It's supposed to be a temporary thing, but MS is progressive. She's not going to get better. She's still sharp, but she needs a lot of help. I can't bear the thought of putting her in a nursing home."

"Sharp is one word for it," Blair says.

Allen smiles at her ruefully. It transforms his whole face. He'll never be handsome, but when he smiles, he looks like someone who could have a bigger life if he wanted it. "I can't leave her alone," he says.

Cam tries to imagine herself stuck in a house with an ailing Irene for the foreseeable future. The thought is appalling. And she actually likes Irene. Most of the time. "That's nice of you," she says.

"She's my mother," Allen says. "My sister lives in Japan, and she has a family. She helps as much as she can, but I don't have any children, and it wasn't that difficult for me to come home. My work let me go remote."

"What do you do?" Blair asks politely, thinking: *Accountant*.

"R&D for a security tech start-up," he says. He laughs at her expression, not unkindly. "It's more interesting than it sounds. You're going to talk to Brad?"

"Yes," Blair says.

"You should be careful," he says.

"You think he's dangerous?" Cam asks.

"I think he doesn't like questions," Allen says.

———

"MAYBE WE SHOULD talk to the sheriff," Blair says the next day after Journalism. Cam, who's rooting around in her locker, emerges in a flurry of papers.

"Oh," she says in dismay, watching them cascade to the floor. "Do you think he'll tell us who funded his campaign?" She shovels papers back in her locker in the same precarious state of entropy that caused their explosion in the first place.

"Not if the money was for something shady," Blair says. "But we could ask him about the investigation. We can try and find someone who was on the cheer squad with her too."

Cam slams her locker door. "Mr. Park said Liechty ran for sheriff a year after Clarissa disappeared. I guess the money could be a coincidence."

"That's a big coincidence," Blair says.

"What's a big coincidence?" It's Sophie, who's just come out of class after them. "How's your podcast going?"

"Hi, Sophie," Blair says. Cam makes a strangled noise. She is, Blair notes, turning pink. "It's good, I guess? We're still doing a lot of background. Trying to figure out who to interview next is hard without more answers."

Sophie leans against the locker next to Cam's. "Yeah, that makes sense. A true-crime podcast is a lot to tackle. Especially for such a sensational crime."

Blair looks at Cam, who is either having a medical emergency or has given up human speech. "It's interesting," Blair agrees, "but it's a lot of work. How's your project going?"

"Oof!" Sophie says, tossing up her hands in a fake-dramatic gesture that somehow manages to be both charming and elegant. "So much research and so many possibilities! Right now I can't decide if I should focus exclusively on projects within the Jamestown S'Klallam Tribe or expand to look at collaborative tribal protection of treaty-reserved resource management rights and co-management with colonial-settler institutions. I might've bitten off more than I can chew."

"I doubt that," Blair says. "You seem pretty able to handle anything." *Does Cam need the Heimlich?* she wonders.

"That's so sweet of you to say," Sophie says. She turns her incredible smile on Cam. "So, what's the coincidence?"

Cam's gone from pink to crimson. "No," she squeaks. "I have to—go." She careens away from her locker, nearly taking out a passing goth.

"See you after practice," Blair says to her back.

"Practice walking, I hope," the goth says, sweeping past.

"She's not always like this," Blair says to Sophie apologetically. "She gets distracted."

"She's pretty cute, actually," Sophie says. "For a junior." She directs that smile at Blair and winks. "Good luck with your background stuff. See you tomorrow."

Blair finds Cam waiting by her car after track practice, laden down with another stack of books. "Library?" she asks, unlocking the passenger door.

"I was listening to a podcast for research," Cam says, climbing in with her finds. "This one called *You're Wrong About*."

"What's it about?" Blair asks, unlocking her own door and getting in.

"Things people are wrong about."

"They must have a lot of ground to cover."

"Did you know in the 1980s people thought Satanists were running daycare centers and sacrificing children?"

"I guess people were wrong about that. What are the books? More true crime?"

"No, these are all about dead girls. I mean, fiction." Cam awkwardly spreads her pile across her lap. A variety of distressed-looking white women stare out from dark backgrounds, titles like *All He Asked of Her* and *The Last Mrs. Parker* hovering over their heads in sturdy fluorescent fonts. Cam picks up *You Saw Me First* and reads the back. "This one is about a husband who turns out to be a stalker," Cam says.

"You think Clarissa had a stalker?"

"She probably didn't have a husband. What if she did have a stalker?"

"Her mom didn't say anything, and neither did Allen."

"Maybe she didn't tell anyone. Or maybe someone else knew. Allen didn't seem all that close to her."

"Jenny?"

"We need to find her somehow."

"If someone was threatening her, she might've been too scared to tell anyone."

"If she did tell someone, the papers never found out about it," Cam says. "Maybe the police knew."

"We can try asking the sheriff," Blair says.

"Maybe that's what the money was for," Cam says. "Maybe someone threatened Clarissa, and the sheriff knew about it and covered it up. That's what he got paid off for later. By then, the national media had moved on, so they never found out about the money."

"Maybe," Blair says. "That's a lot of conspiracy for Oreville, but you never know. What was that about with Sophie, by the way?"

"What was what about?"

"Why were you acting so weird?"

Cam stares at her. "Weird how?"

"Never mind," Blair says. "We should figure out a cover story before we call the sheriff. If someone did pay him off, he's not going to want to talk to us about Clarissa."

Cam fiddles with the dials on the broken car stereo. "Do you think Sophie thinks I was weird?"

"I think maybe she thought you were being—yourself," Blair says, as tactfully as she can.

"Myself? Is that bad?"

"Cameron," Blair says. "What is going on? What is wrong with you?"

"Nothing," Cam says, jerking her hand away from the stereo. She's blushing again.

"What should we tell the sheriff's office?" Blair asks.

"About Sophie?"

"About *us,* Cam. When we call to make an appointment? To interview him?"

"Oh," Cam says. "I guess we could tell them the truth."

"That we're a couple of teenagers trying to solve a mystery the police totally botched decades ago and maybe got paid off to cover up?"

"Yeah," Cam says dreamily.

"Cameron Muñoz," Blair says. "Where are you?"

"Here!" Cam says. "Here. Sorry. Here. Cover story."

"We're teenagers," Blair says. "They're already going to think we're airheads. That might be a good start."

"I'm not an airhead," Cam says. "We're not airheads."

"I know that, and you know that, but they don't know that."

"That's rude of them," Cam says.

"Cam, we can use that to our advantage," Blair says patiently. "It worked with Allen. I don't think he would've talked to us if we were adults. I don't think the sheriff will take us seriously either. We need a good excuse to interview him."

"We can lie!" Cam says excitedly.

"That's the whole point of the cover story, Cam," Blair says.

I give up, she thinks, smiling to herself. Planet Cam is at apogee today; better wait until she's in range of a signal. Blair turns onto the street to her house.

The Johnsons' is nothing like Cam and Irene's shabby, cozy apartment full of mismatched curtains and dried flowers and Irene's semi-ironic collection of milagros, votives, and papier-mâché Virgen del Guadalupes. It's a big split-level in an older development in town. All surfaces are free of tchotchkes and all textiles harmonize.

Blair's family is so normal it makes her teeth hurt. Her mom stays home and irons her dad's shirts while she watches talk shows. Her dad works in an office all day and comes home grumpy. Her brothers are handsome and wholesome and good at (all) sports and smart but not the kind of Cam-smart that makes people nervous. Her family isn't rich like James's, but they have enough money that they don't talk about money. Their expectations of Blair are low. "There's nothing wrong with community college, honey," her mother says at least once a week. There *is* nothing wrong with community college. The problem is that her parents can afford to pay for a four-year school. They just don't think she can get into one.

Sometimes Blair thinks they underestimate her.

Sometimes she thinks they're right.

Being friends with Cam, who is the prickly genius daughter of a borderline-impoverished single mother who has never opened a copy of *The Joy of Cooking*, let alone owned one, is the most rebellious thing Blair's ever done.

It's the only rebellious thing Blair's ever done.

Her two older brothers are at the University of Washington, so now it's just her and Scott. He's a year younger, but he's already had more girlfriends than Blair's had track meets. Plus, he's newly into cologne. He's still her favorite of all her brothers, although she'd never tell him that. Unlike Kevin and Jake, he listens to her sometimes.

Her mom's in the kitchen, making something casserole-y. "Hi, sweetie. Oh, hello, Cameron. Nice to see you. Would you like to stay for dinner?"

"Sure," Cam says. "Lemme text Irene."

"How is your mother?" Blair's mom has never known what

to make of Irene, who not only works but seems perfectly content to remain a single mother, which smacks of disrepute. Irene is a nurse, which is relatively decorous, but she's a psychiatric nurse at the inpatient facility in town—"the loony bin," Blair and Cam once heard Blair's dad call it—which is not. If Blair's parents had any inkling of Irene's renegade antifa past they would never let Blair see either Irene or Cam again.

"She's fine," Cam says.

"Tell her I said hello," Mrs. Johnson says brightly.

"Okay," Cam says. Irene has no more interest in Mrs. Johnson's well-being than Mrs. Johnson has in hers, a fact well known to all parties, but even Cam understands it is inappropriate to point this out.

"Do you need help?" Blair asks.

"Thanks, honey, but this is about to go in the oven."

"We're going to go do our homework, then," Blair says.

She hasn't told her parents about the podcast. They moved to Oreville for her dad's job when Blair was in kindergarten; her parents wouldn't have known Clarissa or any of her friends. And Blair's used to keeping the things she cares about to herself. Her brother does enough talking for the both of them, anyway.

Blair's room is nothing like Cam's. It's always in order, because if Blair doesn't clean it, her mom will. The walls are pastel lavender, a color Blair picked when she was in second grade and hates now. Her pillowcases match her sheets, and her sheets match the bedspread. Her curtains complement the lampshade. Her desk and dresser and bed frame are a matching set.

In fact, it occurs to her, her bedroom looks a lot like Clarissa's.

She has fantasies about pitching the whole setup out the window when her mom's at the grocery store and her dad's at work. But when she tries to think about what she wants instead, her mind goes blank.

"Do you think Clarissa was like that?" Blair asks.

Cam flops onto Blair's bed, pulls her laptop out of her bag. "Like what?"

"Perfect," Blair says.

"I think most people's parents don't know them very well," Cam says. "I mean, look at your parents."

Cam is totally oblivious most of the time, but now and then she comes out with something that makes Blair wonder if she's psychic.

"What do you think we should tell the sheriff's office?" Blair asks.

"We could say we're doing a report on unsolved crime in Oreville."

"Is there a lot of unsolved crime in Oreville?"

Cam opens her laptop and types. "Actually, yeah," she says. "A nineteen-year-old girl was stabbed to death in 2011, and a sixty-year-old woman was strangled in 2013. And somebody murdered a whole family in 2015 and then burned their house down."

"Lovely," Blair says. "Who was the nineteen-year-old?"

"Sara-Jean Rourke," Cam says. "She graduated from Oreville High too."

"Any other connection to Clarissa?"

"I don't think so. The article doesn't mention it."

"Sara-Jean didn't make *People* magazine," Blair says, looking over Cam's shoulder at the *Oreville Examiner* webpage.

"Sara-Jean was a sex worker," Cam says.

"This is sort of depressing," Blair says.

"Yeah," Cam says, closing the computer. "What is it with people?" She looks at her pile of sexy-murdered-white-lady novels. "Are we as bad as everyone else?"

"Everybody loves a dead white girl with good hair," Blair says.

"I deserved that."

"Do you want to stop?"

"I don't think so," Cam says. "I mean, all of this—talking to people, making the podcast, trying to figure out what happened—it's interesting. Honestly, it's fun. Is that bad? Do *you* want to stop?"

"I want to know what happened to her. And I like working on the script."

"You're good at it. I can't write stuff like you."

"I'm not."

"Come on, B. I wouldn't say it if it weren't true."

"I don't see it," Blair says.

"You never do," Cam says. "I knew you were going to be great. You're not as stealthy as you think."

"What do you mean?"

"Writing things down all the time," Cam says.

"I don't write things down all the time," Blair says, panicked.

"Yes you do," Cam says. "Anyway," she adds, seeing Blair's discomfort, "I guess we could say something vague when we call the sheriff. Like, we're working on a school project about crime in Oreville? We don't have to say 'murder' or 'unsolved cases.'"

"Do you want to call?"

"You do it. You're so much better at that kind of thing."

"Now you're trying to get out of doing it." Blair laughs.

"Maybe," Cam admits, "but it's still true. I don't know how to talk to normal people."

"You don't know how to talk to anyone. Especially Sophie."

Cam throws a pastel decorative pillow at her head. "That's the last time I say anything nice to you," she says.

Dinner is the usual Johnson show. Blair's mom makes bright, inconsequential chatter. Scott inhales half the pan of casserole like he's trying for a land-speed record. Blair's dad starts out in a bad mood, but Cam, oddly enough, has always had a positive effect on him. Blair's mom has never known what to make of Cam, let alone how to talk to her. But her dad treats Cam like a miniature businessman with odd ideas about the world, bouncing current events and office problems off her as if she is an eccentric but amusing colleague.

Blair gives Cam a ride home later. The apartment windows are dark. "Irene still at work?"

"Yeah," Cam says. "I'll go over some of this audio and edit the highlights."

"I'll call the sheriff's office tomorrow after first period."

"Cool," Cam says. She doesn't get out of the car. "Do you think Sophie thinks I'm weird?"

"Sophie thinks you're cute," Blair says. "For a junior."

"What?"

"She said so after you ran away."

"I didn't run away."

"After you departed in a rapid manner."

"Cute? She said cute? Not smart?"

"Cameron," Blair says. "Cute is good."

"Cute is for baby animals."

"Get out of my car and go inside."

"Okay," Cam says. "See you tomorrow."

"See you tomorrow."

Cam knocks Blair's shoulder with her fist in a bro-y manner and climbs out of the car. Blair watches until the lights come on in Cam's apartment before she drives away.

———

CAM'S KNOWN SHE'S gay for as long as she's known other entirely self-evident things about herself—her hair is black and her eyes and skin are light brown, one front tooth is crooked, her feet are sort of funny looking, she hates Blair's mom's casseroles. But she's never talked about it with anyone, because it's always been an abstract equation, a function of a complex variable she'll tackle when she is released from high school and into her real life. The idea of finding someone worthy of her attentions in Oreville is absurd.

Until now.

How is it possible that she never noticed Sophie before, and what is she supposed to do now that she has? How do people get other people to like them? Blair's always had boyfriends, but Blair is a lot nicer than Cam is and maybe getting girlfriends is different. Mr. Park is gay, but he is also elderly and into men, which does Cam no good. Irene, although equally ancient, occasionally demonstrates intelligence. But as far as Cam knows, Irene hasn't gone on a date with anyone of any gender in sixteen years. Also useless.

Plus, what if Cam tells Irene she's gay and Irene freaks out? Never mind that freaking out is so antithetical to Irene's nature that Cam has to think about what Irene freaking out might look like. Would Irene cry? Throw plates? Make her go to therapy? They can't afford therapy. Perhaps Irene will send her to live in the loony bin herself, which does not hold much appeal. Cam likes the other nurses, but Irene says the food is terrible.

Cam looks at herself in the mirror. In about three minutes Irene will bang on the door and yell. Cam does not ordinarily bogart the bathroom, but this morning she is trying to analyze what Sophie finds *cute* about her face.

"Cute" is demeaning, Cam thinks. Better would be "interesting" or "brilliant" (both so obvious as to not require comment, she supposes) or "beautiful." But "beautiful" is for people like Blair, not people like Cam. Not being beautiful has never bothered Cam before. Suddenly, it is a crisis of unmanageable proportions. Sophie is beautiful. Why would Sophie want to kiss someone who is not?

"Cameron P. Muñoz!" Irene shouts, banging on the door. Cam doesn't have a middle name. Irene uses the *P* for emphasis when she wants to be severe.

"Sorry!" Cam yells. She opens the door as Irene bellows, "What is taking you so long in there?!" Now they are shouting at each other across a gap of six inches.

"Am I ugly?" Cam asks in a normal voice.

"What?" Irene yells. "What did you ask me?"

"Am I ugly?" Cam repeats.

"Who said you were ugly?"

"No one," Cam says. An enraged Irene is likely to march upon the school and demand blood. "I was just wondering."

"No," Irene says. "You are not remotely ugly, Cameron. Not in the same room as ugly. Not the same building."

"You're my mom, though," Cam says. "You're supposed to say that. You could be lying."

"Have I ever lied to you? What in the name of god has brought this on?" Irene narrows her eyes. "Are you dating?"

"No," Cam says truthfully. "I think I want to be, though."

"Ah," Irene says. "Come into the kitchen with me, my child. I have about fifteen minutes before I have to leave for work."

"I'll be late for school."

"I'll drop you off."

Cam follows her mother into the kitchen, where Irene pours herself a cup of coffee and sits at the scarred wooden table. Kitten materializes in the doorway, looking optimistic.

"No," Irene says to him. "Look how fat you are, old man. No more wet food."

"It doesn't matter if he's fat," Cam says. "He's a cat."

"He'll get health problems and we can't afford the vet," Irene counters. "Who do you want to be dating, Cameron?"

"Well," Cam says. She clears her throat. "I'm gay."

"I know," Irene says calmly. "I meant which girl, specifically?"

"You know?" Cam gapes. "How?" Does Blair know? Do other people know? Is it, like, a smell that she gives off?

"I wasn't totally sure until the year you insisted on covering one wall of your bedroom with pictures of Megan Rapinoe in a sports bra," Irene says.

"Megan Rapinoe is a feminist ico—"

"Cam, you've never *watched* a soccer game. Do you need the safe sex talk?"

"The *what*?"

"If you're going to have sex you need to protect—"

"NO."

"Sex with other women has health risks too—"

"NOOOOOOOOOOOOO," Cam howls.

Irene is not trying to hide how much she is enjoying this. Cam glares at her with murderous intent.

"Sophie," she says. "I like this girl Sophie. She's a senior."

"Does she like you?"

"She told Blair I was *cute*," Cam says with loathing.

"Mmm," Irene says. "I see."

Cam pokes miserably at a crack in the kitchen table. "How does it work?"

"Sex with women?"

"*No,*" Cam says. "Dating."

"You're asking me?" Irene laughs, props her chin on one fist. "My poor child. I'm the last person you want to talk to about dating. You should ask Blair."

"What if Blair thinks I'm going to lez out on her when I tell her I'm gay?"

Irene is struck by a sudden coughing fit that looks suspiciously like laughter. But surely Irene would not find amusement in such a serious predicament. Cam goes to the sink and gets her a glass of water. When Irene recovers, she says, "Blair's not stupid, Cameron."

"What does that have to do with anything?"

"I wouldn't worry about Blair."

"How did you get Dad to like you?"

Irene is quiet for a long moment. "Your father was a special person," she says, which is not the answer Cam is looking for. "A lot like you."

"Cute?"

Irene smiles. "Extremely."

"You never talk about him."

"Would you like me to?"

"I don't know," Cam says. "I can barely remember him. I remember the hospital, kind of."

Irene looks away. "That was a hard time. But we had a lot of good times before that. He adored you."

"I was a baby. Babies aren't interesting."

"You were an exceptionally compelling baby."

"How come you never date anybody?"

"Your father was one of the only people I ever met who was worth the trouble," Irene says.

"It would probably help if you left Oreville."

"I'm sure you're right. Come on, I've got to get to work."

———

CAM FEELS SLIGHTLY better after her talk with Irene, despite the fact that Irene has given her basically no advice and revealed almost nothing. An advice-giving, open Irene would be so out of character, however, that Cam doubts she would find such a version of her mother anything other than alarming.

School is boring; school is filled with troglodytes. *One more year,* Cam thinks tiredly in AP Physics. She watches Kevin Turner spend the class period trying to snap Emily Peters's bra strap without being detected by Mr. Pendergast. Emily endures this harassment with weary resignation. Not consenting; too beleaguered to protest.

Is this how flirting works? Should she ask Blair? Is she supposed to snap Sophie's bra strap? The thought is unbearable.

At last the interminable day disgorges her into the blessed relief of Journalism. The weather is unseasonably warm for October, creating a general atmosphere of cheer. A balmy layer of sunshine pours in through the open classroom windows. Cam is on time for once. Mr. Park has an actual bow tie clipped to his lumpy sweater. Jenna the sophomore sports a festive sundress. Mattmiles look almost confident.

And Sophie! Sophie is radiant in a cap-sleeve blouse and patterned skirt. Sophie's hair shines. Sophie's lipstick matches the sailboats on her skirt. Sophie's delicate gold necklace drapes prettily over Sophie's elegant collarbone.

"Cam," Blair hisses. Cam jumps. "You're staring."

Cam turns around so fast she almost falls out of her chair. Sophie smiles to herself. The bell rings.

"So," Mr. Park says without ceremony, "I thought today we could check in on the status of our projects. Who wants to start?"

Mattmiles shift in their chairs. Mr. Park directs his owlish gaze at them. "Matt? Miles? How are our little green men?"

"Pretty good," whispers Matt. Or Miles. "We're collecting footage from Alienstock 2019 to collate into our documentary."

"You know," Matt mumbles. "The festival."

"Enlighten us, Miles," Mr. Park says.

Mattmiles are turning coordinating shades of pink. "When there was an online call to storm the Area 51 facility? It was a hoax but then it turned into a party in the desert. But that sort of turned into a hoax too. There are a lot of YouTube videos about it."

A long silence follows this disclosure, which Mattmiles seem unwilling to break.

"Glad you're making progress," Mr. Park says at last. "Jenna, anything to report?" He laughs out loud at his own pun. No one else does.

"Just in the research stages still," Jenna says. "And I'm trying to decide on the best format, since podcast is already taken." She shoots a not-entirely-friendly look at Cam.

"No one has a monopoly on podcasts, if you decide to go that route," Mr. Park says. "Speaking of which, Cam and Blair?"

Blair finds herself suddenly mute. Cam sits up straighter. "We're interviewing people who knew Clarissa and can talk about what she was like," she says. "We've recorded and uploaded two episodes already."

"They're good," Sophie offers.

"They are?" Blair says at the same time Cam blurts, "You listened to them?"

"Sure," Sophie says. "It's cool that you have an audience already."

"We do?" Cam is flabbergasted. She's forgotten to check their stats in the last few days, since their stats have been the same every day since she uploaded the first episode and left her anonymous comment on the Clarissa message board: an audience of two.

"Didn't you know?" Sophie asks.

Cam is already pulling out her phone. "Cameron, perhaps later," Mr. Park says, but there's no stopping Cam when she's on a roll.

"Two thousand people!" Cam crows.

"What?" Blair makes a grab for her phone. Cam clings to it fiercely.

"Two thousand people!" Cam repeats. She looks at Sophie. "You thought they were good?"

"They sound like you recorded them in an aquarium," Sophie says. "But other than that, yeah. I can't believe you already got Clarissa's mom to talk to you. And all of Blair's descriptions are so vivid."

"I told you so," Cam says to Blair triumphantly.

Mr. Park clears his throat pointedly. "Any roadblocks you want to discuss with the class?"

"We're *trying* to find *information* about who might have *influenced* the sheriff's campaign, but it's not *going* very well," Cam says, glaring.

Mr. Park nods, unruffled. "Good luck with that," he says. "Sophie?"

Sophie smiles. Cam's stomach does something extraordinary. "I got a bit distracted trying to teach myself the Klallam language online," she says.

"Ah, yes," Mr. Park says. "The famous procrastination tactic of 'research.' The more you look up, the less you have to write."

They spend the rest of the class brainstorming ways to stay focused on long-term projects, but Cam is too elated by *Missing Clarissa*'s sudden fame to pay attention. Lack of focus! Surely a problem for lesser minds, if ever there was one.

Two thousand people! she thinks, the numbers doing circles in her head. Two thousand! What if next week their audience balloons to twenty thousand! Thirty thousand! A million! The whole world! FindClarissa1999 has work to do in the forums!

"How did that many people find our podcast already?" Blair asks after class.

"I have no idea," Cam lies. She is not sure how Blair will feel about FindClarissa1999's promotional activities.

"That's wild." Blair shakes her head. "I guess people are listening to us now. We have to be careful."

"Careful of what?"

"You know," Blair says. "Careful of doing a good job."

"Obviously we're doing a good job."

Blair gives up. "I called the police department. We have an interview with the sheriff next week."

"What did you tell them?"

"That we're doing a Civics assignment on the criminal justice system in Oreville," Blair says. "I made sure to sound extra dumb."

"Brilliant," Cam says admiringly. "Want to come over Saturday and do research?"

"I have a date with James Saturday night, but I can come over in the afternoon," Blair says.

"That should work for my schedule," Cam says magnanimously. "What? Why are you rolling your eyes? Blair? Blair?"

———

"PROMISE ME YOU'LL play this one for Mr. Park before you upload it," Blair says.

The weather is still gorgeous, but they're holed up in Cam's room hunched over her computer. Blair spent the morning on a long training run. Cam most likely built a sentient robot or solved some famous math problem or whatever it is she does when Blair's not around.

"What does Mr. Park have to do with it?" Cam asks.

They've just listened to the final edit of the Allen Dawson episode. They still sound like they're underwater half the time, but Cam's edits are smoother. Blair wonders if she'll ever get over her mortification at the sound of her own voice.

"Because we have a real audience now, and I'm nervous," Blair says. "And because technically, it's for him."

"Technically, it's for Clarissa," Cam says pompously.

Blair refrains from pointing out that a few weeks ago Cam was selling the podcast as their ticket to fame and fortune and Harvard. True to form, Cam is completely unaware of her abrupt pivot to the moral high ground. Blair is sure that if she asks, Cam will insist she was bent on demanding justice for Clarissa from the beginning.

She'll believe herself too.

"What're you laughing at now?" Cam asks.

"Thinking about cat videos," Blair says.

Kitten raises his enormous head from Cam's unmade bed. Sometimes "cat" means "cat food." When no one moves to the kitchen, he utters a disappointed meow and goes back to sleep. Cam scowls but is placated by Blair's answer.

"I'll stay after class on Monday and play it for him."

"Promise promise."

"I promise."

"You promised last time. This time promise on Kitten's eternal soul."

"I think technically he has nine of them," Cam says.

Blair absently reaches up and scratches Kitten behind the ears, feeling his thunderous purr vibrate through her fingers. "Who should we talk to after the sheriff? Do you want to find Brad Bennett?"

"Not yet," Cam says. "I want to know who funded the sheriff's campaign first. If it was Brad, that makes him our primary suspect." She looks back through her notebook. "We could find out who else was on the cheer squad. Or what about her old art teacher?"

"Dan Friley?"

Cam is already typing his name into a search bar.

"Here's that Silverwater place Mrs. Campbell mentioned," she reports. "'A sanctuary in the heart of Olympic National Park for global creatives and digital natives,' whatever that means. Looks more like yoga retreats for bored tech bros."

She clicks on a profile of Friley from a couple of years ago that includes a flattering photo of Clarissa's former teacher. He's standing in front of a big bay window in what looks like an old hunting lodge: high ceilings, timber beams, a fireplace big enough to roast a whole cow. Behind him a lake glimmers through dense forest. His longish hair is a striking shade of silver, but his face is unlined.

Blair's bad at guessing adults' ages, but he looks like he's in his forties. He's dressed in expensive workwear—plaid wool Pendleton, Carhartt jeans, Timberlands—that Blair is sure has never seen either work or wear. His hands are shoved in his pockets, his stance relaxed and confident. He's looking directly at the camera with a faint, knowing smile.

"He's kind of hot," Blair says. Cam makes a gagging noise. "I mean, for an old dude," Blair adds hastily. "Charismatic. You know."

"He looks like a rich prick," Cam says.

"Rich people can be charismatic."

Cam does not dignify this with a response. "This place was built as a hunting resort and hotel in the 1920s," she says. "It closed down in the eighties, and then Friley bought it and remodeled it in 2000. The article doesn't say anything about him being an art teacher."

"He bought it the year after Clarissa disappeared? That means he must have quit teaching at the same time, right?"

Cam sits back, staring thoughtfully at his picture. "That's interesting timing."

"Clarissa's mom said he wasn't one for bureaucracy," Blair says. "What do you think that means?"

"I don't know," Cam says. "Let's find out."

———

TONIGHT'S DATE NIGHT, which means Blair must do her best to look her best. But after a week of late nights researching with Cam, she's exhausted and a bit cranky. Plus, Scott is heading out on a date of his own, and he's been hogging the bathroom for the last hour. Her brother may not be much of one for hygiene on your average day, but his pre-date rituals are Byzantine.

Blair leaves off screaming through the door every five minutes and settles for brushing out her hair and topping off her mascara in her bedroom. She picks out a dress she knows James loves on her as a concession to formality.

"Hey, beautiful," he says, greeting her at her front door with a chaste kiss in case her parents are around. "You look great."

One of the things she likes most about James is that he's never shy about telling her she's pretty. Maybe one of these days she'll believe him.

Blair thinks while James drives. She's never been as confident as Cam. Then again, she's never been special like Cam, so maybe she has no reason to be confident. She's good at track, but nobody's going to offer her a scholarship. She gets decent grades, but she's hardly brilliant. James might think she's pretty, but she's no cover model. The only special thing about her is James, and she can't see for the life of her what it is he sees in her.

Blair is about as normal as it's possible to be, which doesn't bode well for her dreams. Who wants to read the writing of America's most ordinary teenage girl? Cam's the one who should be a writer, but Cam can't sit still long enough to scratch out a paragraph, let alone a book.

But Blair won't let herself think about the idea of writing a whole book.

"Earth to Blair," James says affectionately. He's pulled into the restaurant lot and parked the car, and she's still sitting in the passenger seat staring into space.

"Sorry," she says. "Hanging out in the fifth dimension."

It's an old joke between them. Usually James gets upset when she drifts off into her own inner world. She can't blame him. She shouldn't ignore him when they're together. But tonight he's in a good mood.

The lone Italian restaurant in town that isn't an Olive Garden is James's favorite. Secretly, Blair doesn't think the food is very good. But it's easy enough to make James happy, and if that means downing a plate of overcooked spaghetti drowning in canned sauce once a week Blair is happy to do it.

James is already working his way through the breadbasket, chattering happily about last night's game. As usual, he was the top scorer, which Blair saw, since, as usual, she was there. She makes a point of going to all his games, because that makes him happy too. She's diligently learned the stats for his favorite pro players, roots for his team with him when all the boys are over at his house watching the NBA Finals, downs celebratory shots with them after victories. She can talk basketball like a fan. But when James is on a roll, like he is tonight, he sometimes doesn't notice that she's checked out completely. Which gives her an excuse to wander back into her private thoughts.

Such as: What *did* happen to Clarissa Campbell? Blair thinks of Clarissa's painting, the contrast between the art Clarissa made and the Clarissa her friends and family remember. Did someone know Clarissa's secrets, or did she hold them close? Why did Clarissa choose that particular painting to copy? Why does she look so sad in the picture?

Maybe she told Dan Friley, Blair thinks. *We have to ask him.* She wonders if she can make a note in her phone without James noticing.

". . . isn't that awesome?" James says.

"Totally awesome," Blair replies automatically.

James sighs dramatically. "Do you have any idea what I just said?" Now he's annoyed, and Blair feels a twinge of guilt.

"Sorry," she says. "I can't stop thinking about Clarissa."

"Clarissa who?"

"Clarissa Campbell." He looks blank. "You know, for our podcast."

"Oh, right. Your little project with Cam."

"It's not so little anymore," Blair says with a touch of defensiveness. "We have a pretty big audience. Two thousand people."

James laughs. "Stop the internet!" he says. "My girlfriend is famous! Next thing you know, she'll be on *The Tonight Show*."

"Oh, stop it," Blair says, giggling. The truth is, she's hurt. The podcast isn't as impressive as James's basketball, but she and Cam have worked hard.

I'm proud of it, she realizes suddenly. *I'm proud of what we've done.*

As if on cue, her phone pings with an incoming text. It's Cam, as always. You're coming back over after dinner right?

She flips the phone over, but not before James sees the message and his face clouds over. "What the hell, Blair?"

"She must've gotten the days mixed up," Blair lies weakly. She promised to come back over in exchange for Cam's promise to play the Allen episode for Mr. Park before she put it online. But now she sees she'll have to choose yet again. Tonight is James's night and he's her boyfriend and it's not Blair's fault Cam can't understand that boyfriends are as important as podcasts. More important than podcasts.

Except that Blair is starting to feel like maybe this podcast means a lot more to her than she thought.

"You spend all your time with her," James says.

"This project is important to her," Blair says, feeling like a traitor. To Cam, or to herself?

"It's a school assignment, Blair. She can figure it out herself."

He's right. It is just a school assignment. And Cam is better off without her. The idea that she could do something meaningful, make something good—that she could solve this mystery—is ridiculous. James must think she's pathetic.

Blair Johnson on *The Tonight Show*? What a joke.

But. Two thousand people. That's not a small number.

Her phone pings again.

"Can you please put that away?" James asks, exasperated.

She smiles at him and tucks her phone into her bag without looking at the screen. "Forget Cam, okay? Tell me about the game next week."

His face softens and he smiles back at her. He launches into an analysis of the opposition point guard's weaknesses and strengths.

Blair keeps the smile pasted on her face and nods at all the right moments and wonders how much longer she can keep up the excruciating dance between her boyfriend and her best friend and the school project that is growing into something bigger.

Something that, for the first time, is making her wonder if Blair Johnson, Normal Teen, has something worth saying after all.

ALLEN

She was so beautiful and so kind. I'll keep saying that forever. I'll keep thinking about that forever. She didn't have to be kind, but she was.

I wasn't popular in high school. I was kind of invisible, honestly. I felt like I was a ghost moving through the motions of a boy's life. My father wasn't around, but I knew my mother loved me. I did have a few friends. We played video games, talked about girls. Just talk, you understand. I don't think girls would've had anything to do with us. Nobody bullied me, but nobody noticed me either. So when someone like Clarissa saw me, really saw me—well, you can imagine.

I don't know what else to say. After she disappeared—that was a hard time. For the family, and for the people who were close to her, it must have been horrific. I don't mean to compare myself to that. But it was hard for me too. I was only a junior then. To think of another whole year at school, without

Clarissa to lighten it. It was hard. I guess I was a bit in love with her. Can you blame me? I don't think Brad knew how lucky he was. I'm not accusing anyone of anything. I prefer to think that she's still alive.

I loved all those corny teen movies, you know, where the beautiful girl realizes the nerdy guy is the man of her dreams. It got me through a lot of high school. And when she went missing, I didn't have that anymore. I used to think of what I could say to her to show her how much I cared, how well I'd treat her. I wanted to take care of her. It didn't seem like Brad deserved someone like that.

All that sounds pretty silly now. But we were young. A lot of things seemed possible. I went on to have a good life. A good job. I was married for a while, but it didn't work out. Not that that has anything to do with Clarissa. I moved on from high school, is all. But you never forget being young. You're too young to know that yet. But one day you'll understand what I mean.

MR. PARK

People often think of reporters as vultures, and I suppose in this case that's not entirely unfair. There was so much interest in the story. Yes, always a bit ghoulish when the victim is so—well. Do I need to say it? The Jennifer Bell story, the Lisa Carter abduction, that girl in Texas who did beauty pageants. They never did figure out who killed her. Anyway, Clarissa's was a story like one of those. Not a new story, is what I'm saying, but people do like their reruns.

I wish I had some grand overarching theory of what draws people to crimes like that. I read somewhere that we're always looking for ways to face our most terrible fears without having to go through the trauma of experiencing them. Supposedly women in particular think of themselves as learning something from stories of sexual assault and murder. You know, if you can understand how and why the crime was committed, you can find a way to avoid it happening to you. That's true, I'm sure, but it's not the whole truth. It doesn't explain why we only want to watch girls like Clarissa die. A lot of other crimes happen to a lot of other people. The vast majority of female murder victims are killed by their partners, not some bogeyman with a hunting knife. Nobody makes television specials about them.

To be honest, I can't say I was any different at the time. I thought it was the story that would make my career. One can't help being drawn in when the circumstances are so cinematic. In the early days of the investigation it seemed the case would be solved quickly—there were so few possible outcomes, given the circumstances—and I would be the one to report its unfolding and eventual denouement. I'd be the insider. The expert on a girl I knew nothing about until she was already gone. My name in lights, and so on.

Time has a way of humbling even the grossest ambitions, doesn't it?

THE LOVERS

THE police station is a newer one-story building by the high school. A handful of cop cars are parked in front of a square of lawn edged with an orderly line of fake-looking purple flowers and beauty bark.

Inside, the reception area looks nothing like a television police department. The carpet is gray and institutional, the walls a blinding white. Posters warning against drunk driving are spaced at even intervals. In one corner there's a table with coffee urns and a Costco box of pastries. A man in uniform sits behind a desk with what looks to be a permanently affixed friendly smile.

"Can I help you?" he asks. He looks more like an Oreville High student than a cop, despite the uniform. He is weedily thin and even sitting down it's obvious he's tall, like a tree that's grown too fast toward the light. His bony wrists stick out past his shirt cuffs, and his nose is too big for his face. But his smile is genuine, and he has a calm, confident air despite his youthful spindliness. A plastic badge pinned to his chest reads RELOJ.

"We have an interview with the sheriff," Blair says. Too late, she remembers she was supposed to sound dumb. But Cam is descending on the donuts and coffee with the manic glee of a toddler, so maybe Reloj won't take them as a threat.

Reloj laughs. "Hiring 'em young at the *Examiner* these days, are they? Hold on." He picks up a phone on his desk, dials an extension. "Sheriff? A couple of young ladies here to see you." He replaces the phone in its cradle. "I'll take you back there," he says. "It's kind of a maze."

He leads Blair and Cam down a hallway that branches and turns into more offshoots than they would have thought possible. The police station is like one of those houses from a fairy tale that's bigger on the inside than the outside. He stops in front of a large glass-walled office.

"Here you go," he says cheerfully, opening the door for them after rapping on it briskly.

Sheriff Liechty is a big man, but soft-looking. He makes Blair think of a high-school football player who hasn't done much in the years since. A flamboyant mustache drapes over his top lip. His thinning hair is combed back. The office isn't especially warm, but beads of sweat dot his high forehead. Behind him, a big window gives a view of seagulls wheeling above the bay.

"What can I do for you girls? You're here about"—he shuffles through some papers on his desk—"the criminal justice system? Always happy to talk to the next generation of law enforcement." He smiles at them benevolently.

"No," Cam says through a mouthful of donut. "Can we record our interview?"

"Thanks for taking the time to meet us," Blair adds, trying to sound vapid.

"Sure, sure," the sheriff says, gesturing them to a couple of chairs. The patronizing smile is still in place. "Have a seat, girls."

Blair can feel the contempt radiating off Cam.

"You were the detective in charge of the investigation into Clarissa Campbell's disappearance in 1999," Cam says.

The sheriff looks surprised. "Excuse me?"

"You only focused on one suspect during the investigation. Why?"

Liechty narrows his eyes. "What did you girls say you were here about?"

"Why?" Cam repeats.

He looks at her, considering. "Brad Bennett had motive and opportunity," he says.

"Not that much opportunity," Cam says. "Did he have a reputation for violence? We've heard allegations that he assaulted other students."

Blair is silent. When Cam is like this, she's terrifying. And fun to watch, as long as you're not her target.

"I can't answer questions about an ongoing investigation," Liechty says.

"Ongoing?" Cam pounces. "Are you reopening the case? Why? Is there new evidence? Can we see the file?"

"Don't be ridiculous. And the case was never closed," the sheriff snaps. "But it's not a murder investigation. There was no body. You ask me, that girl was asking for—" He bites down on the rest of the sentence.

"That girl was asking for what?" Blair interjects sweetly.

The sheriff shakes his head. "She was troubled," he said. "What are you girls, miniature tabloid reporters? This is a waste of my time."

"If you screwed up the investigation into Clarissa's disappearance so badly, how'd you get elected sheriff?" Cam asks.

"I don't know what you girls want, but I'm not sitting here and listening to this," the sheriff says. He picks up his phone. "Brian? The interview's over. Come get them."

"Who funded your campaign?" Cam asks.

"*What?*"

"Did the money have anything to do with covering up Clarissa's disappearance? Did someone pay you off?"

The sheriff is flushed red with anger, sweat pouring off him. He points a stubby finger at Cam. "*If* that girl is dead, and that's a big *if*, her boyfriend killed her. No other suspects, no other motives. Are we clear?"

"Did Brad pay you to blow the investigation?" Cam asks.

"Get out of this office," the sheriff says. "Right now. I'm calling your parents."

Cam laughs at the idea of this man trying to take on Irene. Officer Reloj, returned to fetch them, knocks on the glass.

"Nice to meet you," Blair says politely. "Thanks so much for your time."

"Sheriff looked riled up," Reloj says as he leads them back to the reception area. "That must've been the shortest interview in the history of journalism." Something about the way he says it makes Blair think he doesn't have much love for his boss.

"He didn't like my questions," Cam says.

"That so? What were you asking him about?"

"Clarissa Campbell," Blair says.

"Interesting," Reloj says.

"Were you working here when she disappeared?" Cam asks.

Reloj laughs. "I was in kindergarten, miss," he says. "But everybody knows about that case."

"Could we interview you?" Blair asks hopefully.

"Not on your life. I'd like to keep my job. What are you girls working on, if I may ask?"

"We're making a podcast about Clarissa," Blair says.

"Citizen journalists. I like it." He stops so suddenly that Cam walks into him. "Wait, a podcast? *Missing Clarissa?* Is that you?"

"You've heard of us?" Blair asks in astonishment.

"Sure," he says. "We have search alerts for cold cases. I listened to a couple of episodes. Not bad. Do you record in a bathroom, though?"

"You sure you won't talk to us?" Cam is like a terrier. "Do you know who funded Liechty's campaign for sheriff in 2000?"

"Goodness," Officer Reloj says. "You girls aren't kidding around. Be careful, all right? I tell you what." He pulls a card out of his uniform pocket and looks around conspiratorially. "If you run into any trouble, you can give me a call."

"Really?" Cam's eyes light up, and she snatches the card out of his hand.

"Thanks," Blair says, since Cam won't. She takes the card from Cam, who will lose it immediately, and tucks it into her wallet.

Officer Reloj shakes his head, but he's smiling. "Good luck," he says. "But you should know the sheriff's not going to be happy if you keep at this."

In the parking lot, Cam turns to Blair. "Let's go talk to Brad," she says.

BRAD BENNETT OWNS a shooting range out in the county, past acres of farmland and clear-cuts, one new enough that a slash pile still smolders in the stump-scarred wasteland. BENNETT'S GUNS is painted on a wooden signboard so faded they wouldn't have known what it was if they weren't looking for it. Blair turns off the highway onto a rutted gravel road riddled with potholes. A few rattly minutes later, she parks in an empty dirt lot in front of a dilapidated building.

"I'm not going to lie," Blair says. "The serial killer vibes are strong with this one."

"He's not going to kill us," Cam says. "I don't think."

"Cam, this is stupid. We're in the middle of nowhere."

"No risk, no reward," Cam says, and gets out of the car. Blair sighs and follows her.

The inside of the building is as ramshackle as the outside, although, Blair notices, it's also clean. A scratched glass display counter holds a variety of guns. There's an old metal table surrounded by four folding chairs, another table with an ancient coffeemaker and a stack of Styrofoam cups. A small wooden bookcase holds neatly shelved books with titles like *Blacktail Trophy Tactics II* and *Animal Tracks of the Pacific Northwest*. The air smells like stale coffee and loneliness.

The man reading a magazine behind the counter looks up with surprise when they come in. Blair recognizes him immediately. His startling blue eyes have the same haunted quality as his gun shop. He needs a shave and a haircut, and his haggard face is as well-worn as his flannel shirt. But she can still see the photogenic jock from *People* magazine's Clarissa coverage beneath the weathered skin of his face.

"How can I help you ladies?" he asks, half hopeful, half cautious.

"You're Brad Bennett," Cam says.

"Yeah," he says, and now he's all caution and no hope.

"We're doing a school project about Clarissa," Cam says. "We were hoping we could ask you—"

His face closes down like a storm front rolling in. "No. Get out."

"Just a few—" Cam tries.

"I didn't have anything to say about Clarissa twenty years ago and I sure as hell don't now," he says. *"Get out."*

Brad Bennett is tall and massive, and Blair can see the bulk of muscle underneath his faded shirt. His anger makes him larger. She is acutely aware of how alone they are.

"Cam, let's go," she says.

"We'll take a shooting lesson," Cam says.

"Children under eighteen require an accompanying adult," Brad snaps.

"Cam," Blair says again.

"You're an adult," Cam says. She looks pointedly around the empty shop. "We're paying customers."

Brad glares at them, his face a mask of hostility and something else Blair can't identify.

Sadness, she thinks. *Brad Bennett is a very sad man.*

Or a very guilty one.

Cam glares right back. Blair has seen plenty of adults back down under the full force of Cam's will, but Brad is a match for her. Blair half expects sparks. Brad doesn't falter, but Blair can see him come to a decision.

"Fine," he says. He reaches under the counter, finds a set of forms, slaps them down on the glass. "Fill these out."

Blair knows Cam is triumphant, but she has the sense to hide it.

"Thank you," Cam says. She writes down her name and address. "I don't have a driver's license. May I use my friend's?"

Something twitches at the corner of Brad's mouth that might almost be a smile. "Suit yourself," he growls, stalking to the other end of the counter, where he pulls out an alarming assortment of guns.

"Do you know how to shoot a gun?" Blair hisses at Cam as she fills out her own form.

"*How* long have you known me?" Cam asks. "Do *you* know how to shoot a gun?"

Blair writes down her address, wondering if she should use a fake name. But Cam's filled her form out truthfully. Anyway, two teenage girls doing an increasingly famous podcast on Clarissa Campbell won't be that hard to find in a place like Oreville if Brad Bennett wants to track them down.

Brad returns to collect their forms, scanning them with a glance. "Muñoz?" he says, surprised. "You Irene's kid?"

Cam's head goes up like a whippet's. "You know her?"

"Everybody knows everybody in Oreville. How old are you now?"

"Sixteen point five-eight-three years," Cam says.

Brad's mouth twitches again.

"Time flies" is all he says. "Either of you hold a gun before?"

Cam wants to leap into the fields out back and shoot wildly into the tall grass, but Brad is a strict instructor and insists they start on the indoor range with a rifle. He gives them a long lecture on safety, shows them how to hold the rifle and sight down the barrel and load the magazines full of bullets. When he seems satisfied they will not accidentally shoot each other, he sets up paper targets for them, gives them earmuffs, and lets them fire the loaded rifle.

Cam goes first. Most of her shots are wide of the target, but she manages one bull's-eye, which she examines proudly when Brad reels her paper target back in.

"Not bad for a first try," Brad says.

Cam scowls, preferring to be a prodigy. She clears the rifle and hands it over to Blair, who loads it carefully. Brad clips a target to the wire, sends it out.

Blair sets the butt of the rifle against her shoulder, the way Brad showed them, and lets the same focus descend on her that takes over her body when she jumps hurdles or heads into her fifteenth mile. It's just her and the gun and the white square of paper fluttering from the line.

She pulls the trigger, flips the lever, pulls the trigger, flips the lever, pulls the trigger, until the magazine is spent. Brad brings the target back in. Her shots are all grouped neatly in the bull's-eye.

"Let's try again with the target farther out," Brad says. He sends out the white paper twice as far as it was before. She slaps in a new magazine. The calm silence moves through her. Trigger, chamber, trigger, chamber.

This time one shot is shy of the bull's-eye but the others are clustered again at its heart.

Brad gives her an appraising look. "Who taught you how to shoot?"

"I've never done this before."

"Want to try a pistol?"

Blair shrugs shyly.

"Yes, she does," Cam says.

Brad goes through the safety lecture again, tells her that the pistol will have a stronger recoil than the rifle but it won't hurt her.

"Don't anticipate it," he says. "Let it happen."

Blair's in the zone now. She holds the pistol level, focuses on the target, fires again and again and again. Again, Brad sends the target farther out and again she fires.

"You're a deadly young lady," Brad says as he brings in her last target with its cluster of bull's-eyes. The tension has gone out of his body. He's grinning at her the way she's seen teachers smile at Cam when she does something particularly brilliant in class. Being the star pupil is a new feeling for Blair.

I could get used to this, she thinks.

Next to her, Cam is beaming with pride.

"What's this project you're working on?" Brad says, so casually Blair thinks at first she misheard. But Cam is already explaining the podcast, their interviews, how they are hoping to shed a new light on what happened and who might be responsible for Clarissa's disappearance.

Brad listens in silence.

"Why Clarissa?" he asks when Cam is done.

"Because we . . ." Cam begins. She stops and looks him in the eye. "Because at first it almost seemed like a joke. You know? She's so famous in Oreville that she didn't seem like a real person. I thought it would be an easy way to get—" Cam swallows. "To get attention," she says. "It was my idea. I dragged Blair into it. She didn't want to do it."

"And now?"

"And now it's different," Cam says. "Now I know that there are all these people she left behind who are still suffering. It was a story before. Like an urban legend or something. Now it's real. I want to know what happened to her."

"*We* want to know what happened to her," Blair says. Cam gives her a grateful look. "We want justice."

"You know she's dead," Brad says. There's so much pain in his voice that Blair almost flinches.

"Yes," Cam says quietly.

It's the first time either one of them has admitted it out loud, without reservation. Clarissa is dead and she isn't coming back. And that means that somebody killed her, possibly the man standing in front of them.

Although, after this afternoon, Blair doesn't think so. Brad's guilt doesn't seem like that of a murderer.

Not that Blair knows many murderers for comparison.

He takes the rifle and the pistol. Blair assumes the conversation is over. She reaches for the broom to sweep up their shell casings.

"Leave that," he says. "I'll do it later."

They follow him silently back into the main room of the gun shop. "You can sit," he says, pointing to the table.

They sit. He puts on a pot of coffee. All three of them watch the pot fill. The stillness feels almost companionable. Brad pours out three Styrofoam cups of coffee, sets them on the table with a handful of sugar packets, pulls out a folding chair, settles across from Cam and Blair.

"All right," he says.

"All right?" Cam asks cautiously. "Can we record you?"

"No," he says.

Blair expects Cam to protest, but she only nods. "Okay," she says.

Cam tilts her head, birdlike. Her dark hair is sticking up in the back and she has already managed to spill coffee on her decrepit hoodie. Blair is seized by a surge of affection so strong she has to stop herself from reaching over and hugging Cam tight.

"What was Clarissa like?" Cam asks. Her voice is full of compassion. Blair thinks, for the thousandth time, that Cam will never stop surprising her.

Brad was clearly expecting a different question. "She was extraordinary," he says slowly. "I know everybody says that about her. And I know everybody says that about their first—" He takes a deep breath. "Their first love. But she was. She had this quality of attention. When you were around her it felt like you were the only person in the world who mattered." He looks down at his hands. "I was a terrible boyfriend," he says. "I was an asshole when I was a kid. Picked fights, drove drunk. Cocky, spoiled, got away with everything. Being good at sports in Oreville—well, I'm sure it's not any different now. You're like a little god. And you're too stupid to see that Oreville is a nothing town and anywhere else you'd be nobody special."

He looks up at Blair and his blue gaze goes right through her.

"I loved her," he says. "I didn't know what to do with it. And then she—at first, I thought maybe she ran away that night. She wanted to be an artist somewhere real, you know? I never took it seriously. It mattered more to me that she was a cheerleader. All that bullshit. The king and queen of Oreville fucking High. But she was always talking about going to art school, moving to a big city. Clarissa always did what she wanted to do. I didn't think she would've left town without telling me, but that night was . . ."

He trails off.

That night was what, Cam thinks. What, *Brad!*

But Brad has stopped talking, his face closed down again.

"When did you know she hadn't just run away?" Blair asks.

"I think I knew as soon as her parents called me the next day to say she hadn't come home," he says. "But I didn't want to believe it. It was easier to think that she was pissed at me. Blowing off steam somewhere."

"Why would she be pissed at you?" Blair asks.

He shakes his head. "None of your business," he says curtly. "And anyway, it doesn't matter. That has nothing to do with what happened to her. But by Monday, it was obvious. She was— something had happened. Something bad. She might've been mad enough to leave town without telling me, but she never would've done that to her parents. She didn't get along with them, but she was the only thing they had."

Blair thinks of the Campbells' miserable dead house, full of Clarissa shrines. Mrs. Campbell's conviction that Clarissa will be back any moment.

"You know that I was the main suspect," Brad says.

Cam says calmly, "Did you kill her?"

Blair sucks her breath in hard, but Brad isn't thrown by the question. He smiles.

"You're definitely Reenie's kid," he says. "No, I didn't kill her. Not that the truth did me any good back then."

Or now, Blair thinks.

The empty shooting range, the dilapidated building. Oreville still punishing Brad Bennett for his imagined sins.

Brad Bennett is a common enough name. The hysteria over Clarissa died down eventually. He could have a normal life anywhere else.

What is he still doing in Oreville?

"If you didn't kill her, who could have?" Cam asks.

"I don't know."

"We heard you beat a kid up because he was gay," Blair says.

"Sure," Brad says. "I did shit like that all the time." He closes his eyes for a moment, as if he can't bear to look at Cam and Blair. But he opens them again when he says, "I told you, I was an asshole. I can't change what I did. I can regret it. I can apologize. I can try to be a better person. I can't rewrite the past. But I never hurt Clarissa. I never would've hurt Clarissa. No matter what she did."

"What did she do?" Blair asks.

"That was rhetorical," Brad says, but Blair is pretty sure he's lying.

"Why do the Campbells hate you so much?" It's another Cam question, ruthless and direct.

"Clarissa was wild," he says. "Headstrong. She loved trouble. It was one of the things I loved about her. She was always up for anything." He smiles, remembering. "You know that razor wire on the Motel 6 fence on Water Street?" Cam nods. "They put that up because me and Clar used to sneak in there all the time in the middle of the night to go skinny-dipping in their pool. Her idea. All the crazy ideas were always hers.

"She hid it from her parents for a long time. They wanted a princess, and she was—well, she wasn't going to grow up to have a white wedding and a normal job and pump out big fat babies, which was what they expected from her. But by her senior year, I think she stopped caring what they thought. It was easier for them to blame me than to accept that their daughter wasn't what they needed her to be."

Cam's thinking of Mrs. Campbell too. "Her mom doesn't seem to spend much time in the real world," she says.

"You talked to Marian? How'd that go?"

"Not great," Blair says diplomatically.

"I bet. Clarissa's disappearance totally destroyed her," Brad says. "But no, she was never a fan of reality. Clar was an amazing person, but I'm not sure her parents ever saw her for what she was."

Did anyone? Blair wonders. She thinks of the magazine articles, the saintly portraits of the untarnished all-American girl. Maybe Brad is the only person who really knew her.

Maybe he didn't know her at all.

"What about her art teacher?" Blair asks.

Brad's face twists into an expression Blair can't read. "Dan?"

"Did he see her for what she was?"

"I don't know," he says hoarsely.

"We saw her painting," Cam says, when it's clear he won't say anything else. "She was good."

"Yeah," he says. "I think she was. I don't know anything about art. I haven't seen any of her stuff in a long time. Her parents have it all now. I didn't pay attention to her art when we were together. Too caught up in my own petty sports bullshit. Now it's too late."

"Why do you think the police were so focused on you?" Cam asks.

"It's always the boyfriend, isn't it?"

"The police didn't try to find anyone else," Cam says.

"You *have* been asking questions," he says. "No, they didn't. But I don't know who else could've killed her. And I don't know why anyone would want to. It never made any sense. It still doesn't."

"Allen said everybody loved Clarissa," Blair says.

"Allen? Allen who?"

"Allen Dawson," Cam says.

"Allen Dawson? That kid? Where the hell did you dig him up?"

"He's here," Blair says.

"In Oreville?" Brad's surprise is genuine. Blair wonders if that means anything.

"His mom is sick," Cam explains. "He moved back to take care of her. We talked to him last week. He thought you weren't good for Clarissa."

"He was the last person in Oreville who would've known. Clarissa wouldn't have given him the time of day." He catches Blair's look. "Clarissa was a lot of things, but she was no saint," he says. "None of us were. I doubt it's any different now in high school."

"He said she was nice to him."

"Allen Dawson said Clarissa was *nice* to him? That's some wishful thinking. He wormed his way into her parents' house after she disappeared and stayed there for months."

"He said it was basically an accident, that he ended up helping out," Blair says.

"Maybe that's the story he's selling now," Brad says. "But you couldn't have pried him out of that house with a crowbar after Clarissa went missing. Allen and his fucking ribbons. Jesus Christ. Clar hated the color orange."

"Why would he get involved with her parents?" Cam asks. "Even he said he didn't know Clarissa that well."

"I guess it made him feel important. The center of attention. It was the only way he was going to get any. When the cameras disappeared, so did he."

"Rubberneckers," Blair says quietly.

"Lot of that around, after Clarissa disappeared," Brad says. "Everybody was her best friend all of a sudden. Crying on national television. I used to imagine her holed up somewhere in a hotel room, watching the news and laughing. I knew she was dead, but it—" His voice breaks, and he clears his throat. "It was something she would have done." He looks down at his hands again.

"Did she seem different in the weeks before the party?" Blair asks.

"The police asked me that twenty years ago. Look it up."

"Twenty years ago you were a suspect," Cam says.

"You go digging around too hard and they might remember that," Brad says.

"But you didn't do anything wrong."

"You think people around here believe that?"

Cam waits, looking at him with her big relentless eyes.

"Yeah," he says. "Yeah, she was acting weird."

"Did you tell the police?"

"No."

Excitement flares in Cam's chest, but she's careful to keep her voice steady. "Acting weird? Weird how?"

"Like . . ." He shakes his head. "This goes nowhere, you understand me? Keep my name out of it." But Blair can see it in his face. He's desperate for someone to talk to, after all these years out here with no one to share his secrets. She and Cam both nod.

"Like, manic almost," Brad says. "Distracted."

"Distracted by what?" Blair asks.

"I don't know. We got in a few fights about it. We were fighting the night of the party. I thought maybe she was going to go somewhere."

Cam sits up. "Go where?"

"She started talking about leaving town. Like, for real. Maybe she was planning something. She never told me, but I kind of got that feeling."

"You mean she was planning on running away?" Blair asks.

"I don't know. Maybe. But even if she had a plan, that's not what happened to her. She wouldn't have left like that. Like I said, she wouldn't have done that to her parents. I . . ." He takes a deep breath.

Here it comes, Blair thinks.

"I'm done talking," he says. "I think you'd both better go."

"But—" Cam tries.

"I mean it," he says. "I'm done."

Cam slouches back in her chair, unable to keep her disappointment off her face. "One more thing," she says. "Did you donate any money to Aaron Liechty? In 2000, when he ran for sheriff?"

"Are you serious? After what he put me through? I hope that asshole gets run over by a truck. Why?"

"Someone did," Cam says.

"Someone gave *Aaron Liechty* money?"

"Someone made a big donation to his campaign for sheriff after Clarissa disappeared," Cam says.

"How big?"

"We don't know all the details yet."

Brad shakes his head. "That's a hell of a coincidence," he says. "But it wasn't me."

Blair and Cam quietly gather up their things, stand up. Cam pushes the folding chairs neatly back under the table. Brad doesn't move. He's staring into nothing. Lost in memories?

Blair wonders if they should say goodbye or just leave. Cam touches her elbow, and they move toward the door.

"Talk to Jenny," Brad says suddenly. Cam turns around. "Jenny Alexander. She's still in town. She knew Clar better than anyone. Better than I did, that's for sure."

"We couldn't find her," Blair says.

He writes a number down on a piece of paper and holds it out to them. "We're still in touch," he says. "You can tell her I sent you."

"Would you say something on the record?" Cam asks. "So we can use it on the podcast? It doesn't have to be long."

"Do you ever give up?"

"No," Cam and Blair say simultaneously.

Brad laughs. "I'll make you a deal. I'll give you something for your podcast. And if you find out who killed her, I want first crack at him."

Blair looks him in the eye. "We'll do our best," she says. "That's a promise."

———

"*THAT'S A PROMISE*? We can't make promises to *suspects*!" Cam explodes as soon as they're back in the car.

"Oh, come on. Do you think he's a suspect? He's, like, broken-hearted."

"You just like him because he looks like James."

"He does not!" Blair protests, although in truth, the similarities between Brad and James are slightly unnerving.

You're like a little god. And you're too stupid to see that Oreville is a nothing town and anywhere else you'd be nobody special.

But James *is* special.

"He does too! He's like James would be if James got a clue."

"Shut up," Blair says. "Do you think he's guilty?"

"Not really," Cam concedes. "But he seems so miserable. Why did he stick around after Clarissa disappeared if everybody hated him?"

"He's punishing himself," Blair says.

"Okay," Cam says, accepting that Blair understands human motivations far better than she ever will. "He said Clarissa was mad at him about something. What else did we find out? He doesn't know about the money. He thought Clarissa was planning on running away, but she would've told her parents if she'd done it."

"He said she did something bad," Blair says.

"He did?"

"Not in so many words."

"Clarissa did something bad, and then he did something bad to her? Something that made her angry enough to leave Oreville?"

"Something that made him feel so guilty he never left Oreville himself," Blair says.

They both subside into silence, contemplating Brad's potential crimes. If he didn't kill Clarissa, what could possibly be bad enough to send him into self-imposed exile for so long?

"Reenie," Cam says, bringing Blair back to the present.

"What?"

"Brad called Irene 'Reenie.'"

"That must have been her nickname in high school."

"But she wasn't in high school when Clarissa disappeared," Cam says. "She had already graduated. And she told us she didn't know him."

"No, she didn't," Blair corrects, remembering. "She told us she didn't know Clarissa. She didn't say anything about Brad."

"Irene never lies," Cam says. "If she doesn't want you to know something, she forgets to mention it."

Blair sits up straighter, her eyes fixed on the road. "I guess we have to ask her what she left out."

―――――

CAM AND BLAIR spend the rest of the long drive home mulling over how to crack the tough nut that is Irene. They both know from long experience that Irene is immune to flattery, bribes, manipulation, threats, and weeping.

"Let's just ask her and see what happens," Cam says. Blair shakes her head, but she doesn't have a better idea.

Blair parks next to Irene's car in the apartment complex lot.

"Pizza night!" Cam yells, slamming her way into the apartment.

Irene is in the kitchen, staring meditatively at the stove. "Hi, Blair. Would you please tell my child her mother isn't deaf yet?"

"Hi, Irene. Cam, no yelling in the house," Blair says.

"Can we order pizza?" Cam yells.

Irene covers her eyes with her hands. "I need a mental hospital."

"You work in a mental hospital," Cam says in a normal tone of voice.

"We had pizza last week," Irene says.

"That was a different week," Cam points out.

"I suppose it was," Irene says, giving the stove one last look. "I don't feel like cooking anyway."

"I don't feel like eating your cooking," Cam says cheerfully.

"For the love of god," Irene says.

"Cam, leave your mother alone," Blair says, towing Cam out of the kitchen.

"That one!" Irene crows, pointing to Blair. "*That* one is my child! I'm sending the other one back!"

"The warranty's expired!" Cam bellows.

Blair's parents demand family dinners in the dining room, phones off and pleasant conversation mandatory, unless her dad had a bad day at work, in which case he complains throughout the meal though no one else is allowed to.

Cam and Irene don't have a dining room, let alone dinner rules. They eat at the coffee table in the living room like always, an old sci-fi movie playing at an unintelligible volume on Cam and Irene's ancient TV. Cam waits until Irene is halfway through a bottle of red wine and a goat-cheese-and-artichoke-heart pizza before she springs her trap.

"You never told us you were friends with Clarissa's boyfriend," she says through a mouthful of pepperoni, her voice casual.

Irene sets the WORLD'S #1 DAD mug she always uses as a wineglass on the coffee table. "I wasn't," she says.

"That's not what he said," Cam counters.

Irene's face is an absolute blank. Her eyes stay on the screen, where a lady in a jumpsuit is spraying an alien monster with a flamethrower.

"You talked to Brad for your podcast?"

Her voice is calm. Too calm. Blair's heart quails. Danger signals are flaring.

"Yeah, today," Cam says, taking another bite of pizza and watching Irene like Kitten at the refrigerator door.

"Why did you think that was appropriate?"

"He was Clarissa's boyfriend," Cam says. "He had a lot to say."

"I find that hard to believe," Irene says.

"So you did know him," Cam says triumphantly.

Irene picks up WORLD'S #1 DAD, takes a long sip, sets it down again. Cam waits.

"I knew him," Irene says.

"Why didn't you say so?"

"Cameron P. Muñoz," Irene says. "Maybe you should let all of this alone."

"All of what? What do you know about Clarissa? Can I record you?"

"No, you absolutely cannot," Irene says. Cam already has her phone out. "Put that away. Right now."

Cam sets her phone facedown on the table.

Blair wonders if it is safe to breathe yet. Should she flee the scene? Irene doesn't look angry. She looks like Brad looked: very tired and very sad.

"What I am going to tell you does not leave this house," Irene says. "Do you understand me, Cameron?"

"Yes," Cam says.

Irene looks at Blair. "The fruit of my loins, her I do not trust. But you, Blair Johnson, will keep your word. And you will ensure this one"—she points at Cam—"does too. Am I right? Not a word of this outside this room."

Blair nods.

"Fine," Irene says. "I was at that stupid party. I knew Brad from around. I'd had a crush on him since we were kids. We all made a lot of bad decisions that night. I had been drinking, and so had Brad. And—" Irene stops, takes a deep breath. "I am not proud of this, Cameron, and the only reason I am telling you is because you need to understand that what you and Blair are doing has consequences. This isn't some tabloid story about serial killers. You live in a small town, and most of the people who were there that night still live here too, and there is a lot of pain from that time that never went away for any of us. What the two of you are digging up has the potential to destroy people's lives. Am I making myself clear?"

Cameron and Blair nod in speechless unison.

"Brad and Clarissa got into a fight that night. That's not a secret. No, Cameron, I do not know what it was about," she adds, cutting Cam off before she can get the question out. "I don't. Clarissa left. I don't know where she went. No one knows exactly when she disappeared. You know what it's like out in those woods. Everybody was drinking, running around—she could have still been there. I don't know."

Irene's voice is steady, but her hands are knotted together in her lap so tightly her knuckles are white. "Somebody had built a bonfire and I was sitting next to it, alone. After Clarissa left Brad came up to me. We talked for a long time. Not about Clarissa. It was obvious he was upset, but he didn't want to talk about that. We talked about school, our lives, what we were going to do when we got out of Oreville. I had graduated the year before but I was saving up money to move to New York. It got late. A lot of people had left. We were alone for a while by the fire. And then he—" Irene takes another sip of wine. "Then we were kissing," she says curtly. "All right, Cameron? Brad was with me until he went home, and god knows that poor man has suffered enough. Half of Oreville still thinks he killed her. So when I ask you to leave him alone, I mean it."

"And you kept that to *yourself*?" Cam is incredulous.

"It had nothing to do with why Clarissa disappeared, and it is nobody's business. Including yours, Cameron. Are we clear?"

"But you could've been his alibi," Cam says.

Irene is already shaking her head. "No one knows when Clarissa disappeared. How do you think it would have sounded to the police? Brad gets in a fight with his girlfriend, cheats on her, can't prove where he was half the night? Absolutely not."

"You think he's innocent," Cam says.

"I know he's innocent," Irene snaps. "You are not listening to me, Cameron. That man's life was ruined because he was in the wrong place at the wrong time. I will not have you digging through old history to ruin it all over again. Is that clear?"

"But Brad was the only person there who had a motive to kill her," Cam protests. "Maybe their fight was about something serious. Maybe Clarissa knew something bad about him. Or maybe she *saw* you. Did you think of that? What if she saw you and got in a fight with Brad again and he killed her—"

Irene cuts her off. "You are not listening to me, Cameron," she says. "I am *telling* you, Brad did *not* kill Clarissa, and if you go around saying these kinds of things in public—"

"You can't possibly know for sure that he didn't kill Clarissa," Cam says. She's getting just as mad. Blair's eyes move from Irene to Cam and back again like she's watching a deadly tennis match. "You weren't with him the whole night. And you could have told us this when we started working on the project. You're the one hiding things. How do I know you're not hiding something else?"

"And what, you're going to put that on the internet now? Do you understand that accusing someone of a serious crime without evidence has serious consequences? You can't go around libeling people. You know we don't have money for a goddamn lawyer!"

"You're the one who never told the police the truth about what happened!" Cameron yells back. Blair wants to cover her ears. "You have a lot of nerve lecturing me about the truth when you're the one who's been lying!"

Irene thumps her mug down on the coffee table and gets up. Without another word, she walks out of the room. They can hear her bedroom door slam behind her.

"Fine!" Cameron yells after her. "Walk away!"

"Cam," Blair whispers. Cam is sobbing with fury, her shoulders shaking. Blair pets her gently. "It's okay," she says. "Cam, it's okay."

"It's not okay!"

Blair hands Cam a wad of paper napkins that came with their pizza and Cam blows her nose noisily. "I can't believe she lied to me," Cam says, her voice muffled.

"Technically, she just left a lot out," Blair says.

"Right," Cam says bitterly. "Irene doesn't lie."

"You don't think Brad killed Clarissa, do you?"

"No," Cam says, blowing her nose again. "I don't know. Who else could have? Irene?"

"Irene?" Blair asks, shocked. "You think your *mom* killed Clarissa? Why would she do that?"

"If she was in love with Brad or something? She told us she was drunk. Maybe Clarissa did see them and picked a fight with Irene instead. Maybe Irene pushed Clarissa off a cliff and doesn't remember."

"You don't believe that," Blair says. "Come on. There's no cliff out there."

"How am I supposed to know what to believe?" Cam's voice is rising again. Blair makes a noise she hopes is soothing. "Irene never tells me anything!"

You never tell her anything either, Blair thinks.

This, obviously, is not the time. She rubs Cam's shoulders until they come down from around her ears.

"Well," Cam says, sniffling. "That was embarrassing. Want to watch another movie?"

BRAD

She'll always be the one that got away. That's how it works when someone like Clarissa dies young. It's funny, but the thing I remember most about her now was how angry she was. I don't think I knew it for what it was when we were together. But now that I've been angry for a long time myself I can see it. The fire in her, it wasn't only ambition. It wasn't love. Mostly, it was rage.

She wanted so much more than any of us could give her. She wanted more than this town. But we were still from here. None of us had the words to ask for something bigger. We knew there was a world out there, but we had no idea how to find it. And that pissed her off more than anything else.

I mean, this was before the internet. I guess some of the geeks were out there, hanging out in AOL chat rooms or whatever. LiveJournal? I don't know. But it was nothing then like it is now. The news from outside came from magazines, newspapers, MTV. Stuff like that. Yeah, music videos—can you believe that now? You're too young. You have no idea. Clar breathed all that stuff in like it was oxygen, but it still wasn't enough. She knew what we had here was too small for her, but she didn't know how to get anywhere else.

She talked a lot about moving to the city. Seattle first, and then New York. I guess—I guess I know who told her about New York. She never went there. I don't think Joe and Marian have been outside of Washington State in decades. Maybe for a cruise. But probably not. They're still waiting for her to come home. They took her to Mexico once, the summer before tenth grade. I remember because she came back with her hair in cornrows. She was so proud of herself. So tan. She must've kept those damn braids in for a month. These pink plastic beads at the end clacking together. She'd swing her head around so you'd be sure to hear them. That's the closest she got to somewhere that isn't here. That, and dreaming. I know she had big dreams.

Me and Jenny looked for Clar for a long time after she disappeared. I never told anyone, and I don't think she did either, but we did. We used to drive around late at night together. Out to the coast. Out to Seattle. All the way down to Portland once. We got a crappy hotel room and stayed for a couple of days and walked around downtown talking to every street kid we saw. They were pretty nice about it. I guess because we didn't look like parents. We looked lost.

We tried to get her case file—Jenny did, anyway. The cops wouldn't have let me through the door. I was the only suspect. It didn't do any good. The cops wouldn't talk to Jenny either. I knew we weren't going to find her. I knew she was dead. I don't know what Jenny thought. But we couldn't let it go. We couldn't just leave her. Everybody else moved on eventually, except for Clarissa's parents. It felt like a betrayal, though some part of me understood. It's possible to live your life in the past, but it's not a good idea. Not that I'm one to take my own advice. I knew better, but I still hoped one of those nights we'd find her. Walking along the road somewhere, her paintbrushes in her backpack, full of stories about where she'd been. I wanted—

Jesus. It doesn't matter what I wanted. I would have gone anywhere with her. Anywhere she asked me to. But I didn't know how to say that to her when she was alive. And now that I do, now that I can, it's too late.

EPISODE V

THE
REGRETS

WHATEVER Blair was expecting Jenny Alexander to be, Jenny Alexander definitely isn't it. She lives out in the county too, but her place couldn't be more different from Brad's: a cabin in a clearing at the end of a dirt road, surrounded by huge old trees and dappled sunlight. Behind the house Blair can see the rows of a vegetable garden, neatly mulched for winter other than a few rows of greens.

The woman who opens the door to Cam's knock is unrecognizable from the person in the picture with Clarissa. The Jenny on Clarissa's wall was wraith-thin in her tiny shorts and halter, spray-tanned, blond as Clarissa. This person is solid, in faded old overalls and muck boots. The sleeves of her flannel shirt are rolled up to her elbows, revealing muscled forearms wreathed with tattoos that start at her knuckles. She's wearing a wool watch cap; underneath, her head is shaved. An immense dog hulks at her side, tail waving. It looks like a cross between a Rottweiler and the devil.

"Ms. Alexander?" Blair asks.

"Jenny," she says, and grins. Her teeth are still a cheerleader's, white and even. "Come on in. This is Baskerville. He's friendly."

Jenny Alexander's house makes Cam think of a ship. Everything is compact and tidy and stowed away. There's no liberal scattering of Irene detritus, no Mrs. Campbell-esque bric-a-brac, no Brad Bennett shabbiness and sorrow. Jenny points them to the sofa, which is piled with faded old handmade quilts, and brings them mugs of tea that smell like roses and the color green.

"Rose hip and lemon balm from the garden," she says, settling herself cross-legged on a pillow on the floor and looking up at them with her clear gray eyes. Baskerville tries to climb in her lap. "You're too big, doofus," Jenny says. He settles for resting his head on her thigh and gazing up at her adoringly. "Brad must've liked the two of you if he gave you my number. Tell me about your project."

Cam explains the podcast, what they've found so far. Jenny looks thoughtful, but she doesn't say anything when Cam's done.

"You like to garden?" Blair asks to break the silence.

"My girlfriend's got the green thumb," Jenny says. "I kill every plant I touch. I can build a house, though."

Cam starts at "girlfriend," which Blair doesn't miss, and neither does Jenny. "Came out after high school," she says easily. "When I figured out the thing I liked about cheerleading wasn't the cheers."

Blair laughs. Cam looks confused.

"You built this house?" Cam asks, looking around as if expecting cheerleaders to come tumbling out of the woodwork.

"Yes," Jenny says with that same easiness, a quiet confidence that Blair is drinking in. What would it be like, to be so sure in her own skin?

"Why did you stay in Oreville?" Cam blurts at the same time Blair asks, "Can we record you?"

"Yes," Jenny says. "And I didn't, originally." She waits for Cam, still flustered, to turn on her phone's recorder. "I moved to Seattle after high school, lived there for fifteen years, met Ellie." She gestures to a framed picture of her and another woman holding a huge bunch of flowers. Next to it hangs the same picture of her and Clarissa that they saw at the Campbells'. "Ellie wanted more room for a garden and I wanted a forest. Land's still cheap out here."

"I wonder why," Cam says dourly.

"Yeah, I know," Jenny says. "But we stay out here in the woods. I got my party years out of me a long time ago. All I need is my girlfriend and my dog and the outdoors these days." Baskerville woofs softly, tail thumping. Jenny's thigh, Cam notes, is covered with drool. Kitten would never.

"Were you close to Brad in high school?" Blair asks.

"He was my best friend's boyfriend, so we spent a fair amount of time together. But we didn't get close until—after. He understood what I was going through, because he was going through it too. Clarissa's disappearance changed him. Changed both of us." She looks up at the picture of her and Clarissa. "I still don't know if it's better to believe that she ran away and left us all wondering or to think she's dead. There's no option where it doesn't hurt."

"Could she have done it?" Cam asks. "Disappeared?"

"Yes," Jenny says without hesitation. "Clarissa could be ruthless."

"Why would she do that?" Blair asks.

"Clarissa and I fought a lot in the months before the party," Jenny says. "There were always things she didn't tell me. But she was different somehow. More closed off. More secretive. She'd pick fights with me about nothing. Looking back, I think she was trying to push me away. But when it was happening, I couldn't see that. I said some horrible things to her at that party. That tore me up for years."

"And you thought that was why she might leave town?" Cam asks.

Jenny shakes her head. "Nothing I said to her mattered by then. She was already gone somewhere I couldn't reach. We had been close for so long, and then it was like someone flipped a switch. It took me a long time to get over it. That someone I loved so much could change like that, practically overnight." She looks straight at Cam. "I was in love with her," she says. "I didn't have the language then. I was a cheerleader. It was the nineties. In *Oreville*. And even if I had been able to talk about it, there's no way I would've said anything. I hated myself for how I felt. I didn't know anyone else like me. I thought I was a freak. Clarissa didn't feel the same way about me, but I think she knew."

"Is that what you fought about?" Cam asks.

"No," Jenny says. "We fought about—something else."

Blair feels something barely out of reach, a puzzle with one piece missing.

I guess—I guess I know who told her about New York.

And then the final piece is in her hand. She knows.

"You fought about Dan Friley," Blair says.

Jenny looks at Cam's phone. "Turn that off," she says.

"But—" Cam protests.

"Turn it off and give it to me," Jenny says.

Cam powers off her phone and hands it to Jenny, who puts it in her lap.

"Yes," she says. "We fought about Dan Friley."

"Her art teacher? Why?" Cam says.

Oh, Cam, Blair thinks. How can someone so smart fail to see all the things that are bad in the world?

"They were—" Blair begins, but she can't finish the question.

"Yes," Jenny says. "They were."

"They were what?" Cam again, still bewildered. "They

were—" And then it connects in her giant brain and she sits, staring, totally speechless.

"There are teachers everybody knows not to end up alone with, right? Dan Friley wasn't like that. He was a real artist. Handsome, charismatic. He was from a big city. Sold his paintings in galleries. Wore nice clothes. Knew about wine. That kind of thing. All the girls loved him."

Cam makes an appalled noise.

"Easy for you to say now," Jenny says. "He treated us like adults. Told us to call him by his first name. Swore in front of us, told dirty jokes. He encouraged us to talk about our lives. He said his office was always open—it was a joke, you know? He didn't have an office. But he let us come into the art studio anytime we wanted. He asked us about who we were dating, paid attention to the details. He had us keep sketchbooks—he'd collect them once a week, write personal notes to us, encourage us to write back. He told us what books to read, what movies to watch, what painters to love. He told us to go to Europe after we graduated, before we went to college. He told us which museums to go to. He had a list. We worshipped him. When he and Clarissa started—whatever you want to call it—it seemed glamorous. I was jealous."

"Of him?" Blair asks.

"Of her. Of both of them. I don't know. I was so young and so confused. I didn't know if I wanted Clarissa or if I wanted to *be* Clarissa. I wanted to be special enough for Mr. Friley to pick me. But I wasn't. You don't think about what kind of thirty-year-old man wants to sleep with a seventeen-year-old girl when you're seventeen. You assume it's because you're so sophisticated. Because you're so mature for your age."

Blair can see it: the dazzling teacher, telling you you're special. That you have something other girls don't. Something irresistible.

If that happened to her, who's to say she wouldn't believe it too?

"Clarissa told you?" Blair asks.

"She didn't tell anyone, as far as I know," Jenny says. "I think it had been going on for a while by the time I figured it out. They were—he was—careful."

"What happened the night of the party?" Cam asks.

"Clar and I—" Jenny stops. Her voice is thick. She clears her throat, wipes tears out of her eyes with the back of one hand.

Cam leans forward. Blair puts one hand on her shoulder.

"I told Brad that night," Jenny says. "About Clarissa and Dan."

"Why didn't you tell a teacher or something? How could Brad help?" Cam asks.

But Blair is way ahead of her.

"You didn't tell Brad because you wanted to help Clarissa," Blair says. "You told him because you wanted to make him jealous. Because you thought if you blew up her relationship—relationships—you might have a chance with her."

"I'm not sure I thought it through that clearly," Jenny says. This time she doesn't try to stop the tears running down her cheeks. "Clarissa was so talented, but all her life she'd only gotten attention for being pretty. Nobody saw past her face. Dan was this big-deal artist. He didn't say she was beautiful. He said she was a painter. When I told her I knew about them—she laughed at me. She said they were going to run away together. Move to New York. That he was going to get her a show in a real gallery."

"They had a plan? She was going to run away with him?"

"Maybe she thought so. But him? Come on. I told her that was a crock of shit, that he wanted to get in her pants. She was furious. And then the night of the party I got drunk and told Brad about Clarissa and Dan. He totally lost it. He went tearing

through the woods after her. Screaming her name. It was awful."
She stops again.

"And then she disappeared?" Cam asks.

"No," Jenny says. "Then she found me. She knew. That I was
the one who'd told him. She told me—" Jenny stops, her voice
breaking, and takes a deep breath. "The last thing she said to me
was 'I will never forgive you for this.' And then she walked away
from me into the woods, and I never saw her again."

"I'm sorry," Blair says quietly.

"Yeah," Jenny says. "Me too. For years I . . ." She trails off.
"Let's say for a while after high school I made some pretty bad
decisions. Ended up in rehab a few times, the whole dog-and-
pony show. Who knows, maybe I would've gone that way anyway. Like I said, I hated myself in high school, was terrified of
coming out. But carrying that around didn't help."

"But it wasn't your fault," Cam says. "It was his. Dan Friley's."

"Maybe," Jenny says. "I went over it so many times in my
head. If I hadn't told Brad. If I'd tried to talk to her differently.
If I hadn't been so jealous. If I'd told her how I felt. Nothing
changes what I did."

"But you wouldn't have fought with her in the first place if
he hadn't—"

"Cam," Blair says.

"You sound like my therapist," Jenny says.

"You should listen to your therapist," Cam says.

"*Cam,*" Blair says, and Cam shuts her mouth on whatever
she's about to say next. "Did you see Dan Friley at the party?"
Blair asks.

"No," Jenny says.

"Do you think he could have killed her?"

"Theoretically, sure. I mean, all that stuff about running
away together? Maybe she pushed him too hard or he got tired

of her. But I don't see how it would have been possible for him to kill her that night. He had no way of knowing where we were."

"Maybe they were going to meet up at the party," Blair says.

"Why?" Jenny asks. "Why that night? Why would he drive all the way out there? She didn't have anything with her. It doesn't make any sense. If they did have a plan, they would've picked a different time to leave."

"Could Clarissa have called him from the party?" Cam asked. "After you fought with her?"

"With what? Back then we used pagers and pay phones."

"Oh," Cam says. "Right." She looks confused. "Pagers?"

"Never mind," Jenny says. "Anyway, she disappeared that night, and he didn't. They didn't leave together. I don't know why he would've gone all the way out there to hurt her."

"What if Clarissa was going to go public about their—" Cam pauses, trying to find the right word, but Jenny is already shaking her head.

"You have to understand, this was the nineties," she says. "Teachers got away with things like that all the time. There had been rumors about Dan for years. Clarissa never wanted to hear any of it; for her, he walked on water. The school didn't do a thing. I don't know what she could have threatened him with. I doubt anyone would have believed her. Or if they had, they would've blamed her."

"How could they not believe her if they already knew it was true?" Cam asks.

Jenny looks at her. "You're young," she says. "No offense. You still believe that people will do the right thing when it's harder than doing nothing."

"But he was her *teacher*," Cam says. "He was an adult. She was our age."

"I hear things are different now," Jenny says bleakly.

"Why did he quit teaching after she went missing?" Blair asks.

"I don't know."

"Why didn't you tell the police?" Cam asks.

"I did."

"What?" Cam sits up straight. "What happened?"

"I didn't want to say anything. If it got out—that's all people would remember about her. Some teenage seductress, screwing her art teacher. I already felt like her disappearance was my fault. Maybe it was. Trashing her name after she was gone felt like the worst thing I could do. But the cops were hounding Brad. For a while there, it seemed like he might go to prison. I knew it wasn't him. He never would've hurt her. So I went in to see that horrible detective. Aaron Liechty. 'You can't possibly prove that,' he said. And I couldn't. He told me to keep my theories to myself. That there was no reason to ruin an upstanding man's life with idle gossip."

"And he gets to . . . live his life?" Cam asks. "Like nothing happened?"

"At least he's not teaching high school anymore," Jenny says.

"We saw her painting," Blair says. "The one where she's sitting in a field in front of the high school. She looks so sad in it."

"I remember that one," Jenny says. "Marian has her paintings now. They're all pretty sad, from what I remember."

"She said you lost touch," Blair says.

"That's one way to put it. Marian's not exactly a crusader for LGBTQ rights," Jenny says sharply. But then she sighs. "Forget I said that," she says. "That's not fair. Marian's a piece of work, but I used to show up drunk at her house after Clarissa disappeared. She had to call the cops on me once to get me to leave. I don't blame her for writing me off after that."

"Maybe she could put together a show of Clarissa's paintings," Blair says.

Jenny shakes her head. "She'd have to admit Clarissa's gone. And she'd have to let people see that Clarissa wasn't all sunbeams and butterflies. Those paintings are dark. Marian doesn't like to think about that version of Clarissa."

"The real version?" Blair asks.

"The whole version," Jenny says.

"Clarissa was a good artist," Cam says.

"She was," Jenny says. "I think she could have been—oh, who knows. Who knows what she could have been? She was so young. She could've been anything. Or nothing."

"What do you think happened to her?" Blair asks.

"That's the worst part," Jenny says. "No matter how many times I go over it. I can't think of who or how. Where she would've gone. If she hurt herself in the woods somewhere and we left her there—"

"They would've found her," Cam says. "If that had happened."

"I guess by now they would've," Jenny says. But she doesn't sound sure.

"How did Clarissa get to the party?" Blair asks.

"The cops were all over that. Brad gave her a ride there," Jenny says. "He brought back a couple of guys from the football team around three in the morning. Nobody else drove her anywhere."

"Nobody else said they drove her anywhere," Cam says. "It was a big party, right?"

"I can't imagine anyone had a reason to hurt Clarissa. Not Brad, that's for sure. If he was going to kill anyone, he'd kill Dan Friley. No way would he hurt Clarissa."

"Irene said the same thing," Cam says thoughtfully.

"Irene?" Jenny looks hard at her. "You're *Reenie's* kid? Oh, hell."

"Small town," Cam says.

Jenny laughs, a hard, broken sound. "You have no idea," she

says. "You know Brad and I used to look for her together, after she disappeared."

"He told us," Blair says.

"Did he? He really must've liked you."

There's the noise of a key in the lock, the knob turning. Jenny's dog leaps to its feet and runs to the front door, tail wagging. The door opens, revealing a slight figure carrying reusable grocery bags.

"Hey, babe," Jenny says. She gets up and helps her girlfriend carry in their groceries. "No, it's fine, stay there," she says to Cam and Blair before they can get up too.

Ellie is a tiny, sprite-like Black woman, her angelic features topped with a puckish Afro dyed white-blond. She looks curiously at Cam and Blair. Jenny introduces them as Ellie settles the groceries on the kitchen counter and makes herself a cup of tea.

"They're making a podcast about Clarissa," Jenny explains. Ellie gives them a sharp look.

"Did you know her?" Cam asks hopefully.

"I'm from Alabama," Ellie says, her voice a syrupy golden pour. "Didn't move up to Seattle until a few years ago."

Jenny smiles down at her, kisses the top of her head. Her sadness has lifted.

She's glowing, Blair thinks. They both are. Their love charges the whole room.

"Thanks for your time," Blair says, getting to her feet. She doesn't want to bother this woman anymore with old ghosts.

Cam gives her a dirty look. "I have one more question," she says. "Do you think you could show us where the party was?"

"You mean, drive out there with you?" Jenny asks.

"No, like with a geotag," Cam says. "But you still have my phone."

"Right, sorry," Jenny says. She hands Cam's phone over. Cam pulls up a map and gives her phone back to Jenny.

"I don't know," Jenny says, dubious. "It's been a long time." She looks at Cam's screen, her face thoughtful as she moves the map around. "Maybe here?" She taps the phone and hands it back to Cam again.

"People still party at that exact spot," Blair says.

"Seriously?" Cam asks. Mr. Park was right.

"Sure," Blair says, checking Cam's phone again. "There's a party out there this weekend."

"I'm not surprised, honestly," Jenny says. "Why wouldn't they?"

"I don't know," Blair says. "Respect?"

"It's Oreville," Jenny says.

Cam looks again at the photo of Jenny and Clarissa hanging on Jenny's wall. "Can I take a picture of this?" she asks.

"Sure," Jenny says.

Cam leans in with her phone. Jenny and Clarissa, smiling into the sunlight. She pauses, a strange sharp feeling screwing its way into her brain.

She's missing something. What is it?

Sunny smiles, white teeth, tan cheerleader skin, colorful bikinis, ordinary cutoffs. Too-skinny Jenny jewelry-less, Clarissa wearing a blue necklace.

The forest? The water?

And then it's gone.

She frowns, snaps a picture, turns around. "Who took this?"

"Brad," Jenny says.

Brad.

Does it mean something? How could it? It's just a picture. He must have gone to the beach with Clarissa and Jenny all the time.

Cam turns back to the picture one last time. Someone she missed in the background? Had Jenny had a boyfriend? She hasn't said anything. If she did, why would he have killed Clarissa?

"Thank you," she says. "We'll stop bothering you now."

Jenny smiles. Her eyes are sad.

"Y'all be careful now," Ellie says suddenly. "Sometimes it's better to let sleeping dogs lie."

"Is that a Southern thing?" Cam asks.

Ellie gives her an amused look.

"Naw, honey," she says. "It's common sense."

"Why do people keep telling us all this stuff?" Cam asks in the car.

"What do you mean?"

"All these secrets. Jenny confessed that she was in love with her best friend and knew Clarissa was sleeping with a teacher and told Brad to try and—I don't know what. Even Brad told us all kinds of personal things. Why us? Why now?"

Blair thinks about this for a while. "I think secrets are hard to keep for a long time," she says. "I think Jenny and Brad have been dragging this around with them since Clarissa disappeared, with no one to talk to about it except each other. Maybe it's all ready to come out. Like one of those zits, you know? The kind that are all red and painful for weeks until they get to the surface and you can pop them?"

Cam laughs. "Is that a writer metaphor?"

Blair laughs too. "No, that's just a zit metaphor."

"How do you know so much about people? Is that a writer thing?"

"I don't know anything about people," Blair says. "You're the smart one."

"Well, yes," Cam says. "But not about people. I couldn't figure out Clarissa's art teacher was—you know. How did you know?"

"Didn't you see the way Brad looked when we asked about him? And then Jenny too. How do you know when a math problem is right?"

"When I've solved it," Cam says.

"There you go," Blair says.

"I see," says Cam, who doesn't. "You can tell all that from looking at people's faces? Sometimes I can't tell people apart. Not the people I love. But other people. Is that bad?"

"It's different," Blair says. "A different way of seeing."

"Sometimes I hurt people's feelings," Cam says.

"Yes," Blair says.

"Is that why you're such a good writer? Because you understand why people do bad things?"

"I'm not a good writer," Blair says automatically.

"Stop arguing with me. I don't think I would be a good writer."

It's the first time Blair has heard Cam admit she might not be good at something. She wishes she had her phone on record.

"What if we do find out who killed her?" Cam asks. "What if it's someone we like? I *like* Brad and Jenny."

"Do you think one of them killed her?"

"No," Cam says. "I sort of hope she ran away."

"She would have to be a pretty terrible person to do that to so many people who love her," Blair says.

Cam thinks back to when she said the same thing to Mr. Park.

But everyone involved in Clarissa's story is starting to look like an occasionally terrible person. Which maybe means they're human. Except for whoever killed Clarissa. But almost any one of the people they've talked to could have killed Clarissa, which makes it all a big confusing circle.

"Being a terrible person is better than being dead," Cam says. "Right?"

"Yeah," Blair says. "I guess it is."

But Blair thinks of Brad and Jenny, and years of broken hearts, and wonders if that's true. They've been waiting for Clarissa longer than Blair's been breathing.

What would it do to them if Clarissa did come back?

Or if she was still alive, and didn't?

———

CAM HAS NEVER been to a keg party in the woods. The thought has never occurred to her. The last thing she can imagine wanting to do on a weekend night is stand around in the dark voluntarily with people she is displeased enough by every weekday at school.

"What am I supposed to do?" she asks Blair.

"Wait here," Blair says. "Take notes or something."

"Take notes on what?"

"Atmosphere," Blair says.

"It's dark and we're in the woods," Cam says.

"Not very evocative, Cameron."

"Where are you going?"

"To get you a beer."

"I don't want a beer," Cam says, but Blair is already trotting away through the undergrowth, toward where Cam can see the keg shining like an idolatrous object in the light of the campfire. She imagines she is an exobiologist observing the arcane religious rituals of an alien species. It does not make her feel any better.

She pulls her notebook out of her pocket. It is too dark to write. She finds her phone. No signal. Not a surprise out here.

"It's dark and we're in the woods," she records. She looks about her. "There are a lot of trees."

How would Blair describe the scene? What does Blair's brain have that hers does not, to make Blair so adept at that sort of thing? Does Cam need to learn more adjectives?

"It's a . . . thick dark," she says into her phone. "I assume there are forest animals."

What sorts of animals live in the forest here? She has never considered this. Bears? Cougars? Frogs? Dragons?

"Look up forest animals," she adds.

She listens carefully, but can hear no indication of bears, only football players hooting inarticulately. What do bears sound like? Do bears make noise? Do they roar? No, she decides. It has been a while since she watched a nature show, but bears certainly do not roar.

Irene is always after her to go hiking. Perhaps she should take her mother up on the offer, for research.

There's a noise in the dark behind her. Too small to be a bear, she hopes.

She turns, but out here beyond the flicker of the campfire the darkness is almost solid.

She thinks suddenly of a story Irene once told her, about a patient at the hospital who liked to sneak up on the nurses. How Irene could feel him behind her sometimes, even when he wasn't making any noise. How her whole body would go into a kind of animal alertness.

The hospital administration told the nurses not to worry about him. He wasn't hurting anyone. The nurses were terrified of him, but the administration didn't think that was a problem. Cost-saving measures meant no special care for patients just because they made the staff feel funny.

And then he tried to strangle one of the nurses on night shift.

Sometimes your body knows things your brain doesn't, Irene had said, but Cam had barely listened, because there was nothing in the world her brain couldn't know. Now, she wishes she'd paid more attention.

"Hello?" she says. "Is someone there?"

It's like the silence itself is breathing. And then she knows what Irene meant. There's someone out there. Someone she can't see.

Someone, she is pretty sure, who is not a nice person.

"Hello?" she says again.

"Hi, Cam," says a familiar voice.

Cam jumps. But it's only Blair, who has returned at last, with—

"Sophie?" Cam says. "What are you doing here? Did you guys see someone out there?"

Sophie looks as out of place as Cam feels, in another sweater set and a wool skirt, but she does not seem nearly so uncomfortable.

"It's a party, Cam," Blair says.

"No, I mean—" Cam turns around again, but the feeling is gone.

Blair hands her a red plastic cup.

"What is this?" Cam says.

"It's your beer," Blair says.

"I don't want a beer," Cam says again.

"You've never had a beer," Blair says.

"You don't know that," Cam says.

Sophie observes this exchange with what seems to be amusement. "I hate beer," she offers, in a supportive sort of way.

"They didn't have champagne," Blair says. "I'll be back." She lopes off into the woods again.

"Where are you going?" Cam yells at her back, panicking.

Blair is leaving her! Blair is leaving her alone with Sophie!

"Probably to find James," Sophie suggests.

"I hate James," Cam says instinctively.

Sophie laughs. "Not much to love there," she says.

"What Blair sees in him I will never know," Cam grumbles. She looks down at her plastic cup and sniffs, takes a cautious sip.

"This is disgusting," she says sadly.

"Afraid so," Sophie agrees.

"What *are* you doing here?" Cam asks again.

"Blair said you would be here."

"She did?"

Sophie smiles and Cam's stomach lurches as though it is trying to fling itself out through her feet.

"For research," Sophie says.

"I would never come to one of these for *fun*," Cam says in horror. What Sophie has said suddenly registers. "You came because I would be here?"

"You run away from me at school," Sophie says.

"I do not," Cam protests. "I didn't—are you—why would you think that?"

"I listened to the new episode," Sophie says, instead of answering. "It's good." She is standing so close that Cam is in Paris.

Cam closes her eyes, opens them again. Sophie is still there, watching her quizzically.

Cam is standing in the dark in the middle of the woods with Sophie!

Sophie smells incredible!

Sophie is very, very, very pretty!

"Thank you," Cam says desperately.

"And the forum!" Sophie says.

"The what?"

"You didn't know?"

Cam shakes her head, realizes belatedly her mouth is slightly open, shuts it.

"There's a whole discussion board about your podcast now," Sophie says. "You should look it up. People have some wild ideas about what happened."

"Sasquatch," Cam says.

"Sorry?"

"This one guy thinks a Sasquatch took her. He has a whole website."

Sophie cocks her head and looks up at Cam. Sophie is so small! "Sasquatch is an Anglicization of Sasq'ets, from the Halq'eméylem language of the Stó:lō group of First Nations. Sasquatch is a colonial caricature of an important figure in many coastal peoples' religious beliefs, and an example of the way white people romanticize the cultures they are responsible for trying to eradicate and dismiss Indigenous knowledge as 'primitive' superstition," Sophie says.

"That's a good idea," Cam says. "How is—um—your project going?"

"Not as exciting as your podcast, honestly."

"I bet it's good, though," Cam says. "Your project. I bet your project is good."

"We'll see," Sophie says. "Cam?"

"Yes?" Cam can barely breathe. Why is Sophie *looking* at her like that?

"Are you doing anything tomorrow night?"

"I don't know!" Cam says.

"Do you want to go to a movie?"

"With who?" Cam squeaks.

"With me, Cameron Muñoz," Sophie says, laughing. "Would you. Like. To go. On a date. With me."

"Oh," Cam says. "*Oh.*" It is not so dark that she cannot see Sophie's flawless face glimmering faintly. A foreign power takes hold of Cam and she takes one step forward until she and Sophie are almost touching. The top of Sophie's head barely comes to Cam's nose, which means that Cam has to lean down, and then she is kissing Sophie, she is absolutely totally kissing Sophie Jenkins and it is totally *amazing,* it is like all the adjectives she does not even know, it is the most—

A shirtless personage barrels past them in his basketball shorts, shrieking piteously as he crashes through the underbrush. He runs into a rhododendron and falls over abruptly, where he commences industriously vomiting. He takes no notice of them as they spring apart.

"Yes," Cam says breathlessly. "Iwouldliketogoonadatewith. You."

Sophie smiles like a cat in cream. "I thought you might."

"Oh boy," Blair says, reemerging from the dark with another red plastic cup and, unfortunately, James. The four of them gaze at the thrashing inebriate, briefly united across their disparate interests by pitying contempt.

"Brent's gotta learn to hold his Jäger," James says with Vedic calm.

"Someone should give him a shirt," Blair says. "It's getting cold."

"Why did you tell Sophie Jenkins I would be at that party?" Cam asks later in the car. James has elected to remain with his comrades, but Blair has practice in the morning and Cam is only too happy to be transported away from her anthropological exercise.

Except Sophie, she thinks. Sophie! Sophie, who reached out and gave her hand a surreptitious squeeze that James missed entirely!

Sophie, with whom she has a date tomorrow!

"Because you like her and you'll never do anything about it unless someone makes you," Blair says, turning onto the freeway back into town.

"What?" Cam asks.

Blair grins at the road. "Come on, Cam. I've known you since we were twelve. I've never seen you act like that around anyone."

"How do I act?"

"Like you like her," Blair says.

"Like in an embarrassing way?" Cam asks frantically.

"Like in a you-like-her way," Blair says. "It's okay to have feelings for people, Cameron."

"Do you think she knows?"

"She knows now," Blair says, smirking.

"You saw us?"

"Only because I was checking. Nobody else noticed."

"We have a date tomorrow," Cam says. "I don't know what I'm supposed to do."

"Want me to come over before?"

"Yes," Cameron says. "Oh my god. Please, yes."

Suddenly, she remembers what Sophie said about the podcast, gets her phone out. She has enough of a signal now to look up the online forum.

"Whoa," she says. "We have fans."

"What?" Blair yelps.

"And haters," Cam says. "We already have haters. 'PumpkinH8_988' says we are dumb cunts who should get raped."

"*What?*"

"That's his thing," Cam says, scrolling. "He went through and replied to everyone who commented so far with the same line."

"Cam, what are you talking about?"

"This forum thing," Cam says. "Sophie told me about it."

"Forum? About *us?*"

"About the podcast," Cam says. "'Teenage girls think they knoe everything but Clarisa isnnt dead,'" she reads. "All the people who don't like us can't spell, so that seems good. Here, this is a nice one. 'I thought it was interesting. I hope they find out what happened to Clarissa.' Kind of boring, but at least the grammar is solid."

"How many people are on this forum?" Blair asks.

"Not that many. Like . . . fifty?"

"Wow," Blair says.

"Yeah," Cam agrees. "Wow. I guess we're making a splash. Blair?"

"Yeah?"

"There was someone out there."

Blair squints at the road. "It's so dark out here. I can barely see the center line. What do you mean?"

"When you went to find Sophie and I was alone. There was someone there."

"It could have been someone from the party," Blair says.

"It wasn't," Cam says.

"Are you sure?"

"Yeah."

"Maybe we should call that nice cop. Officer Reloj."

"And tell him what?" Cam says. "I had a bad feeling while surrounded by underage drinkers on private land?"

"Do you think . . . do you think it was about Clarissa?"

"Why else would someone follow us to the exact place in the middle of the woods where she disappeared?"

Blair looks worried. "You know," she says. "If Clarissa's dead. Whoever killed her is probably still around."

"Yeah," Cam says. "I think he probably is."

"Or she," Blair says.

"Or she."

"Sometimes it's better to let sleeping dogs lie," Blair says.

"I don't know if it's better," Cam says. "But I guess it's safer."

They drive the rest of the way in a not very comfortable silence.

———

CAM HAS HAD many occasions over the years to appreciate Blair's largely uncomplaining friendship, her seemingly endless tolerance of what Cam is able to admit on occasion may be a personality somewhat off-putting to persons of lesser character, but the Saturday afternoon of her date with Sophie marks a new high bar for her gratitude.

Blair finds her in her room, which is more chaotic than usual. Every item of clothing Cam owns—not much, but enough to create a small disaster—is strewn across the bed and floor. Cam stands at the tornado's eye, looking panicked.

"I don't know what to wear," she says instead of hello.

Blair clears a spot on the bed, unearthing Kitten from a nest of mismatched socks. He greets her with an agreeable yawn before going back to sleep.

"Wear what you like," Blair says.

"But what do girls like?"

"I think what Sophie likes is more relevant," Blair says.

"What does Sophie like?" Cam asks.

"Sophie likes you, Cam," Blair says.

"She does? How do you know?"

Blair summons the vast reserves of patience she has accumulated over the course of their friendship. "Because she drove fifteen miles to a heinous party in the middle of nowhere to ask you out on a date after you spent the last month and a half running away from her every time she tried to talk to you at school, and then she made out with you," Blair says.

"It *was* a heinous party," Cam says, holding up a sweater that is more pill than knit. "Are they all like that?"

"Yes. Not that one," Blair says. "Maybe start with something manufactured in the twenty-first century."

Cam rummages through her pile of clothes again. "Blair?"

"Yeah?"

"What is it you like about James?"

Now Blair is truly astonished. "Um," she says. "He's funny."

Cam holds up another sweater, this one slightly more presentable. "He is?"

"Cam," Blair says. "That one's better. Keep going."

"What else?"

Blair thinks. "He's—well, I mean, he's good-looking."

"Not to me," Cam says.

Blair smiles. "I get that he's not your type," she says dryly.

"No, I guess—" Cam laughs. "I guess I can see that," she says. "Girls are always freaking out around him."

"That's the whole basketball star thing too," Blair says. She does not like to be reminded that James could have his choice of any girl at school.

Except Cam, she thinks, smiling to herself.

"What?" Cam asks. "What's funny?"

"Nothing," Blair says. "He makes me feel special, I guess."

"You are special," Cam says instantly.

"But he makes me feel special. You know?"

"I don't make you feel special?"

"Oh, Cam." Blair scratches Kitten's immense upturned belly to give herself something else to look at other than Cam's open, honest face. "It's not that. Of course you make me feel special. But you're my best friend."

Cam sits dispiritedly on her pile of ratty T-shirts, holding up one with a picture of the Milky Way and a large arrow labeled YOU ARE HERE pointing at a spot on one of its arms. "Sophie's smart," she says.

"Yeah, she is," Blair agrees.

"And she's pretty."

Blair nods.

"Blair, you *are* special. I don't know why you need some jock to tell you that."

"Cam," Blair says. "Don't start."

"But I—" Cam stops. Blair has never listened to her before about this, and badgering her now won't change anything. But it infuriates her sometimes, Blair's total refusal to see her own brilliance.

"You're not going to have sex with a writing teacher, are you?"

Blair laughs. "We don't have a writing teacher at Oreville."

"But you thought Dan Friley was handsome. What if a handsome writing teacher said you were special to get in your pants?"

"Are you trying to say I'm special or that I'm not special?"

"I'm trying to make sure you don't run away with any creepy old men," Cam says. "Because you *are* special."

"I promise I will not run away with any creepy old men who tell me they like my writing," Blair says.

"Thank you. How did you know you liked James, though?" Cam asks. "Like, really liked him?"

"At first? I felt like I was going to throw up whenever I was around him," Blair says.

"Yeah, that sounds right. Blair?"

"Yeah?"

"I think I like . . . I think I might . . . like, really like Sophie. Like, a lot." She looks up at Blair from the floor, her expression as helpless as a child's. "How do I not mess this up? I always mess things up with people and I never know why."

Blair gets down from Cam's bed, puts her arms around her best friend, and holds her tight. "Sophie already likes you," she says again. "You're starting from a good place. Keep being yourself. You're special too."

"I know I'm special," Cam says, her voice muffled by Blair's shoulder. "But what if Sophie doesn't?"

"Then she's an idiot," Blair says.

"You just said she was smart," Cam says.

"You are impossible," Blair says, but she can tell Cam is smiling. She lets Cam go.

"Thanks for not freaking out," Cam says.

"About what?"

"About me being gay."

"Cam, I already knew. It's no big deal."

"You did? How?"

"That whole Megan Rapinoe wall you had going on in here in eighth grade was a pretty solid clue," Blair says. "Come on, let's find you something to wear for your hot date with Sophie, who totally likes you, so stop freaking out and asking me questions about feelings. You're scaring me."

"Okay," Cam says meekly.

Blair could get used to this.

AT FIRST IT bothers Blair that Sophie's suddenly spending every waking moment of her non-school time at Cam's. She doesn't leave when they're recording, sits quietly on Cam's bed with her headphones in, writing furiously on her computer and taking breaks to scratch an ecstatic Kitten behind the ears.

Blair knows Cam wouldn't tolerate five seconds of James's company if their positions were reversed.

But when she says something about it to Cam, Cam doesn't bristle the way she expected.

"I know," she says. "I'm sorry. But she's not out to her parents. They're, like, hard-core Catholic. They make her go to *church* twice a week. She doesn't have anywhere else to go. I can tell her to leave, though, if you don't like her being around."

What can Blair say to something like that? She's not a monster.

Besides, if Sophie truly upset her, she could always insist Cam come to her house. But Cam's is an easier place to work. No brother, no prodding parents. Irene is at the hospital most of the time, and when she isn't, she leaves them in peace.

Blair's dad wouldn't notice them unless they burned the house down, but Blair's mom would never let the two of them shut themselves in her room for hours. She'd ask questions, bring snacks, eavesdrop, make not-so-subtle comments about how Blair has more than one subject to study for if she wants to raise her grades.

Cam's is an oasis, their own world. If Sophie's going to join them on their private island, so be it.

And Cam in love is an easier, far less prickly version of herself, almost gentle at times. The way she looks at Sophie when she thinks Sophie doesn't notice, with palpable awe, makes Blair's heart contort with a mixture of love and envy.

Has James ever looked at Blair like that?

Surely he must have.

At least in the beginning.

Blair has to admit that Sophie is easy to be around. She's quiet. She doesn't interrupt them. She doesn't offer advice on the podcast unless she's asked directly, and then she's always careful to defer to Blair and Cam's opinions. She does her work with a concentration that makes Blair want to focus more too.

And it's true that Blair can't imagine James behaving himself so admirably if she and Cam were to try to work around him, even if Cam would allow such an unlikely parley to occur. When she talks to him about the podcast, brings up the increasingly active message board, their growing audience, her tentative pride in their work, he's always either patronizing or dismissive.

Sophie, she knows, is a firm supporter of what they're doing. Maybe even thinks it's good.

As far as she knows, James has never listened to a single episode, no matter how many times she hints how much she'd like it if he would.

It doesn't take long for Blair's irritation to fade.

"So that's the girl," Irene says.

She'd made lasagna, an uncharacteristic effort that Blair and Sophie heaped with praise. Blair and Sophie left after dinner. Cam and Irene are doing the dishes.

Irene washes. Cam dries. Kitten lurks, laser gaze on the fridge.

"What girl?" Cam says.

Irene raises an eyebrow. "Cameron. You think your mother is stupid?"

"No," Cam says sullenly. "That's her."

"You don't have to start with the U-Haul quite yet, you know," Irene says. "You're sixteen."

"Almost seventeen," Cam says automatically. "What U-Haul?"

"Old lesbian joke."

"What?"

"You think your father is the only person I slept with?"

"*What?*" Cam says, almost dropping a plate. "Irene. That's disgusting."

"I had a life once," Irene says, soaping a steak knife. "Before I was saddled with my most beloved burden. That's you, if you were wondering," she adds, handing the knife to Cam. "Don't stab your mother, you don't know the bank account password."

"You told me you couldn't give me any dating advice," Cam says. "When I asked."

"Oh, Cam." Irene straightens up from the sink to look her in the eyes. "You know, I'm doing the best I can. But I'm terrified for you. I remember what it's like to be a teenager. Most days I still feel like one. But I can't begin to imagine what it's like to be your age in this world. I can tell you what it was like for me. But—" she gestures with one sudsy hand. "I might as well have grown up in the Middle Ages, for all I know about what it's like to be a kid right now."

"I'm not a kid," Cam says.

"A young adult."

"Mostly you do okay," Cam says.

"Mmm," Irene says. "I'm flattered beyond belief."

"Irene? Did you know about Clarissa and Mr. Friley?"

Irene doesn't pretend not to know what Cam's talking about. "I heard rumors, but nobody knew anything for sure. If he was having sex with his students, he was quiet about it."

"Is that why nobody did anything?"

"I like to think so."

"What do you mean?"

Irene looks like she wishes she hadn't said anything, but she answers Cam's question. "You know, I want this to be a safe world for you, Cam. I want to believe that things have changed. Maybe they have. But in 1999 . . . it would've been a teenage girl's word against a respected"—Cam makes a noise—"I know, baby, but he was—a respected older man. The pressure a girl would've been up against, even if she realized at the time what he was doing was wrong—"

"Of course it was wrong!" Cam blurts.

"I know that, and you know that, thank god, but relationships can be complicated. People can believe things that aren't true, especially when they're young. They can believe they have power in situations where they don't. They can fall in love with people who don't love them back or care about their well-being. If it's true—and that's a big *if*, Cameron, so don't go putting anything in your podcast—if it's true, who knows what he might have said to get what he wanted? He was a big star back when he taught at Oreville. Parents loved him, the other teachers loved him, his students loved him. It would've been hard—maybe impossible—to go up against that."

Cam is quiet for a while as she dries the rest of the dishes.

"Did you know him? I mean, personally?"

"I knew who he was. But I've never been much of an artist."

"Do you think he could have killed Clarissa?"

"Cameron," Irene says. "Please. *Please*. This is not a game. Do you understand?"

"Yes," says Cam. "But I wish you'd told us about Brad."

"I'm not sorry I didn't. Do you understand why?"

"I don't know," Cam says. "Yes. I guess."

"I'll take what I can get," Irene says. "I know you think I lied to you."

"You did lie!"

"I didn't lie. I left some things out. That's an important distinction, and you know it." Cam grunts. "But you met him, Cam. You saw what his life is like now. He's been through hell. I didn't want you to put him through anything else."

"Too late now, I guess," Cam says. "But people don't think he did it anymore. Killed Clarissa, I mean."

"How do you know?"

Cam tells Irene about the message board, the warring forums. "Sasquatch is leading over Brad these days as the chief suspect."

Irene shakes her head. "Still," she says.

"Sophie says Sasquatch is racist."

"She's a sharp one, that Sophie. You like her a lot, don't you?"

"Don't change the subject."

"You're almost an adult. We can carry on a multifaceted conversation."

"I like her a lot."

"I like her a lot too."

"You hardly know her!"

"Some people, you can just tell."

You can? How? Cam doesn't know what this means. "If it makes you feel any better, I don't think Brad did it either."

"It's not me you have to make feel better," Irene says.

"It doesn't matter anyway," Cam says. "We don't know who to talk to next. We could talk to Mr. Friley, but we don't know anything for sure. I think we're stuck."

"Talk to Dan Friley?" Irene says, alarmed. "That's not a good idea."

"Not to accuse him or anything," Cam says unconvincingly. "But maybe he can tell us more about her."

"Cam, you've done your homework. You and Blair have poured your hearts into this. I'm sure you'll get an A. Let it go."

"We want more than an A. We want justice."

Irene heaves a sigh that seems to come from her toes. "Justice doesn't happen to men like Dan Friley," she says.

"You're probably right," Cam says. Cam knows Irene well enough to know Irene knows she's lying. But she also knows what Irene wants to believe: *Maybe it's over. Maybe Cam will let this go.*

Sorry, Irene, Cam thinks.

Not this one.

It feels too much like she's made a promise. Not to herself, or to Blair. Not to Mr. Park.

To Clarissa.

And she's not going to let Clarissa down.

JENNY

She was her own self, even that young. I can't think of another way to describe it. So terrible and so beautiful and so real. I'm sure she knew I was in love with her before I did. She knew everything, it felt like sometimes. She could be a monster, but she was also only a girl.

When you're a teenager, everyone around you feels more than real. Everything matters so much. Adults tell you this time in your life won't be so important one day, but they're full of shit. I still listen to the same music I did then. One song on the radio and everything comes back, what it felt like, the two of us driving down the freeway, windows open, the whole universe in front of us full of golden light. I'll never not be the person I was with her, the person she made me.

I've changed. I'll keep changing. But the hole in the heart of me will always be the size and shape of her.

You get older, you learn about disappointment, you learn about letting go, but you never do. Some part of you is always back in that limitless night, that open road, that moment where anything is possible, with the girl who knows you better than anyone else in the world, the girl you love better than anyone else in the world, the girl who'll be in your life for the rest of it, for always. Except she left, and I'm still living here without her.

I used to buy things for her, after she disappeared. Books I thought she'd like, a silver bracelet shaped like a bird. When I got into woodworking, I made her shelves, a wine rack, a jewelry holder. My first girlfriend, I told her about Clarissa on our first date. That was a mistake. Four months later, her screaming *How am I supposed to live up to a dead girl?* on her way out. My second girlfriend I told about Clarissa a few months in. It didn't go any better. I kept that up for a while. When I met Ellie, I knew if I messed up I'd never have another chance like her again. Ellie was the first person I met since Clarissa disappeared who made me feel like one day I could be someone other than the shadow I was. A person whose first love was gone, but a person who was no longer so haunted by it.

I waited a year to tell Ellie about Clarissa. When I did she said, "Jenny, we all have our own awful ghosts," and I understood for the first time in my life that I wasn't the only person with something following them, I wasn't the only woman in the world who'd blown her own future over and over again because she couldn't find her way through the past. That's when I went to rehab the final time, for real.

And now when I think about Clarissa—it's sunlight and water, open skies, it's laughing together over some dumb secret joke, it's convincing older guys to buy us beer at Safeway and running away before we had to drink it with them, it's that open road without so many ghosts. The thing is, white women's pain isn't special. It's real, but it doesn't need to be the center of every story. It's not Ellie's job to make me think about that, but I think about that a lot more since I met Ellie. That's not something I'm proud of. It's something that's true. That's what almost broke us up. Not Clarissa. Me, having my head up my own ass. Letting my grief be an excuse for not learning how to live.

Ellie's no picnic either. The best people never are. But we found our way. I think we'll be finding our way together for a long time. That's all you can ask from another person. That's more than I had with Clarissa. Probably more than I would've had with Clarissa if she was still here. I understand that now, but the impossible still hurts. Love isn't enough to live a long time with another person. You have to be willing to grow together. To build something together. A garden. A house. A future. An ordinary, beautiful life.

What happened to Clarissa happens every day. It happens a lot more often to women and girls who don't look like her. You know over five thousand Native women and girls have been reported missing since 2016? I want to live in a world where that doesn't happen. I want to live in a world where everybody is safe. What can I do to help bring that world into being? That's what I think about now.

I had this therapist back in rehab—early rehab, one of the ones that didn't take—who told me to focus on a growth-oriented mindset. I didn't want to hear it, believe me. It still makes me laugh. I'm a person, not a stock market. But now I understand better what she meant, even if that's not how I would've said it. I can see something bigger than what Clarissa's disappearance did to me. I can see something more important than my own pain. I can see the whole picture.

Clarissa was incandescent, and now she's gone. I don't think I'll get over her. But in this time, in this life, I've learned how to live with what she'll never be.

THE BETRAYERS

CAM'S phone rings between first and second period. It's a number she doesn't recognize, but she answers anyway.

"Hello?"

"Is this Cameron Muñoz?"

The speaker is a woman who sounds as though she's spent the last century breathing through a respirator. She pronounces Cam's name Munn-oz.

"Muñoz," Cam says.

"Don't hold much with political correctness," the woman says. She emits a grotesque wheezing noise that Cam realizes belatedly is a laugh. "This is Elsie Potts from County Records. You wanted to know about fundraising for the sheriff's election in 2000?"

"Yes," Cam says, her outrage instantly forgotten.

"Not many people asking about that sort of thing, I gotta tell you. Anyway, not a hard question. Few people donated fifteen dollars or thereabouts here and there, but I'm guessing you want to know the big one."

There is a silence. Is Cam expected to respond? Elsie Potts must not have much to do.

"Yes," Cam says.

Silence.

"Please?" Cam tries.

"Daniel R. Friley," says Elsie Potts.

It's him, Cam thinks. *I knew it. It's him.*

"How much?"

"Twenty-five big ones," Elsie Potts says.

Cam isn't sure she's heard correctly. "Twenty-five thousand dollars? Is that normal?"

Elsie cackles. She sounds like she's on the verge of a medical emergency. "In Hoquiam County? Are you kidding? Want to know about the election in 2004?"

"Yes! Please!"

"Thought you would," Elsie wheezes smugly. "So I looked it up."

Silence again. "Thank you?"

"You're welcome. Another twenty-five grand from Daniel R. Friley in 2004. And again in 2008. And then it stops."

"Why?"

"You'd have to ask Daniel R. Friley that," Elsie says. "But after 2008, nobody tried running against Aaron Liechty again."

"Thank you," Cam says. "Thank you so much."

"That's my job," croaks Elsie Potts, and hangs up.

———

THIS TIME IT'S Cam who makes the call. She uses the voice she's heard Irene affect for collection agencies: brassy, friendly, vacant.

"Hi! I was hoping to talk to someone about renting the Silverwater for a private party? Yes, the whole thing! It's my mom's birthday and we want to surprise her? Thank yeeewwww! My name? Oh—uh, Sophie? Sophie—Smith? Yes, Sunday works! A tour? Fabulous! Okaaaay, bye!"

"Wow," Blair says. "That was kind of scary." Sophie's eyes are wide. Even Kitten looks unnerved.

"You did sound like someone with a lot of money who does a lot of yoga," Sophie says.

"Good," Cam says. "We have an appointment for Sunday."

Blair looks at Sophie. "Want to come?"

Cam looks startled, then pleased. But Sophie shakes her head.

"Church," she says. "Plus, this is your big interview. You don't want a third wheel."

"You're not a third wheel," Blair says, surprising herself. Even more surprising, she realizes she means it.

Sophie blushes, ducks her head—a gesture totally unlike the breezy, confident, beautiful Sophie she is at school. Blair understands her initial dissatisfaction with Sophie's presence was not as subtle as she thought and feels bad about it.

"What are you going to ask him?" Sophie asks.

"We need to figure that out," Cam says. "We can't blow this one. And we can't go in unprepared. So, what do we know for sure?"

"The only things we know for sure are that he quit teaching after Clarissa disappeared and funded Liechty's campaign for sheriff a year later," Blair says.

"And he was having sex with Clarissa," Cam says.

"We think we know that," Blair says. "But we can't prove it. And we can't say it on the podcast."

"Why not?" Cam says.

Blair and Sophie, in an unexpected alliance, give her a look of total disbelief.

"Libel laws?" Sophie says.

"We're minors," Cam says.

"He'll go after our parents," Blair says. "That is not a conversation I want to have with my dad. Or Irene."

"What are you hoping will happen?" Sophie asks.

"We'll get him to confess," Cam says without hesitation.

"And then?"

"Then we'll call the police."

"What good will the police do?"

Cam looks at Sophie with suspicion. Has she been conferring with Irene behind Cam's back? "Arrest him," she says. "Take him away. Put him in jail forever where he can't hurt anybody else."

"Do you think that's how it works?" Sophie asks. "Do you know who goes to prison?"

Cam senses a trap. "Bad people?"

"No," Sophie says fiercely. "Marginalized people. Poor people, Native people, Black people, brown people, immigrants, queer and trans people. That's who goes to prison, because that's who the system is designed to hurt. If Dan Friley goes to prison, that'll be an aberration. And jail doesn't have anything to do with justice. There are better ways to address harm within a community. You're obsessed with Clarissa's story, the same way so many other people are. But you know who comprises the highest percentage of murder victims? Young Black men. Weaponizing stories of imperiled white women serves to enforce political repression. The prison industrial complex isn't interested in protecting people from harm. It's founded on the principle of harming people who are already vulnerable. All these dead white girl stories? All this fixation on sexualized violence against white women? Those narratives normalize structures of oppression that don't do anything to prevent more violence from happening. That *foster* violence."

Cam sits with her mouth slightly open. "You don't think Dan Friley should go to jail?"

"I don't think there should *be* jails," Sophie says.

"What should we do instead?" Blair asks.

"Build a new society," Sophie says. "One based on mutual aid and community. One where everyone has what they need. Food, shelter, safety, art, healthcare, clean water, rest. Jailing people doesn't solve problems. The police don't solve problems. Look at what they did when Clarissa disappeared. Dan Friley bought their silence. Do you think someone like that is going to rot in prison for the rest of his life? Do you think that's the answer? It's not going to bring Clarissa back. If he killed her, it's not going to undo the damage he caused to her family and her friends."

"I guess I never thought about it that way," Cam says.

"Most people don't," Sophie says. "But they should."

"Do you think we should stop doing the podcast?" Blair asks.

"That's up to you," Sophie says.

"You're right," Cam says. "The dead white girl thing. I know that." She glances over at her metastasizing pile of murder books. "But I want to know what happened to her too. Maybe you're right about justice not meaning anything. But it feels like we're close."

"I don't think justice doesn't mean anything," Sophie says. "I don't believe that putting people in cages is justice. Including Dan Friley." She smiles. "That's the thing about being an abolitionist. You don't get to wish prison for anybody, even if they really, really suck."

"I still want to talk to him," Cam says. "Blair?"

"Me too," Blair says.

"Do you think that's safe?" Sophie asks.

"He's not going to murder us at his resort," Cam says with more confidence than she feels.

"We'll be careful," Blair says. Sophie raises an eyebrow. "Seriously," Blair says. "But Cam—maybe you should let me do the talking."

"Why?" Cam asks, aggrieved.

"I know you hate him," Blair says. "But—"

"And you don't?"

"Sure, I hate him," Blair says. "But that's what I mean. I can hide that I hate him."

"You can't," Sophie says. "Sorry, Cam. No poker face."

"We're not playing poker!"

"You kind of are," Sophie says. "Right? You need him to show his hand. Tell you something you don't already know. You're not going to get anything out of him if you go in guns blazing. You should let Blair ask the questions."

"You think I can't do it?" Cam bristles. Sophie and Blair exchange glances. Cam relents. "You're right. Blair is better at this stuff. She's a nice person."

"You're a nice person," Sophie says.

"No, I'm not," Cam says.

"You're a good person," Blair says.

Cam grins at them. "That's not the same thing."

THE DISTANCE FROM Oreville to the Silverwater isn't far mileage-wise, but the two-lane highway out to the edge of the peninsula is so winding the drive takes almost two hours. Cam is uncharacteristically quiet for most of it, looking out the window as the landscape shifts from big-box stores and parking lots to farmland and then bigger and bigger trees.

The narrow old highway ribbons past huge stands of old-growth forest garlanded in moss, crosses broad rivers swollen with fall rains, twists through the looming foothills of the Olympic Mountains.

This time of year, the road is clear of tourists, and Blair can almost believe they're the only two people in the world. That they've been driving forever through this deep-green and dreamy world, the trees so dense they meet overhead and transform the highway into a dim-lit emerald tunnel.

"I never come out here," Cam says.

"Yeah, me neither."

"Irene always says we should go hiking, but she never has time."

Blair can't imagine Cam traipsing around the wilderness, Irene or no Irene. Knowing Cam, she'd bring a calculator instead of a raincoat and get lost on a marked trail while trying to triangulate her exact latitude and longitude from the position of the sun.

They stop for gas at a tiny station on the border of the Quileute Reservation. A wooden sign in front of the single pump reads TREATY LINE NO VAMPIRES PAST THIS POINT, and another sign outside the store is painted like a fire danger rating that warns instead of vampire threat levels. The arrow on the sign points to HIGH. Cam makes Blair take her picture underneath it.

Glass cases by the cash register display beaded earrings made by a local artist and glossy hunks of smoked salmon. The cashier is a cheerful, portly Native woman wearing a hot pink sweatshirt festooned with puffy-paint cats.

"You girls here to do the Twilight tour?" she asks as she rings Blair up for her gas. "You can get the map at the tourist center in Forks. They got a whole museum now with an animatronic Renesmee and everything. Creepiest baby you ever saw."

"We're on our way to the Silverwater," Blair says.

The cashier's voice shifts into an entirely different and far more cautious register. "Oh, yeah? What you want out there?"

"We're interviewing Dan Friley," Cam says. "You know him?"

"We all know Dan out here," the woman says without enthusiasm.

"He used to teach at our school," Cam says.

"What do you want to talk to him for?"

"He was Clarissa Campbell's art teacher," Blair says, and tells her about the podcast.

"Clarissa Campbell, sure," the woman says when she's done. "I remember her."

"You knew her?" Cam asks.

"Not personally. But she was all over the news for months. You think Dan knows something about what happened to her?"

"Yes," Cam says. Blair steps on her foot. "We're not, like, publicly accusing him of anything." She looks at Blair. "We think he—"

"We're just asking questions," Blair says. Cam subsides.

The cashier hands Blair her change. "He's an interesting one, that Dan," she says. She clearly does not mean "interesting" as a compliment. She looks them both over as if she's trying to decide something. "You girls be careful out there," she says.

"Careful?" Cam asks. "What do you mean?"

The woman shrugs. "Wouldn't want to accuse him of anything publicly," she says with a wry grin.

"Off the record," Cam says. "Cross our hearts."

"I don't know anything about any missing girls. But he's got a lot of money and a nasty reputation, if you want to know the truth. Not on good terms with his neighbors, which isn't such a good idea in this area. Bringing rich city people out here for who knows what. I know it's good for business, but you should see how some of them behave. Like we're all out here turning into werewolves." She rolls her eyes. "I'll take their money, but I don't have to like their attitude. Speaking of which, can I interest you in some earrings? This pair here would look awfully nice with your coloring."

"Sure," Blair says. "Why not?"

The entrance to the Silverwater is marked by a huge wrought iron gate like something out of a Gothic novel. Flowering metal vines spell out SILVERWATER in ornate lettering over the arch. The effect, surrounded by looming trees and the lowering early twilight of late fall, is not so much classy as sinister. Blair can easily imagine a basement full of Bluebearded wives.

"Whoa," Cam says.

"Seriously," Blair says, turning down the driveway. Her palms are clammy.

The lodge itself is massive, erupting out of the earth like some giant fungal growth. Twin two-story wings flank a three-story central building. It's sided with cedar shingles, and the main building is dominated by a stone chimney. But the floor-to-ceiling windows give the structure a modern look. A totem pole towers by the main entrance, carved with ravens and orcas. At its peak a wooden eagle stretches vast wings.

"I wonder what Sophie would have to say about the totem pole," Blair says.

"Something about how messed up it is to steal people's land and then stick their art on it where they'll never see it again," Cam says. "But with more big words." She rubs her own sweaty palms on her faded jeans. "We should have dressed up. No way is this guy going to believe our cover story."

"He wouldn't have believed us if we showed up in Prada," Blair says. "We're teenagers."

"Great," Cam says. "I should have said my mom was an Amazon billionaire."

"Too late now," Blair says, parking the car. "You ready?"

"I don't know," Cam says.

She's as scared as I am, Blair thinks. She finds the fact oddly heartening. Maybe it's her turn to be the brave one for a change.

"Come on," she says, with more conviction than she feels. "He's just some old guy. He can't do anything to us."

"He's an old-guy millionaire rapist who's probably a murderer," Cam mutters. But she unbuckles her seat belt and gets out of the car, taking a deep breath of the clean damp air. "It smells good out here."

"And we saw an anti-vampire gas station," Blair says. "Even if we blow the interview, we still had an adventure."

She's not sure if she's trying to reassure Cam or herself. But Cam's already striding toward the front door of the lodge, her long legs moving fast, and Blair has to hurry to catch up.

The heavy wooden front door opens onto a vaulted expanse of space stretching the entire length of the main building. Blair recognizes it from the picture in the profile of Dan Friley: the fireplace, the heavy beams, the beautiful rugs strewn casually across what seems like acres of wood-plank flooring burnished to a honeyed glow. Today the lake beyond the windows is a flat, angry silver. A storm front is rolling in.

A pretty woman sits behind a big wooden desk that looks like it came out of a catalog selling faux battered furniture for thousands of dollars. She's carefully made up, wearing a creamy wool blazer over a white blouse that makes Blair think of Sophie. She has diamond studs in each ear and her smooth blond hair is pulled back in a chic chignon. Even her eyebrows look like they cost a lot. But under the armor of her clothes and makeup, Blair realizes, she's not much older than Blair and Cam.

"Can I help you?" she asks.

"We have an appointment scheduled with Dan," Blair says, trying to sound the way James does when he walks into a restaurant: benevolent, disdainful, content in his own superiority and wealth.

"Welcome," the woman-girl says. She lifts the receiver of a stagily old-fashioned phone, dials. "Dan, your three o'clock is here," she purrs.

"Does he have a lot of appointments?" Cam asks.

The receptionist looks her over, as if she's surprised that someone dressed like Cam can speak. "Dan is a busy man," she says. "But he always has time for guests."

She gives them a dazzling smile, revealing the most expensive teeth Blair has ever seen in person. Where did she get them done? Seattle? Not out here, that's for sure.

"I'll walk you back to his office."

She clicks across the vast room, graceful in her perilous heels. *How does she get to her car?* Blair wonders. Even Dan Friley can't do anything about the perennial Northwest mud. Blair and Cam follow her like dutiful sheep. Blair glances over at Cam. Her face has the grim set of someone marching to their own execution.

Dan Friley's office is another huge room with dazzling windows. A leather sofa at one end is heaped with Pendleton blankets. Soft Oriental rugs cover the floor. An easel is set up next to the floor-to-ceiling windows with a half-finished painting of the lake. Outside, the storm is gathering. Sheets of rain gust across the choppy water. A carpet of mist creeps down the green-black foothills. Blair's heart thumps in her chest.

Dan Friley's desk is a more massive sibling of his receptionist's. Like her, he looks like money. He's dressed as he was for his profile: wool shirt, carpenter's pants that have never seen the inside of a workshop, heavy brown work boots without a single scuff. His hair is longer now, but his face is the same. His eyes are so blue they're almost silver, his gaze so intense that Blair feels flayed open and pinned like a butterfly in a specimen collection. Jenny made Dan Friley sound charming, but charm is not the word his predator's stare brings to mind. Up close, he smells like sandalwood and smoke.

If Sophie smells like Paris, Cam thinks, *this guy reeks of bank vault.*

This, Blair thinks, *is the scariest man I've ever met.*

Dan Friley stands up to greet them, shaking each of their hands in turn. His huge hand dwarfs Cam's broad palm. If he's surprised by how young they are, he doesn't show it.

"Please, sit," he says, gesturing to the leather chairs facing his desk. "Can I get you something? Coffee? Tea?" He doesn't wait for their answer. "Angela, can you bring us some coffee, please?"

The "please"s are for show. This man gets what he wants, whether he asks for it or not.

"Happy to, Dan," the receptionist says, and clicks back out the door, leaving it open behind her.

"Welcome to the Silverwater," Dan Friley says, spreading his massive hands out as if to encompass the entire lodge. "You're interested in booking for a private event?"

Blair and Cam rehearsed this interview endlessly with Sophie in Cam's bedroom. But now, faced with Dan Friley himself, his money, his terrifying charisma, his hunting-lodge palace in the woods, Blair finds herself at an utter loss. Everything she meant to say has fled from her brain. Next to her, Cam seems equally paralyzed.

It's my turn to be the brave one, Blair reminds herself. "Yes," she says, as solidly as she can. "For our mother's fiftieth birthday. We want to surprise her."

"You two are sisters?" Friley asks.

Shit, Blair thinks. She and Cam don't look anything alike. Why didn't they think of that? "Yes," she says. "Sisters."

"How thoughtful of you," Friley says. "You'll be booking for the whole weekend, correct?"

"Yes," Blair says again. "Can you—uh, can you tell us about—the facilities?"

"Naturally, Miss Smith," Friley says. "Or should I say Misses?"

He knows, Blair thinks. *He knows we're here for something else. He just doesn't know what it is.*

"Sophie," Cam blurts. "I'm Sophie. This is my sister, uh—Janeifer. Jennifer."

"Sophie," he says. "And Janeifer. Ah, here's Angela with the coffee."

The receptionist brings in a wooden tray with handmade ceramic mugs big enough to be soup bowls, a pitcher of milk, sugar, a plate of biscotti. She pours each of them coffee without asking, though Blair's so jittery she wants to refuse. She adds milk until the coffee is almost white; still, when she takes a sip, she can taste how strong it is.

"The beans are roasted nearby," Friley says, watching her. "Small batches. There's a local artisanal movement building here."

"Wonderful," Blair says weakly.

"I'll give you the tour. Let's drink as we walk." Friley doesn't wait for their answer, standing smoothly and gesturing to the door. Angela gives them another ten-thousand-dollar smile and clicks away again.

"Sure," Blair says, but he's already walking past them, certain they'll follow.

Friley leads them back across the great hall, through one wing and the other, up and down staircases, in and out of an endless series of rooms. A billiards room, green-felted pool tables standing under the pensive gaze of a national park's worth of taxidermied bears and deer and mountain goats and a melancholy-looking mountain lion; a lounge with more leather-upholstered couches and soft rugs and Pendleton blankets and a bar with shelves upon shelves of liquor bottles; a sauna, smelling richly of cedar; a big empty room with one mirror-covered wall and a tidy pile of yoga mats; a library with floor-to-ceiling shelves of leather-bound books and newer paperbacks, their spines uncracked.

Bedroom after bedroom, some furnished with bunk beds made up in matching plaid flannel sheet sets and shelves of beautiful wooden toys; others with immense four-poster wooden beds piled high with more flannel. Leather armchairs and big fireplaces; oil paintings of mountains and loggers and shirtless

Native men on horseback staring out at buffalo-laden prairies in feather headdresses or battling equally generic-looking cowboys.

Sophie would have a field day, Blair thinks. The thought gives her a jolt of courage.

As they walk Friley keeps up a smooth patter, telling them about individually tailored yoga classes, painting and ceramics offerings (this as he shows them through a cement-floored studio with a kiln and a small forest of standing easels), seaweed facials, something called "therapeutic spiritual sessions," meditation, archery, discovery hikes, kayaking, canoeing, plant medicine, wine-tasting, coffee-tasting, ten-course meal offerings using only locally sourced meat and produce, team-building courses ("Surprisingly popular with families," Friley says), wilderness overnights with shaman-designed exercises to facilitate the identification of one's spirit animal.

"Which tribe?" Cam says to this, rallying at last.

"Sorry?" Friley stops, caught off guard.

"Which tribe's practices are you appropriating?"

"The ceremony integrates a variety of Native spiritual traditions," Friley says.

He's about to slide back into his sales pitch, but Cam's broken the near-hypnotic spell Blair has fallen under.

"This is such a beautiful place," she says. "How long have you been here?"

Friley leads them back to his office, calls to Angela for more coffee, settles into his chair.

"The lodge was built in the twenties as a hunting resort by the lumber baron Andrew Jackson Talbot," he says. "It closed in the late thirties because of the Depression, but it stayed in the Talbot family for another twenty years. The National Park Service bought it after World War II and reopened it as a hotel. The property went back on the market in 1995. I fell in love with it the moment I saw it. I spent the next five years or so renovating it, and we opened as the Silverwater in 2000."

"That must have been expensive," Cam says.

Friley looks at her from under half-lidded eyes. "I've been fortunate," he says.

"You're not from out here," Blair says.

"No, my family is on the East Coast," Friley says. "I moved here from New York in the early nineties."

"Why?" Cam asks. "Weren't you a famous artist?"

"I came out here for a change of pace. To reconnect with nature."

"You didn't come *here* here, though," Cam says. "Not at first. Why Oreville? Why not Seattle? Or the coast? There's not a lot of nature in Oreville."

"I found myself drawn to the small-town life," he says.

"You taught at Oreville High School before you opened the Silverwater," Blair says. Her throat is so tight with fear her voice comes out breathy and strained.

"I enjoyed giving back to the community and working with talented young people who might not have otherwise had the opportunity to engage with a professional artist," Friley says. Cam shifts in her chair but stays silent.

"You quit teaching in 1999," Blair continues. "Why?"

"I never intended to teach forever."

Blair's heart is pounding so hard she wonders if she's going to pass out. "Nineteen ninety-nine was the same year one of your students disappeared," she manages.

"I'm afraid I can't keep track of all my former students."

"Oh, you remember this one," Cam says, unable to keep it in any longer. Her voice is tight with rage. Friley smiles blandly.

"Clarissa Campbell," Cam says, when it's clear he's not going to say anything. "She disappeared. And then you quit. And now you're here. Why did you buy this place? Did you kill her? Did you bury her under the parking lot?"

Dan Friley laughs. He reaches for the phone on his desk. "Angela, darling, can you do me a favor? Can you have Aaron run our guests' license plate for me?" He hangs up, leans back in his chair, interlaces his fingers on his desk. Nothing Cam's said has thrown him off in the slightest.

"We're done here," he says easily. "In about five minutes I'm going to find out your real names. And then I'm going to make you both wish you'd never been born."

Blair's legs are trembling so badly she can barely get out of her chair. Cam's breathing hard and her eyes are wild as she stands, but she doesn't give up. "Why did you give Aaron Liechty seventy-five thousand dollars?" she asks. "Is it because he knows you killed her?"

"Good afternoon, *Sophie*," Dan Friley says. "And I'd have my parents call a lawyer, if I were you."

———

"HE DID IT," Cam says in the car, over and over. "He did it. Did you see his face? Did you hear him laughing? Blair, he killed her. He *killed* her. She's *there*, B. I *know* it."

"Cam," Blair says. "*Cam*." Cam's shaking like she's going to shiver apart. Blair pulls over, grabs her in a hug. "Cam, it's okay," she says into Cam's hair. "Breathe. It's okay. Count to ten with me, okay? You're okay. You're okay."

She counts through Coach's breathing exercise until Cam calms down enough to do it with her. After two rounds, Cam gently pushes Blair away.

"I'm fine," she says tightly.

She isn't, but Blair restarts the car and pulls back onto the highway. It's not yet five p.m., but this late in the year it's dark already. It's still raining hard. She turns her high beams on. They only make the darkness around the car denser.

It's going to be a long drive home.

A light winks in her rearview mirror: the headlights of a car behind her. There's no one else on the road, hasn't been since they left the Silverwater.

"We forgot to ask him about the painting," Cam says.

"I think that's the least of our problems right now. What are we going to do? What if he calls our parents?"

"What *can* we do?" Cam cries. "You saw him. He's rich, he's got the sheriff on speed dial, he's gotten away with it for who even knows how long. Who are we going to tell? Who's going to believe us?"

"We could tell Mr. Park, at least."

"He already knows," Cam says.

"What do you mean?"

"He knows as much as we do. He found out Friley funded the sheriff's campaign back when it happened, remember? If he could've done anything, he would have."

"So what?" Blair asks. "We give up?" The headlights behind her loom larger and brighter. Someone's impatient. She's already five miles over the speed limit.

"No," Cam says. "We don't give up." She's thinking hard. "Clarissa couldn't have been the only one, right? I mean, I assume she was the only girl he murdered. But she wasn't the only one he had sex with. Raped. I don't know what to call it. Jenny told us as much. So did Irene."

"Jenny and Irene said there were rumors. How would we find out for sure if there were more girls?"

Whoever is behind them is almost on their bumper now. Blair taps the brakes. Cam twists in her seat.

"What's going on?"

"I don't know why they don't just pass me," Blair says. "There's plenty of—"

The car behind them rams into Blair's rear bumper. Her shoulder explodes with pain as the seat belt jerks across her chest. Dimly, she's aware of a loud, high-pitched noise. The car slides forward, skidding across the rain-slicked highway. The car behind them is accelerating, pushing them forward. She pedals the gas hard, wrenches the steering wheel desperately to the right. Her rear wheels spin uselessly. The road is covered with water.

Blair realizes the noise is coming from her. From her and from Cam. She's screaming, Cam is screaming, the car is sliding across the highway into the other lane and an engine is roaring behind them and the white lights are swallowing her rear windshield and the car skids off the highway and into the ditch and suddenly the screaming stops.

It takes a long moment for Blair to decide she isn't hurt. The car engine's ticking, the hood steaming in the pouring rain. Cam is crying quietly.

"Cam? Are you okay?"

"I think so," Cam says, hiccupping. "Are you?"

Blair moves her arms, her legs. Her shoulder hurts from the seat belt, but otherwise she's undamaged.

"Yeah, I'm fine."

"What happened? Did that car—did someone run us off the road? Where did they go?"

"I don't know," Blair says, an answer that applies more or less to all three questions. "I think they ran us off the road. Yeah, they ran us off the road."

She turns the key in the ignition, taps the gas cautiously. "At least the engine starts. But I'm just spinning the wheels. I think we need a tow truck."

"Hold on," Cam says, unbuckling her seat belt. "I'll go see how bad it is."

"Cam! They could still be out there!"

"They drove away," Cam says, climbing out of the car. She makes a startled noise.

"What's wrong?"

"I'm fine," Cam says crossly. "The ditch is full of water, is all."

Blair rolls down her window, sticks her head out, watches anxiously as Cam splashes around the car. "We definitely need help," Cam yells over the storm. "But back here it looks like— what the hell?" She disappears below the rear end of the car.

"What?" Blair shouts. "What is it?"

Cam splashes back to the passenger seat and climbs in. Her legs are muddy nearly to the knees and her sleeves are soaked. She's holding a filthy piece of black plastic about the size of the deck of cards.

"What is that?"

Cam swipes the plastic with her thumb, but her hands are so dirty she only spreads mud around. "There's something here," Cam says. "A brand name and I think a serial number. Do you have a signal? Can you look this up? My hands are too muddy."

"Cam—"

"Clarity Valiant X9009," Cam says.

Blair sighs and pulls out her phone. "It's a GPS tracker," she says. "A four-hundred-and-ninety-five-dollar GPS tracker. Cam, we're in over our heads. We need to call the police."

"The police?" Cam says. "Are you kidding?"

"Our parents, then."

"If Irene finds out about this, she'll kill me."

"Cam, someone *did* try to kill us."

"That was a warning," Cam says. "We're fine. If he wanted to hurt us, he would've done it at the Silverwater."

"Cam, this is insane. It's a Journalism assignment. Come on."

Cam turns to look at her. "It's not a Journalism assignment anymore and you know it," she says. "Don't call the police. Call James."

"What?"

"I'd call Sophie, but she doesn't have any way to get out here. The back end of your car isn't in the ditch. James can probably help us push it out."

There are so many different things Blair could say to this. The person who ran them off the road is still out there in the dark. She does not want to die, and she does not want Dan Friley to sue her parents. She wants to graduate high school and go do something else. Something brighter and bigger, a life she cannot picture as anything other than sunlight coming through windows and a desk of her own somewhere. Learning how to write books.

Here, now, in this heavy rain-soaked dark, water still hammering on the roof of her car, Cam covered in mud, looking at her as if the whole world hangs on her answer: This is not what she signed up for.

Who knows what she could have been? She was so young. She could've been anything. Or nothing.

Did you kill her? Did you bury her under the parking lot?

Clarissa, a girl like anyone.

A girl like Blair.

Goddammit, Cam, Blair thinks.

This is not what she signed up for. But she's here now.

Blair decides. She dials.

"Hey, babe," James says. "Are you on your way over?"

"Not exactly," she says. She tells him part of the story. Running off the road, the dark, the ditch.

"Are you alone?" he asks, alarmed.

"Cam's here."

"Oh," he says, his voice cooling. "Another date with Cam, huh?"

"Can you— I need you. We need your help."

"'We'?" James says. "Cam doesn't need much of anything, does she?"

"James," Blair says in disbelief.

"You're with Cam. Call a tow truck. You'll be fine. I'm supposed to meet up with Luke and Weber to watch a game."

"A game?" Blair echoes. "Can't you—can you come get us?" She is trying to keep the hurt out of her voice. She's not fooling anyone. At least, she's not fooling Cam.

"What good would I be? Sit tight with Cam."

"Have fun with the boys," Blair says inanely. She ends the call.

"We'll think of something else," Cam says, her voice steady. She reaches over to give Blair's shoulder a squeeze, stops before her muddy hand touches Blair's sweater. Her palm hovers for a moment like a benediction.

"We could call a tow truck," Blair says shakily.

"We don't have enough money. And they'll probably make us call our parents." Cam thinks. "What about that cop who gave us his card? Do you still have it?"

"I thought you didn't want to call the cops."

"Not the cops," Cam says. "A cop. He seemed okay."

Blair sorts through the bits of detritus in her bag with trembling fingers, finds the card, dials. She feels like she's dreaming. But her voice is clear when Officer Reloj answers the phone and she tells him what happened—the same story she told James, leaving out the tracker, Dan Friley's deadly eyes, his broad, strong hands capable of closing around a girl's neck and—

stop Blair stop it now

—Officer Reloj is quiet for a long time when she finishes.

"What are you girls doing out there?" he says finally.

"Hiking," Blair says. Cam covers her mouth so he can't hear her laugh.

"This isn't procedure," Officer Reloj says. Blair doesn't know if he's referring to what she's asking of him or the state of the world in general.

"You said we could call you if we got into trouble," Blair says.

"This isn't what I meant," he says. "You girls need to call 911."

"We're not hurt. We didn't want to call an ambulance away from someone who might need it."

"Isn't that altruistic of you," Officer Reloj says. "Why don't you call a tow truck?"

"We don't have any money."

Officer Reloj sighs heavily.

"Please?"

"What mile marker are you at? It'll take me a while to get out there."

"Thank you," Blair says. "Thank you so much."

Officer Reloj mutters something under his breath and hangs up.

Cam's teeth are chattering. "Are you cold?" Blair asks. "You're all wet." She turns on the ignition again, cranks up the heat. The car smells strongly of wet Cam and Blair's brothers' old gym socks.

"Do you think he'll come back?" Blair asks.

"I don't know," Cam says. "I don't think so."

"What will we do if he does?"

"Hit him over the head with a rock," Cam says fiercely.

"We don't know it was him," Blair says.

"Who else would it be? Who else could afford a five-hundred-dollar GPS tracker? Who else would want to scare us?"

"What about the person you thought was there in the woods that night? That was two weeks ago."

"Maybe he's known who we were all along. Maybe he's been

following us this whole time. Maybe I was wrong, and no one was there." Cam shifts restlessly. "I don't know, Blair. But we both know he did it."

"Cam?"

"Yeah?"

"I'm scared."

"I'm not," Cam says. "Not anymore."

They wait.

LATER: HEADLIGHTS.

"I hope that's Officer Reloj," Blair whispers.

It is.

"Here you are, the Nancys Drew," Officer Reloj says. "Aren't you in a pickle. Want to tell me what you're really doing out here?"

Cam stares daggers at Blair. Blair does not have to be psychic to receive the signal. *DO NOT TELL DO NOT TELL DO NOT TELL.*

"Hiking," Blair says. "I told you. We ran off the road in the storm."

"You girls been drinking?"

"No!" Cam says.

"Pretty close to the Silverwater out here, aren't you? Happen to do any hiking past Dan Friley?"

"No," Cam and Blair say together.

"Because that would be a bad idea, if you were to go bothering him."

Silence. Blair looks at Officer Reloj in what she hopes is an innocent manner. Cam looks at her feet, presumably so he cannot see her extremely-non-poker face.

"Your parents know where you are?"

"We're eighteen," Cam says.

"And orphans, I imagine," Officer Reloj says. He looks at them, his jaw working. "All right," he says. "Here's what we're going to do. I think the three of us together can push this car onto the road. And then you're going to drive back home, and I'll follow you to make sure there's nothing wrong with the car. And then you're never going to do anything as stupid as go out to the Silverwater to harass Dan Friley again. Are we clear?"

"I don't—" Cam begins.

"Yes, sir," Blair says, cutting her off.

"Don't make me regret this."

"We won't," Blair says.

Officer Reloj shakes his head. "I think you girls should let this whole podcast thing go," he says.

CAM HAS BEEN angry before. She's gotten in fights with Irene. She's battled school administrators who wouldn't let her take high-school math when she was in sixth grade. She's gotten mad at James, at Oreville, at teachers; since Sophie, she's gotten mad at police violence, at racism, at poverty, at injustice.

But she has never, not ever, not once in 16.583 years felt a fury like the one that burns through her now, white-hot and purifying.

She has never hated anyone or anything with the all-consuming focus with which she hates Dan Friley.

Her rage is so powerful she can do anything: set buildings ablaze, bring cities to the ground, destroy whole worlds.

Destroy a man.

But what Dan Friley did to one girl long ago, Cam knows from watching television and from her serial killer books, won't make people pay attention.

They need a blood-soaked kill room, a case of torture tools, a car trunk refitted for kidnapping, a trail of body parts.

A girl is not enough. They need a pattern.

It's Sophie's idea to go back to the library.

"What are we looking for?" Cam asks. She and Sophie are sitting in front of the microfiche again, looking through binders of blue film.

"I'm not sure yet," Sophie says. "Start with the summer she disappeared."

Cam slides a sheet under the glass, turns on the projector. It's the graduation special issue of the *Examiner* from June 1999, the one she's already looked at.

Parents: Joe and Marian Campbell. GPA: 3.86. Favorite subject: Art. Most influential teacher and why: Mr. Friley, who taught me to see the world differently. What I do for fun: Learn new cheer stunts, go to movies and concerts. Future plans: Move in with my amazing boyfriend!!!!!

"Most influential teacher," Cam says. "God."

"Wait," Sophie says. "I have an idea." She digs through binders, finds the June 1998 graduation issue, scans the graduation announcements. "Nope," she says. "Try 1997."

"Why?"

"Trust me." Sophie's eyes flit across the screen. "There," she says, triumphant. She points.

Alicia Dearling. Parents, Mark and Candy Dearling. GPA: 3.5. Favorite subject: Art. Most influential teacher and why: Mr. Friley, who opened new doors. What I do for fun: painting!!!!

"Sophie," Cam says. "You're brilliant."

It takes them two hours and innumerable sheets of microfilm, but when they're done they have a list of six girls.

"What are you going to do?" Sophie asks.

"Call them."

"They might not want to talk to you. I think you should think about this. Talk to Mr. Park. Talk to Irene."

"I have to try," Cam says.

"Why you?"

"Who else?"

There are many possible answers to this question, but it's clear from Cam's expression that she is not interested in hearing any of them.

"Aren't you at least going to tell Blair?" Sophie tries.

"She's scared."

"I don't blame her."

"I know," Cam says. "But I have to do something. I can't . . ." She raises her hands helplessly and drops them in her lap. "I don't want to put Blair in danger. Or get her in trouble. I'll call them myself."

"Cam," Sophie says, taking one of Cam's hands in hers and leaning close. "I don't think that's a good idea. At least talk to Blair before you do anything."

"I don't want to get her involved in this."

"She already is."

Cam looks down at Sophie's fingers, interlaced with hers.

"Not this," Cam says. "Not an actual accusation."

"You have new information." Sophie gestures at the screen.

"Mr. Park can't do anything. I can't tell the police. What are they going to do? Listen to a teenager with a list of girls who liked the same art teacher? You think Aaron Liechty is going to go after the guy who put him in office?"

"Do you think he killed her?" Sophie asks.

"Who else could have? Why else would he have paid off the sheriff?"

"Cam, you can't just call these women up out of the blue and interview them for your podcast."

"Why not?"

"Because it's not your story to tell," Sophie says. "It's theirs. What makes you think you can do it for them?"

"What else am I supposed to do? How else am I supposed to prove what he is?"

"This isn't about him, Cam. It's about them. At least talk to Blair first."

"I told you. She's scared of him."

"If he killed Clarissa, maybe she should be."

"Why are you helping me if you don't think I should do anything?"

"Cam," Sophie says, her voice hard, "that's not what I said. You aren't listening to me. This isn't a situation where you get to barge ahead and do whatever you want."

"You're the one who isn't listening. You're not trying. You don't understand," Cam says, pulling her hand away from Sophie's and standing up. "You don't understand anything."

"Cam—"

But Cam's stalking away from her, across the library, out the door.

Sophie watches Cam go without trying to stop her. She slots the film back into its binder, gives the binder back to the librarian, and walks home, her beautiful mouth set in an angry red line.

ALICIA DEARLING AND Danya Caudwell have disappeared into the ether. No social media, no online traces. Or else they've gotten married and changed their names. Either way, they're impossible to find.

Three of the women from Sophie's list no longer live in Oreville. Ashley Reese is a travel blogger and yogi who leads women's empowerment retreats in places like Bali and Tulum. She has white lady dreadlocks and posts a lot of pictures of herself looking fit on white-sand beaches. Cam grimaces and writes down her email. Lauren Freeman lives in Florida and has a lot of children. She has recently welcomed her third grandbaby, although she's only a few years older than Irene. Cam finds her phone number easily; Lauren is not good at online data protection. She, Cam thinks, looking at a picture of her smiling like a maniac and saddled with infants, has not aged well. Ariana Reyes is a personal trainer in Colorado who recently set a local record for the marathon. Cam writes down the number for her business.

And then there's Brooke Barbour, who lives within walking distance of the high school. Hard to believe she would've stayed here, but she did. From what Cam can tell, she's divorced, one small son, one baby. She uses a lot of exclamatory emojis in her captions but her eyes are sad in every picture. Cam finds her phone number too.

She tries Lauren first. Lauren doesn't look scary, or like her emotions will be difficult to read, even over the phone. Lauren answers on the second ring.

"Hello?"

In Cam's haste, she forgot to think of what to say. "Uh, hi, my name is Cameron, and I'm—"

"No thank you!" Lauren says. "Please take my number off your list!"

"I'm not—" Cam says, but Lauren has already disconnected the call. She calls again. "I'm not selling anything," she says, as soon as Lauren answers. "I was hoping I could interview you."

"What is this? Is this a poll? I don't talk about who I vote for with strangers."

"No, it's not a poll," Cam says. "I'm from Oreville. I'm in high school. I'm—my friend and I—we're making a podcast about Clarissa Campbell."

"The cheerleader who went missing? That was after I graduated."

"I wanted to ask you a few questions," Cam says.

"About what? I didn't know Clarissa."

"Not about Clarissa. About Dan Friley."

There is a long pause. When she speaks, Lauren's voice is so flat and deadly even Cam can get the point. "I don't know who you are or what you want," she says. "But I have nothing to say to you. Don't call me again."

Ariana takes a moment to figure out Cam isn't trying to book a training session. She hangs up on Cam too, the minute Cam mentions Dan Friley's name. Cam crosses Ariana's number off her short list.

What would Blair do? she thinks.

Blair would know what to say. Blair would be warm, and gentle, and persuasive, and kind.

Cam isn't any of those things.

All she can do is lie.

When Brooke answers, Cam says she is writing an article for her Journalism class about former Oreville students who stayed in town. Brooke is interested. "You want to interview me for the paper?"

"Yes," Cam says. "For the paper."

"I guess so. Now?"

"Since you're in Oreville, I thought maybe we could talk in person."

Brooke thinks about this. "I guess," she says again, more cautiously this time.

Cam names a coffee shop that usually isn't crowded. "When is good for you?"

"I don't know," Brooke says. "Charles is at kindergarten right now."

"Right now is fine," Cam says.

Brooke Barbour looks tired and sad in person too. But maybe that's because of the baby, who is asleep in a broad fabric sash wrapped elaborately around Brooke's chest. Brooke's hair is bleached a brassy yellow. Her roots are long and oily. Her jeans don't fit her well, and her shoes are cheap.

Cam remembers Dan Friley's casual piles of expensive Pendleton blankets and the receptionist's costly teeth, and rage floods her veins.

Careful, she thinks. *Act like Blair.*

So instead she smiles brightly. When she introduces herself Brooke looks surprised, as if Cam wasn't at all what she expected. Probably Cam isn't. She doesn't look much like a chipper journalism student. She should've borrowed some clothes from Sophie, but then she would have to tell Sophie what she was doing, and she can't do that either, so here she is in her fraying jeans and pilly old sweater and funny hair and awkward elbows, self-conscious, doing her best. She buys Brooke a vanilla latte with her scanty allowance, gets the cheapest drink on the menu—plain coffee—for herself.

"Can I record you?" she asks, setting her phone on the table between them. Brooke takes a sip of her latte, her eyes darting around the near-empty coffee shop. Cam wonders if she's having second thoughts.

"Okay," she says uncertainly.

"Great," Cam says, as Blair-like and cheery as she can manage. "Thanks so much for talking to me! For my article! So, um, when did you graduate?"

"Nineteen ninety-four," Brooke says.

"And then?"

"And then?" Brooke repeats, looking confused.

"And then what did you do?"

"Oh." She falls silent, considers. "Well, I went to the community college for a while. Wanted to go to UW, but couldn't afford it. So I thought I would do some of the requirements here and then transfer." She stops again, looks expectantly at Cam.

"Great," Cam says. "Um, did you?"

"No. I stayed here."

"I see," Cam says. She takes out her notebook, pretends to make notes, buying herself some time.

"What are you writing?"

"Making notes for the interview," Cam says. "Uh, what did you study? At community college?"

"Business management," Brooke says apologetically. "Not very interesting. You don't have to put that in your article. It was helpful, though. I got a pretty good job at a property management company after I finished my AA."

"Business management," Cam says. "That sounds fun."

"Not really," Brooke says. "But I like the people. It pays the bills. Mostly. You have kids?"

"I'm sixteen," Cam says.

"That doesn't always stop people. Anyway, they're expensive." She looks down at the sleeping baby with affection. "Worth it, though," she says with a sad laugh.

"Right," Cam says. She has no idea what to say next. How to ask what she's here to find out. What does Blair do to get all these people to talk to them? Cam remembers the times Blair's stopped her from talking herself in their interviews. It's not the question, Cam realizes. It's the silence.

Blair waits, Cam thinks. *She waits and lets them fill in the empty space by themselves.*

Cam waits. It's a lot harder than it sounds.

"I wanted to study art," Brooke says suddenly. "More than anything. I wanted to be a painter. They have art classes at the community college. But I didn't have the time to take any. Or the money. And I knew I could never make it as an artist. I wasn't good enough. You have to be good. You have to have something special that I don't have. When I was young I thought maybe I had it. But then I realized I didn't." She stops short after this unexpected monologue, her cheeks flushing. "I didn't have it," she says again softly.

"You were an artist?"

"Nobody is a real artist when they're in high school." Cam sits on her own hands to shut herself up. Brooke doesn't notice, keeps talking. "Nobody's much of anything in high school, right? I mean, you think you are. You think you're special, or good at something, but then you find out it's not true. There are a million girls like you. You're not special at all. For a moment you thought . . ."

Her eyes are filling with tears. She trails off and looks at Cam. "Why am I telling you this? This isn't what you want to know. Sorry." Cam hands her a clean paper napkin and she blows her nose.

"It's okay," Cams says in her best Blair voice. "It's okay. Did you have a, um, favorite art teacher?"

"Yeah, he was—Mr. Friley—he told me—" Brooke stops. She's looking not at Cam but through her, at something that isn't there.

"He was nice," Brooke says dully. "He taught me all I know about painting. What artists were best. What museums I should go to. That kind of thing. I never went to any of them. They're all in Europe or New York. I only went to Idaho. But I still have that list somewhere. He helped me get better at painting."

"Is he the one who told you that you weren't special enough?"

Brooke looks down at the crumpled napkin. "It's important to be realistic in the end," she says.

"I think secrets are hard to keep for a long time," Cam says.

Brooke starts, looks back up at her. "What?"

"Something a friend of mine said. It's hard to carry things around by yourself."

Brooke's eyes narrow. She is breathing hard, like she's trying not to start crying again. "You're not here to interview me about staying in Oreville," she says.

"I think he hurt someone," Cam says. "I think he killed a girl and got away with it."

"No," Brooke says. "No. I can't talk to you about this. You have no idea what he can do."

"I'm not scared of him," Cam says.

"I don't know who you are. I can't. I'm sorry, but I can't."

She backs her chair away from the table so violently the baby wakes up and makes a mewling noise. She stands up, and the baby starts to cry.

"Please talk to me," Cam says. "You're the only person who will talk to me. Someone has to make him pay for what he did."

"I can't help you. Please leave me alone."

"Brooke—" Cam says.

But it's too late. Brooke is almost running out of the coffee shop, the baby howling in protest. Cam watches through the window as Brooke hurries to her car, tucks the baby into a car seat, gets in, drives away.

Her phone is still recording, her notebook open in front of her.

Now what, she thinks.

One left.

She picks up her phone and writes an email to Ashley Reese.

And then she walks home. She uploads the audio file from the Silverwater, listens to it.

The quality is worse than usual, because her phone was in her pocket. But Friley's voice is clear enough.

Mr. Park has hammered into the class from day one what happens to people who record conversations without consent. He didn't bother to cover what happens to people who publish them. He assumed none of them would be that stupid.

But Cam is past worrying about that now. Somebody has to bring Friley to justice. Nobody else has tried.

She settles in and starts to edit.

CAM

Blair's the one who's good at telling stories. Not me. I'm good at things like math and science. Things that have rules. I like knowing how to make the world make sense. I like looking at a star and knowing how it burns. I like looking at a tree and knowing how it breathes.

I can't do that for people. Blair can. But she's not here, because I'm doing this on my own. I'm taking full responsibility. I'm going to tell you things I shouldn't, and I'm going to play a conversation for you that I recorded without consent. I want to admit to that up front, so there isn't any question. And I want you to know this is all me. None of this is Blair. She didn't know. She doesn't know. So come after me, not her.

When we started out this whole thing was kind of a joke. It didn't seem real. I didn't think of Clarissa as a person. Which is the whole problem with her story. That's something I understand now. That people didn't see her for who she was when she was alive, and they didn't see her at all after she died. And I want to apologize for that too. For being part of it. For being part of the world that turns girls like Clarissa into stories they can't tell themselves. It may not seem like it, but I did learn something. And I saw a lot of people in a lot of pain. And I started to understand that a single person is always connected to so many other stories. So many other lives. We're all tangled up together. Blair would have a good metaphor. I guess symbiosis is a good metaphor. Except that symbiosis is an ongoing inter-action between biological organisms of different species and human beings are all the same species, so that isn't a good metaphor at all. I hope you know what I mean anyway.

I should also say we can't prove anything. We—I don't have evidence. But I know I'm right. I know what he did. And Clarissa deserves the truth. I think that when you know what I know, you can't keep it quiet. Not everybody agrees with me. My—uh, my girlfriend—she says this isn't my story to tell. That's true. None of this happened to me. It happened to other people, and most of them are still alive. All of them except Clarissa, I think. So I'm not going to tell you the names of anyone else I talked to about him. About what he might have done. I think you should know Clarissa wasn't the only one. I'm sure about that. And Clarissa can't tell anyone anymore.

My girlfriend says going to jail isn't justice. I mean, because the whole system doesn't work. Or I guess, because the system works the way it's supposed to, and the way it's supposed to work is to hurt people. I thought about that a lot, because I wanted to see him suffer. I wanted him to be punished. I still want that, to be honest. My girlfriend is a better person than I am. But I think the truth is something people should be able to know. And then they can decide what to do with it.

That's another thing my girlfriend says. She says we don't have to figure everything out on our own. We can decide together how to build a better world. I hope you can understand that's what I'm trying to do. Maybe I'm doing it wrong. But I couldn't hold this inside. I'm giving it to all of us, to figure out together.

EPISODE VII

THE APOLOGIES

"GODDAMMIT, Cameron! What did I tell you? I told you not to push this!"

It's Saturday, the morning after Cam posted her episode, and Irene is storming into Cam's room angrier than Cam has ever seen her.

"What?" she says sleepily, sitting up in bed. Kitten grunts in protest and thumps to the floor, stalks out with his tail waving in reproach.

"What in god's name have you done!"

"Stop yelling at me," Cam mumbles, rubbing her eyes. "It's too early for you to yell at me."

"What am I supposed to do now?" Irene shouts. She slams out of Cam's room without waiting for a response.

"Now what did I do?" Cam says out loud. And then she sits bolt upright, fear flooding through her.

There's only one reason Irene could be this pissed at ten

o'clock on a Saturday morning. Cam checks her phone. She has thirty-three missed calls and seventy text messages.

"Oh no," she says.

She pulls on a pair of jeans and a T-shirt and goes into the kitchen.

Irene doesn't only look pissed. She looks exhausted, and she looks scared. There are dark hollows under her eyes.

"Do you know who I just got off the phone with?" she says without preamble when Cam enters the kitchen. "Dan Friley's lawyer, Cameron."

"Shit," Cam says.

"Yes, 'shit.' What the hell were you thinking? Do you have any idea how much trouble you're in? How much trouble you've put *me* in? He's filing the paperwork for a defamation lawsuit, Cam. I had to call in sick to work to deal with this. Where do you think I'm going to get the money for a lawyer? I can't even pay the goddamn court fees!"

"It was my fault," Cam says. "I said so on the podcast. I said it was my idea."

"You're *a minor*, Cameron. Blair's mother called me right after the lawyer did. She's hysterical."

"Blair didn't have anything to do with it!" Cam protests. "I'll figure something out. I'll talk to Mr. Park. I'll—"

"Don't you so much as open your mouth, Cameron. I don't know what to say to you right now." Irene, horrifyingly, starts to cry. "Go back to your room. I have to call Blair's parents back."

"Why?" Cam asks.

"Because they're named in the lawsuit too!" Irene shouts.

"Oh no," Cam says. "No, they can't be. I said Blair had nothing to do with it. I swear."

"That doesn't matter right now, Cam," Irene says. "Go to your room."

"But—"

"Please," Irene says. "I can't look at you right now. Just go."

Most of the text messages are from Blair. Cam scrolls through, feeling sick. What were you thinking? My parents are going to kill me. I don't know what to do. Some from Sophie: What were you thinking? Cam, I told you to wait.

Some are from strangers who've gotten her number somehow. We will find where u live u cunt. Good job you got him. She isn't dead you dumb bitches. You know it was Brad!!!! Cam deletes them all, blocks the numbers, considers throwing her phone in the toilet.

The first voicemail is from Mr. Park, asking her to call him immediately. She deletes it. The next one is a reporter from *USA Today*, asking her to call him immediately. She deletes it. The next is a reporter from the *New York Times*, asking her to call her immediately. Cam deletes that one, and the one from the *Oreville Examiner*, and the one from *People* magazine, and the one from a prime-time talk show. Her stomach is in knots. It's possible she is going to throw up. She wants to crawl back into bed and pull the covers over her head and never come out again. She wants to disappear.

But is she sorry?

No, she thinks. *I'm not. I'm not sorry at all.*

Still. She has to deal with what she's done. She knew it might blow up in her face.

But she didn't expect the *New York Times*.

Her phone rings.

Blair.

"Hi," she says, answering.

"I can't believe you did that," Blair says. "I can't. Cam, he's suing us. He's suing my parents."

"They'll have to reopen the case now," Cam says. "Really reopen it. Not just pretend it's still open."

"Why?"

"Because we found new evidence," Cam says.

"No," Blair says. "*We* didn't. *You* found a list of girls who said Dan Friley was their favorite art teacher and you accused him of murder and statutory rape on a podcast that three hundred thousand people listened to."

"Three hundred *thousand*?"

"Since last night," Blair says. Her voice is cold. "Do you not understand what a big deal this is?"

"People keep asking me that," Cam says.

"Yeah, I wonder why," Blair says.

"I'm sorry I did it without telling you," Cam says, which is true, even if she isn't sorry she did it.

"It's a little late for that," Blair says.

"Are you mad at me?"

Blair makes a noise somewhere between a laugh and a sob. "What do you think?"

"Is that a yes?"

"Yeah, Cam, that's a yes. You don't ask. You don't think. You charge ahead without caring what it does to anyone else. I can't do this anymore."

"Can't do what? The podcast?"

"I can't be friends with you," Blair says.

"Are you serious?"

"Yeah," Blair says. "Even if my parents let me see you again. Which they won't. But that's fine, because I don't want to."

"Ever?" Cam asks, feeling her heart constrict. "You don't want to see me again ever?"

"Not for a long time," Blair says.

"Blair," Cam says. "Blair, don't go. Blair, don't say that. Blair, I'm trying to do the right thing."

But the line is silent. Blair hung up on her.

And then, finally, Cam starts to cry.

MR. PARK FINDS a lawyer who will help them for cheap. A friend of a friend who owes Mr. Park a favor.

Mr. Park does not want to offer Cam advice.

"Talk to the lawyer about this, not me," he says.

Cam has not been to school in four days. Irene is too upset to care. Cam spends most of her waking hours staring at her phone. It won't stop ringing: reporters, lunatics from the internet, people from school who Cam is pretty sure hated her guts up until the moment she got famous, more reporters. Cam lets them all go to voicemail until her voicemail is full. Cam does not want to talk to reporters or lunatics from the internet or people from school. Cam wants Sophie, saying she's sorry she got mad at Cam in the library and Cam was right and Cam did the right thing. Cam wants Blair, saying she's sorry and Cam can be her friend again. Cam wants Mr. Park, saying the last week has been a bad dream and everyone believes her and Dan Friley is going away forever to a non-jail abolitionist place of restorative justice where he can never hurt any more girls and has to give all of his money and his stolen land back to the Quileute people.

And if a frog had wings, Irene says in her head, *he wouldn't bump his ass when he hopped.*

At night, Cam puts her phone under her pillow and lies awake in the dark, looking up at the ceiling, waiting for the relief of sleep to wipe out the present for a few hours. It rarely comes.

So far the lawyer has sent a lot of emails, none of which seem to have changed anything. Irene goes around grim and silent. Cam is grateful for the hours she's at work. Once a day Cam searches her own name online to punish herself. The story is only getting bigger. She makes herself read every article and all of the comments. At least a few of them are almost on her side. Not that that helps.

She called Mr. Park back on the first day, when he gave her the phone number for the lawyer, and she calls him again on the fifth day to ask what she should do to get her life back, and that's when he tells her he can't help her. Like she's poison he can't touch.

"It's not that," Mr. Park says. "Cameron, I can't give you advice here. Don't you understand that? I'm a journalism teacher, not a legal expert. What you did broke every journalism rule there is, not to mention the law. I don't want to tell you something that will end up creating an even bigger disaster."

"You're mad at me too," Cam says. "Everyone is mad at me."

"A number of people have good reason to be mad at you, Cameron. But no, I'm not mad at you. I think you made a serious mistake. That's not the same thing as being angry."

"Blair isn't talking to me."

Mr. Park is quiet for a moment. "I'm not sure I blame her," he says.

Cam's throat hurts, but she's cried so much in the last four days she's not sure she has any crying left in her.

"What if I apologize?" she asks.

"To Blair?"

"To—him."

Cam isn't sorry. That's the thing. She isn't sorry, because she wasn't wrong. But maybe if she can find a way to get Blair out of this, Blair will forgive her.

Maybe she'll work up the nerve to call Sophie.

Maybe Irene won't look at her with an expression Cam has

never seen before. Something more than fury, more than disappointment. Something painfully close to disgust.

"I could make another podcast," Cam says.

Mr. Park makes a noise. "I think the last thing you want to do right now is make another podcast," he says.

"I mean an apology. A public apology. To him." Cam can't bring herself to say his name. "Maybe then he would leave Blair's family alone. She didn't have anything to do with this. We have a big audience now. People would listen."

"People would listen," Mr. Park agrees. "I don't know that Dan Friley would."

"I know you can't give me advice," Cam says. "But what would you do? If you were me? He did something really bad, Mr. Park. He did something bad to a lot of people. I *know* that. I think he killed Clarissa too."

"What you know to be true and what you can prove are not the same thing," Mr. Park says. "And that difference is essential in journalism, Cameron. You don't publish something you can't back up. I'm sorry you're learning that the hard way, but that's how it works." He sighs. "I don't know if it would help to apologize. I don't know Dan Friley."

"There has to be evidence," Cam says. "I mean, there has to be *something*. Maybe I'm not asking the right people. Or the right questions."

"You've drawn so much attention to yourself that you've blown your own investigation. You can't keep digging around without Friley coming after you even harder. This is why we counsel a certain degree of patience in our field."

"I'm not patient," Cam says.

"Yes, I've noticed. Talk to your lawyer. She's there to help you. She can tell you if an apology is a good idea."

"But what if he gets away with it?"

"What if he's innocent?" Mr. Park counters.

"He's not!" Cam says, furious.

"I'm not saying you're wrong. I'm saying you need evidence, which you don't have."

"Yet. If an apology gets Friley off our backs, that will buy us some time to investigate," Cam says excitedly.

Mr. Park sighs again, heavily. "Cameron. You are in a world of trouble right now. Do what the lawyer says, and leave this alone. The last thing you need is to give Dan Friley more ammunition for his lawsuit. Do you understand me?"

Cam grunts.

"Cameron?"

"Yes," she says. "Yes, I understand you."

"Good," says Mr. Park.

THE LAWYER THINKS an apology might help. Or, at least, won't do any harm.

Cam doesn't call Blair; she won't be able to bear it if Blair hangs up on her again. So she texts, phrasing it as carefully as if she's addressing a cherished elderly relative who's easily offended.

Blair calls her back a few minutes later.

"Hi," Cam says. "Um. How are you?"

"Fine," Blair says.

"I'm fine too," Cam says, although she isn't, and Blair didn't ask, and Blair probably isn't either.

"So, what about this apology?" Blair asks.

"The lawyer thinks it could help. If I—we—are sincere. That maybe Friley will settle with us. I mean, with me and Irene. If I say it was all my idea. That he might leave your family alone." Cam is stumbling over herself.

"It *was* your idea," Blair says coldly. "This whole thing was your idea."

"I'm sorry I got you into this," Cam says. "But you worked hard on it too."

"So this is my fault?"

"No!" Cam says. "No. That's not what I meant. I mean, the good parts. The good parts were because of you. Because of your writing."

"I wish I'd never said yes."

"You do?" Blair doesn't answer. "You're the fan favorite," Cam says. "On the forum. Everybody likes you the best. They think I'm annoying."

"You are annoying," Blair says, but the chill has thawed slightly out of her voice.

"Will you do it?"

"Irene's lawyer thinks it will help?"

"I mean, it's not a guarantee or anything. But maybe."

"Let me talk to my parents about it. Have you talked to Sophie?"

"Sophie's not talking to me right now," Cam says. "I don't think. She hasn't called me."

"Have you called her?"

"No," Cam says. "I don't know what to say. She told me I shouldn't make the episode. Not without talking to you."

"She was right."

Cam takes a deep breath. She has a hard time getting the words out. "I know. I'm—I'm sorry, B. What I did was dumb. No. Not dumb. That's not the right word. I should have talked to you. It's our podcast. Not mine. I, uh, made a big mistake. And I hurt you."

Blair is quiet for a while. "Thanks," she says. "I know that was hard for you. You messed up, Cam."

"I know," Cam says quietly.

"Well," Blair says. "That's something."

"How is James, uh, dealing with it?"

"He told me so," Blair says tiredly. "I mean, that's what he said. 'I told you so.'"

"Oh," Cam says.

"Aren't you going to tell me how much he sucks?"

"I'm just glad you called me," Cam says. "I don't want to do anything to make you mad."

"Do you think he's right?"

"No," Cam says immediately. "B, you didn't do anything wrong. The podcast was good. Really good. I'm the one who screwed it up. Not you. You should be proud of the work you did."

"You're only saying that because you want me to help you with the apology."

"I'm saying that because it's true," Cam says.

"I don't think James listened to it," Blair says.

"The—my—episode?"

"The podcast," Blair says. "I don't think he listened to a single one." Cam is silent. "You can say that's shitty," Blair says. "I think it's shitty too."

"It's shitty," Cam agrees.

"So I broke up with him."

Cam is not sure she heard this correctly. "You *what*?"

"I broke up with him," Blair says. "I guess I figured—I mean, you're not the only person in the world with a backbone."

"You think I have a backbone?"

"Not, like, an intelligent backbone," Blair says. "A backbone with no sense of self-preservation."

"Do you—uh, do you want to come over? I already asked Irene if it was okay. If we recorded an apology, I mean. She says we have to let the lawyer listen to it before we post it. And your parents. And Mr. Park."

"That's fine," Blair says. "That seems like a good idea."

"Yeah."

"You should call Sophie."

"Okay," Cam says.

"She loves you. She knows you. She'll get it."

"She loves me?" Cam asks, astonished.

"Just call her."

"I'll call her."

"As soon as you hang up."

"I promise."

"Sophie's a keeper, Cam. Say you were wrong."

"I wasn't *wrong*. Just—impetuous."

"Cam."

"Okay, okay," Cam says.

"You still think he did it, don't you?"

"Yes," Cam says. "Do you?"

Blair sighs. "Yeah, I do. Too bad he's going to get away with it."

"No, he's not," Cam says.

"You're never going to let this go," Blair says. It's not exactly a question.

"I don't want to get anyone else in any more trouble," Cam says. It's not exactly an answer. "B? Did you mean what you said about not wanting to be friends with me anymore?"

"I meant it when I said it."

"What about now?"

"If you record another podcast without telling me I will never speak to you again, Cameron P. Muñoz," Blair says.

"Deal," Cam says.

"I'm coming over," Blair says. "This doesn't mean I'm not still pissed."

"Understood."

"This is only for damage control."

"I know."

"Call Sophie."

"I will."

"Right now. I'll be there in half an hour."

"I'm not going anywhere," Cam says, her heart singing hymns of joy in her chest. "I'll wait right here."

EPISODE VIII

THE
FINAL GIRLS

THE lawyer calls Irene two days after the apology drops. Half a million people have listened to it in forty-eight hours. Cam and Blair both changed their phone numbers, but the reporters still find them.

"He's willing to meet," Irene says to Cam when she gets off the phone.

"What does that mean?"

"She's not sure," Irene says. "There's a chance he'll drop the suit."

"He wants us to beg."

"You're not in a position to argue, Cameron."

"I'm not arguing," Cam says. But. Grovel? For Dan Friley? Dan Friley, who is a murderer and a rapist and a sheriff-briber? She's not sure she can do it. Not even for Irene. Not even for Blair.

Irene makes them a pot of coffee, lights a cigarette. She's worked her way up to half a pack a day since the lawsuit was filed. "I know how hard this is for you," she says, when the coffee's poured and they're sitting at the kitchen table. "Especially if you're right about him."

"I am," Cam says.

"I think you are. But that doesn't change what you did."

"What else was I supposed to do? Let him get away with it?"

"You could've done any one of a number of things," Irene says. "You could have talked to Mr. Park. You could have talked to the police—"

"The police!" says Cam. Irene has about as much love for the police as Sophie does.

"All right. You could have talked to a real reporter. You could've talked to *me*, Cameron."

"Sophie told me it wasn't my story to tell," Cam says.

"I told you Sophie was a smart one."

"I'm sorry I got us in trouble," Cam says. "I'm sorry I got Blair in trouble too."

"You're lucky she's speaking to you."

"I know."

"You're lucky I'm speaking to you."

"You're my mom."

"That doesn't mean I'm required to speak to you."

Cam tries a smile. Irene shakes her head. "You are an impossible child," she says. And then she says, "You know, your father would be proud of you."

"He would?" Cam sits up. "Really?"

"Yes," Irene says. "He was a fan of speaking truth to power."

"And you?"

"The first time I got arrested I was tagging ACAB on the side of the Manhattan-bound three train," Irene says. "But I was twenty-one years old and the NYPD didn't file a libel suit against my parents. Am I making my point clear here?"

"Yes," Cam says happily. "Use chalk instead of spray paint."

"Get out of my sight, you monster," Irene says. Neither one of them moves. Kitten sits next to the refrigerator, purring like the idiot he is.

THE APOLOGY IS scheduled for Friday afternoon at the Silverwater. Blair, her parents, her parents' lawyer, Irene, Cam, Irene's lawyer. Cam thinks they should invite Mr. Park. Perhaps the whole class. Make a party out of it. Mattmiles can screen their film. Sophie can tell Dan Friley to go fuck himself in Klallam.

"Cameron," Sophie says. "You need to go into this with an attitude of humility if you don't want Irene to end up in the workhouse."

"They don't have workhouses anymore," Cam says.

"Right. Now people get sent to prison, where they have to work."

It's the night before the big event. Rain pounds against Cam's windows. Kitten is buried in Cam's unmade bed, invisible but snoring so loudly his presence is unmistakable. Sophie is still distant, but she's here. Sophie helped Cam pick out the closest thing to a professional ensemble Cam owns. Now, Sophie drills Cam on her facial expressions so she can look appropriately contrite in Friley's office.

"You look like you ate a lemon. No, not that one. Nope, now you look ill. *Cameron.* You're not trying!"

Sophie's ponytail has come loose and strands of brown hair drift across her perfect face. Cam wants to push her hair out of her eyes and kiss her, but having a girlfriend is still a new experience, let alone making up after a fight with one. Is this an inappropriate time?

"Sophie?"

"Yeah?"

Cam's heart is huge, a feeling she has never before had to name. She doesn't know how.

"I love you," Cam says.

Sophie looks up, her brown eyes alight. She smiles.

"That face," she says. "Freeze it like that."

"You want me to tell Dan Friley I love him?"

"No, silly," she says. "I want you to look at me like that for the rest of our lives."

———

LATER—

Cam and Sophie make dinner for Irene: spaghetti with marinara sauce out of a jar. Sophie sautés mushrooms, onions, finds basil in the cupboard. Cam's already burned the garlic. Irene watches them from the kitchen table, smiling a private little smile to herself. Kitten snores under her chair, replete at last.

Blair stays late after practice, running loop after loop on the track behind the high school under the buzzing glare of the arc lights, ignoring the light, steady rain.

We did a good job, she thinks. *I did a good job. I could be good at this.*

I could have something to say.

James watches clips of famous basketball games on his iPad. One video ends. In the ad break before another begins, he thinks of Blair.

Thinking of you, he texts.

She won't see the message for another hour. When she does, she won't respond.

Brad Bennett cleans a shotgun, all alone in his trailer. He looks down the barrel, thinks about bullets.

Not tonight, he hears Clarissa say in her clear bright voice.
He puts the shotgun in a cabinet and locks it away.

Jenny Alexander's marinating tofu while Ellie picks winter greens from the garden. Jenny looks out the window over the kitchen sink, but it's dark outside and she can only see her own reflection. Behind her, a flash of blond hair, a white smile, an echo of a laugh.

"Clarissa?" she says, turning around.

No ghost. Only a trick of the light.

Dan Friley sits at his desk, making notes. He's not worried about the girls, but he thinks they should be punished. Cam and Blair, that is. The other girls he doesn't think of anymore. He stopped thinking about them the moment he left them behind.

Angela walks into his office, unbuttoning her blouse.

"Perfect timing," he says. "I was getting ready to take a break."

Allen Dawson watches *Murder, She Wrote* with his mother. She knows all the episodes by heart.

Marian Campbell looks through an album of Clarissa's baby pictures. Her husband's in the garage. He says he's vacuuming the car.

But the truth is, he can't bear to watch.

Mr. Park drinks an after-dinner whiskey with his husband on their front porch. The clouds have briefly cleared; Orion chases the tree-tops in his glittering belt. Mr. Park thinks of Cam. He thinks of dead girls. He thinks of stories he never got to tell. He thinks of re-vising the Journalism syllabus for next year. He must add laundry soap to the grocery list. And toothpaste.

"Thomas," his husband says, taking his hand.

"Sorry," Mr. Park says, bringing his husband's knuckles to his mouth. "Here I am."

"Here you are," his husband says.

They are quiet together in the dark, hoping for shooting stars.

Brooke Barbour listens to an episode of *Missing Clarissa*. And then she listens to another. She pours a slug of vodka into one of Charles's sippy cups, doesn't bother with tonic. The baby's asleep. So is Charles. She's sitting alone in the dark with all those voices.

The apology. Cam's voice, thin and shaky.

I'm so sorry for—uh. For what I did. I was—I shouldn't have—it wasn't the right thing to say.

Brooke pours herself another drink, looking out into the night. Orion's moved across the sky. Her eyes are full of tears.

Before she can think too hard about it, she gets out her phone and writes an email.

CAM CAN'T SLEEP.

Sophie's gone home. Irene is in her room. She took a bottle of wine and WORLD'S #1 DAD with her, so Cam doubts she's asleep either, but her closed door means she doesn't want to talk.

Cam pulls out her phone, scrolls idly through her photo roll. Blair laughing. Blair at track. Blair in her new beaded earrings. Sophie making a facetious duckface. Sophie when she doesn't know Cam's taking her picture, her face lit radiant by a stray beam of sun. Sophie in a pretty dress. Sophie in another pretty dress.

Clarissa and Jenny on the beach.

Cam and Blair never asked Jenny when it was taken. Before Dan, Cam wonders, or after? There's no way to tell from their smiles. But they are both alight with joy. Cam can see it coming off them like a halo. Before Dan, she decides. Maybe the last picture of them together, before everything went wrong.

White teeth, tan skin, the flash of turquoise at Clarissa's throat.

The flash of turquoise at Clarissa's throat.

The faint stab she felt at Jenny's house, looking at this picture on Jenny's wall, explodes into recognition.

And then she knows.

All along. She should have known all along.

What they've found already is true. But it's not the whole truth.

Not even close.

"Oh, shit," she says. "*Shit.*"

Brad's number rings and rings. Voicemail. Cam ends the call, tries again. The third time, he answers.

"Who the hell is this? Do you know what time it is?"

"I'm sorry," Cam says. "It's Cam. Cameron. Cam Muñoz."

"Why the hell are you calling me at three o'clock in the morning? After what you did? There are reporters beating down my goddamn door. Twenty years of peace, and now you—"

"I'm sorry," Cam says again. "I'm so sorry. Please don't hang up. I have to ask you a question. It's important."

"I told you already. I don't know anything about Dan."

"It's not about Dan," Cam says. "Clarissa had a necklace. A blue necklace. I think it was turquoise, but the picture I have is too blurry. Do you know what I'm talking about?"

"Yeah," Brad says. "I gave it to her."

"Can you describe it?"

"It was a pendant. A turquoise pendant. Big. Kind of a teardrop shape. The stone had a dark streak down the middle, like a lightning bolt. Set in silver."

"Did she have it at the party? The night she disappeared?"

"She never took it off. What is this about?"

"Thank you," Cam says. Should she apologize again? Is that too much?

"Why is that important?"

"Because now I know who killed her," Cam says, and hangs up.

What does she need? What do you take with you, when you confront a murderer? In the movies she would have a gun, but she doesn't own a gun, and nobody is going to give her a gun at three in the morning, even in America. She doesn't have a car. But if she starts now, she can get to where she needs to go and back home before it's time to leave for the Silverwater. She puts on black pants and a black sweater and a black beanie, like a cat burglar.

She will be fine. It's not like Clarissa's murderer is a frightening man.

Confront a killer, patch up her life. Pass Journalism, hopefully. Go to college and never come back. That's it. That's all she needs.

These days, Cam's to-do list is concise.

This late at night the crosstown bus runs once an hour. Cam stamps her feet at the stop, her breath blooming white in the cold. At least it's stopped raining. She waits in the dark, strangely calm.

Before, she was sure.

But now, she knows.

Blair can't sleep. There's too much in her head: the in-person apology tomorrow, which technically should be Cam's alone, but Cam in her habitual recklessness has dragged everyone she loves along with her. James, who won't stop calling her, though she never calls back. Her parents, who are treating her with a kind of mute, uncomprehending condescension. It's easy enough for them to blame Cam too, Cam with her weird excuse for a family, her broken home, her insane schemes.

"I hope this means you won't be spending so much time with that girl in the future," Blair's mother actually said, as if Cam was some stray she'd brought home and not her best friend of years.

She doubts Cam's sleeping either. She's still angry with Cam, but the anger is fading into something else. Pride? She's not sure. Whatever she's feeling, it's new. She thinks of Cam's relentless insistence that her work on the podcast was good. She thinks of hundreds of thousands of people, listening to her words. No matter how dumb her voice sounds. It's what she's said that's brought them in.

That, and Clarissa.

Everyone still loves a dead girl.

It's not fair, Blair thinks. Nowhere near this many people would have bothered to listen to Clarissa speaking for herself. If Clarissa hadn't disappeared. If Clarissa were still alive. If Clarissa were any other ordinary girl, prettier than most but still a dime a dozen.

But if Clarissa hadn't died, no one would be listening to Blair either.

So what does that say about her?

She dials Cam without thinking about it. Cam, who's been on the other end of the line for as long as she's had thoughts that need a listener. In middle school they used to fall asleep still talking, their phones pressed between their ears and their pillows. Waking up in the morning with the battery dead.

Blair can't stay mad at Cam. It's like being angry with the only fearless part of herself.

But Cam doesn't answer. The call goes straight to voicemail. Either Cam doesn't want to talk to her or her phone's off.

Maybe she's trying to sleep.

Maybe she *is* asleep.

Blair looks out her window, where a faint scatter of stars gleams through a dark scrim of trees.

She knows Cam better than that.

"Cameron P. Muñoz," she says out loud, "what are you doing?"

The sky's going gray with dawn by the time Cam gets to her stop. She checks her phone, which she's set to silent. Seven missed calls from Brad and one from Blair. It's six in the morning and she has more than enough battery for what she needs to do.

His neighborhood is silent, but already the lights are on in a handful of houses. Ordinary people, getting ready for work. Drinking coffee, reading the news. The news is always bad.

But tomorrow, Cam thinks, the news will be new.

She pounds on his door. Waits. Knocks again. No answer. A third time. And then it swings open, and he's standing there, blinking at her from behind his round glasses. The most ordinary man in the world. His soft white hands.

Did he strangle her? Did he hit her? How did he do it?

What did it feel like, to look at a girl you loved and watch her die?

"What are you doing here?" he asks. "What is this? Do you know what time it is?"

"I'm recording this," Cam says in a rush. "For the podcast. And in case anything happens to me. So don't get any ideas."

She's learned her lesson. More or less.

"Excuse me?" he says.

"Where did your mom get her necklace?" Cam asks.

"What necklace?"

"You know the one I mean."

He stands there looking at her for an eternity.

"I think you'd better come in," Allen Dawson says.

Blair's thrashed around in her flowered sheets for long enough. There's no point. She gets out of bed, calls Cam again.

No answer.

She takes a long shower, extra hot. Spends longer than normal on her hair, her face. This early in the morning, she doesn't have to worry about her brother or her parents demanding the bathroom. But her mom's awake when she comes out, and the kitchen smells like coffee.

"Do you want breakfast, honey?" her mother says. As if this is a normal day. As if she's heading off to school, instead of into the belly of the beast.

"Toast," Blair says, although she doubts she can eat anything at all. She texts Cam again while her white bread browns in the toaster. Still nothing.

> Cam, what are you doing?
>
> Where are you?

She tries Irene.

"Would you like coffee? Or tea?" Allen Dawson asks, as if she's making a social call. "Why don't you sit?" He gestures to the flowery couch. She doesn't sit. She doesn't want to touch anything in this house again.

"No, thank you," Cam says. "This won't take long. Where did your mother get her necklace?"

Allen stares at her, his soft white hands dangling at his side. He looks older than he did the first time she saw him.

"It was a gift," he says. He licks his lips.

"From who?"

"From me," he says.

"You took it from Clarissa," Cam says.

"I think you should sit down," Allen says.

"Why did you give it to your mother? Why is she still wearing it?"

"My mother is ill," he says.

"Does she know you killed Clarissa?"

Allen takes a step toward her, and Cam backs away. "I'm going to call nine-one-one," Cam says. "But I want to hear it from you. I want to hear you say it."

"Allen?" his mother warbles from another room. "Allen, dear, do we have guests? Isn't it awfully early?"

Instinctively, Cam turns her head toward the sound. And Allen Dawson moves faster than she would've thought possible. She whips back around, but it's too late. He's holding something big and white.

"I wish you hadn't come here," Allen says, and brings his mother's ceramic Pegasus lamp down on her head.

"She's not answering her phone because it's six thirty in the morning, Blair," Irene says. It took Blair four tries to get her to answer, and Irene still sounds groggy and cross.

"Would you do me a favor? Would you check?"

"I know you're nervous, but you'll see her in a couple of hours."

"*Check her room*," Blair says, with Cam-like force.

Irene makes an aggrieved noise, followed by several thumps and what sounds like a door slamming. "Cam?" Irene yells. "Cam, are you in the bathroom? Cam? *Cameron P. Muñoz!*" She brings the receiver back to her mouth. "Where is she?"

"I don't know," Blair says.

"What the hell is she doing?"

"Stay there," Blair says. "I'm coming over." She hangs up. "Mom!" she yells, grabbing her car keys off her dresser. "Going out to check the mail! Be right back!" She slams the front door behind her without listening for a reply and runs to her car.

In books when someone hits you over the head the world goes dark and you wake up in a different scene.

That's not what happens to Cam. Her legs collapse underneath her, and she falls over like a log. She's trying to move her arms and legs, but it's like she can't organize herself. The pain is incredible. For a long moment the question of whether she is going to throw up takes all her attention, and that's enough time for Allen to tie her arms behind her back with a piece of clothesline and half drag, half frog-march her into his mother's basement.

"*Really?*" she tries to say, but moving her mouth makes the pain in her head worse, and now she is definitely going to throw up, and she does, all over Allen Dawson and Allen Dawson's mother's basement stairs. Allen Dawson shoves her between a deep freezer and a washing machine and ties her feet together, and she is so angry she wants to scream at him, but if she screams she will almost certainly throw up again. Her vision is blurry. Does she have a concussion? How do you know if you have a concussion? Does she need to go to the hospital?

Allen Dawson, Cam realizes, is probably not going to take her to a hospital.

Allen Dawson leans forward and fumbles around in her coat pocket, pulls out her phone. He puts it in his own pocket.

"You wait here now," he says. He backs away from her, thumps up the stairs, shuts the basement door. She hears a key turn in the lock. Allen Dawson's mother's basement is small and dark and smells like Cam puke and damp clothes that have been left in the dryer too long. Cam's head hurts too badly for her to think. Her mouth tastes like vomit. She can hear a dull, tinny noise that she knows is coming from her broken head.

Something that is likely blood trickles down her face, but she can't check, because her hands are tied behind her back.

It's possible, Cam acknowledges, that confronting Clarissa's killer on her own without telling anyone where she was going has maybe not been one of her best ideas.

Irene calls the police. The police tell her Cam is not missing. Not yet.

"What do you mean, my daughter is not missing!" Irene screams into the telephone. "My daughter is not here! That is the literal fucking definition of missing!"

Irene hangs up on the police. Irene calls her lawyer. She calls Dan Friley's lawyer. She calls Dan Friley's office. She calls Blair's parents' lawyer. The lawyers and Dan Friley do not answer, because it's seven o'clock in the morning. She starts to dial Blair's parents, but Blair points out that she just left her parents, who know absolutely nothing about where Cam is.

Blair still has Officer Reloj's card in her wallet. But he doesn't answer either.

Because it's seven o'clock in the morning.

Irene is pacing the kitchen, chain-smoking. "Where would she go? What is she doing? Is this about the podcast?"

You think? Blair thinks, but does not say aloud. Irene does not need her sarcasm. Blair does not need to freak Irene out any more than Irene is freaked out. She has never seen Irene freaked out before, not in all the years she's known Irene, and the tiny part of her brain that is not also freaking out is marveling at the spectacle.

"She was serious about the apology," Blair says. "She wouldn't have screwed that up. Whatever she's doing, she thinks it will help."

"Help us? Or help the podcast?" Irene snaps.

"I think she thinks that's the same thing," Blair says.

"What could have happened last night? What changed?" Irene stops her pacing. "Did someone call her? A reporter? Did she get some harebrained idea?"

Knowing Cam, she absolutely got some harebrained idea, but Blair doesn't say that out loud either.

"She would've told me if she talked to a reporter," Blair says. "I mean, I think she would have. She promised me she wouldn't make another episode without telling me."

Irene snorts.

"Yeah, I know," Blair says. "But she meant it when she said it. Besides, why would a reporter call her so late? Or so early?"

She thinks some more. Who could Cam have talked to? Not the Campbells, who are clueless. Not Mr. Park; not in the middle of the night. Certainly not Dan Friley. It's possible one of the women Cam and Sophie found called her, but that's also unlikely, given the timing.

Which leaves Jenny and Brad.

"I have an idea," Blair says.

First she tries Jenny, who answers right away, sounding as perky as if she's been up for hours. "No," she says in response to Blair's mostly incoherent question, "I haven't heard from Cam. Did something happen?"

"I'm sorry to bother you," Blair says. "Never mind. Thank you."

Brad, too, answers immediately. "What the hell are the two of you up to?" he barks as soon as Blair identifies herself. "What's going on?"

"She called you?"

Irene's head whips around. She looks like she wants to snatch the phone out of Blair's hand.

"Yeah, she called me, asking about Clarissa's necklace, and then she said she knew who killed her and hung up on me."

"Clarissa's necklace?" Blair echoes.

"Why would she ask me about it?" Brad is yelling. "What do you know? Who killed Clar?"

"I don't know!" Blair says. "I don't know. She didn't talk to me. I have to figure out where she is. I think she's in trouble."

Irene looks stricken.

"Okay," Brad says. "Okay." He takes a deep breath. Blair does too. "She called me. In the middle of the night. Like, three a.m. I, uh, yelled at her. Because of the reporters. They won't leave me alone."

"Sorry," Blair says uselessly.

"Then she asked about Clarissa's necklace. This necklace I gave her. It was an antique. She loved it. She never took it off. Cam asked me about that. She asked if Clarissa was wearing it the night of the party. The night she disappeared."

"Wait," Blair says. "She knew about it already? She asked you about a necklace she knew Clarissa had?"

"She said she had a picture," Brad says. "She said she needed me to describe it because the picture she had was too blurry."

"What picture?" Blair asks.

"I don't know," Brad says. "I'm sorry. She didn't say."

And then Blair remembers. Jenny and Clarissa on the beach, on the wall at Jenny's house. Cam leaning in with her phone, asking if she could take a picture.

What necklace? she thinks. *What does a necklace have to do with anything?*

"Why would she ask you about Clarissa's necklace?"

"I don't know," Brad says.

"What did it look like?"

"It was a big piece of turquoise. Like a teardrop shape. I don't know why she cared."

"What happened to it?"

"Clarissa was wearing it that night," Brad says. "Whatever happened to her, that's where it went."

"That's it? That's all Cam asked you?"

"That's it," Brad says. "She said she knew who killed Clarissa, and then she hung up on me. She hasn't answered since. Is she all right?"

"I don't know," Blair says. "I don't think so."

"What did she mean? Who killed Clarissa?"

"I don't know yet," Blair says again. "But I'm going to find out."

What did you figure out, Cam? she thinks.

What did you see that I didn't?

Cam tries to move her head. The feeling of nausea is like a shock wave rolling through her entire body. Blair is always telling her to take deep breaths and count things for a calming effect. *One,* she thinks, inhaling. *Two. Three.*

By the time she gets to ten, she does feel a bit better. The pain in her head has sort of localized to a single throbbing orb behind her ear. She wiggles her fingers and toes experimentally. The nausea doesn't come back. She lifts her chin again and takes a cautious look around.

No puking: that is a plus. No basement window: that is a minus. The only light comes from a lint-thick vent over the dryer that is far too small for her to crawl through, even if she could untie herself and pry away the grating, which she can't. Beyond the metal grille she can see a patch of sky, bright enough to suggest it's fully morning.

Irene will almost certainly have noticed by now that she's not at home, but that doesn't do her much good, because Irene has no idea what she's doing.

Irene will call Blair. But Blair won't know anything either.

Cameron P. Muñoz, she tells herself sternly, *you are a genius. Think.*

Her eyes have gotten used to the basement's grimy light. There's not much clutter, nothing that looks like it could make a useful weapon. No hammers or large rocks or trusty old revolvers lying around. Just an old mop with a broken handle, which theoretically she could use to stab Allen Dawson upon his eventual return, except that the plastic is cracked and brittle-looking with age and her hands are tied behind her back. A plastic bucket. A bottle of laundry detergent and a package of Fresh Dawn–scented dryer sheets sitting on top of the washing machine, next to her head. Too bad Allen Dawson isn't a vampire; she could battle him with Fresh Dawn.

She looks around again. Washing machine, dryer, freezer, mop handle, stairs. A rusty old stepladder leans against the wall across from her. That's it.

Rust, Cam thinks. Rust means metal. Metal means possibly sharp. Possibly sharp means maybe she can cut the clothesline tying her hands and feet. Which doesn't give her much, but it gives her something.

She leans back on her knuckles, pushes her butt forward. The movement sends an explosion of stars across her vision. She breathes. In, out. Moves her bound ankles toward the ladder, pushes herself another few inches. More stars.

Cam has never been a patient person.

But this journey is going to take her a while.

Blair calls Officer Reloj again. It's 8 a.m. now, two hours before her parents and the lawyers are scheduled to meet them at Cam's apartment.

This time he answers. "Reloj," he says cheerfully.

"Officer Reloj," she says. "It's Blair."

"Nancy Drew," he says, sounding less than enthusiastic now. "What's going on?"

Blair wishes Irene would stop pacing. "It's Cam," Blair says. "She's missing."

"Missing? Since when?"

"Since this morning."

"Blair, it *is* this morning."

"I know, but I think she went somewhere dangerous. I think she figured out who killed Clarissa and went to confront them."

"You can't file a missing persons report—"

"I know!" Blair yells. "Irene—her mom—already called the police. That's what they said. That's why I'm calling you. We're supposed to go to the Silverwater today to—"

"Absolutely not," Officer Reloj says. "You need to leave that man alone."

"You don't understand! We have a meeting with him and all the lawyers, to apologize. We're trying to fix this. Cam wouldn't skip out on that. Something's wrong. She's not answering her phone. You have to help us find her."

"Blair," Officer Reloj says in the soothing voice a parent uses with a small, unreasonable child, "Cam is fine. She probably got nervous. She'll turn up."

"Cam doesn't get nervous!" Irene reaches for Blair's phone, but Blair shakes her head, keeps trying. "You have to believe me. Someone already tried to hurt us. That afternoon we called you. Someone ran us off the road. That's why we were in the ditch."

"What?" Irene says loudly. *"What ditch?"*

"Blair, give it a rest," Officer Reloj says. "No one is trying to hurt you or Cam. You're all wound up, and that's understand-able. But—"

"Forget it," Blair says, and hangs up. She wants to throw her phone at the wall, but if it breaks, Cam can't call her.

"Who tried to hurt you?" Irene shouts. "What is going on here? Blair Johnson, you tell me the whole story right this minute!"

"Someone ran us off the road when we were driving back from the Silverwater," Blair says. "Cam found a tracker on my car."

"*What?*"

"Cam didn't want to worry you," Blair says miserably.

"We're well past that point now," Irene says. She sinks into a chair. "I want to talk to that cop. Give me your phone."

Officer Reloj is not going to listen to Irene any more than he did Blair. "I have to think," Blair says. "I have to *think.*"

Turquoise, she thinks. *Clarissa had a turquoise necklace. Brad gave it to her. Why is that important? Why now? Does that mean Brad killed her? Is Cam with him?*

She closes her eyes, goes through everything they know. Mrs. Campbell and Clarissa's painting. Mrs. Campbell hadn't said anything about a necklace. Neither had Jenny. Nor had Brad, until they asked. Not even Allen Dawson and his mother—

Allen Dawson and his mother.

Her bright turquoise leggings.

The matching necklace.

"I know where she is," Blair says. "I know where she is!" She snatches her phone, dials Officer Reloj again. Irene jumps to her feet, grabs her coat and car keys.

"Cam went to Allen Dawson's house," Blair says as soon as Reloj answers. "Allen Dawson killed Clarissa. And you might as well head there too, because that's where I'm going now, and if nobody answers the door I'm going to break in, and then you'll have to arrest me anyway."

"Blair—" Reloj begins.

"You have to believe me," she says. "You have to." She hangs up on him and puts her phone in her pocket.

"Allen *Dawson?*" Irene says. "*That* kid?"

"Yes," Blair says.

"Let's go," Irene says.

Cam's made it halfway across the basement, a journey of long, agonizing minutes, when she hears the knob of the basement door rattle and turn.

Not now! she thinks. *I need more time! I need more time!*

The door swings open. Allen Dawson fumbles for the switch. The basement lights blaze on, a long strip of fluorescent bulb.

"What on earth are you doing?" Allen says.

Cam's in too much pain to speak, even if the question were worth answering.

"I didn't know what to do with you," Allen says, taking the first few steps. "But I think I've come to a decision. I want you to know I'm not a violent person. I never have been. But I like my life as it is. I hope you can understand that."

Cam groans. "Clarissa," she manages.

Allen Dawson stops on the stairs. "I loved Clarissa," he says. "I loved her so much more than her boyfriend did. Or her art teacher, for that matter. I've been listening to your podcast. Is all of that true? That must have been awful for her. If I'd known, I could have done something to help her. She should have told me."

"You *killed* her," Cam grunts.

"It was such a long time ago."

"You were—at—the party," Cam says.

Keep him talking, she thinks. *Keep him talking, keep him talking, keep him talking.*

"I knew about it," Allen says, sitting on the stairs. "Everybody did. I think half the school was there. That wasn't my thing. I was home that night—here in this house. My mother has lived here for fifty years. But I missed Clarissa so much. I hadn't seen her since graduation. So I borrowed my mother's car and drove out to the woods. And there she was. Can you believe it? Walking down the road toward me, all by herself. It was a sign."

Cam makes a noise meant to convey her skepticism.

"You can think what you want," Allen says serenely. "But I knew she was looking for me. She was crying. I pulled over and asked if she needed a ride. She got in my car. She wouldn't stop crying. I asked her what was wrong, but she wouldn't tell me. It wasn't the moment I had dreamed of, but it was the only moment I had. I said, 'I love you, Clarissa. You're so special. I'll always be here for you.' That's what I said to her. I kissed her. My first kiss." He pauses.

Cam would rather throw up again than listen to this, but she also doesn't want to die. "And then?" she croaks.

"She laughed," Allen Dawson says. "She was overcome, I suppose. She was hysterical." He pauses again. "I just wanted her to stop crying," he says.

"She laughed at you, and you killed her," Cam says. Fury burns through her pain. "You kissed her and she said no and she laughed at you and you killed her? You're a monster."

"I drove her home with me. I thought she could rest here for a while. My mother was awake. She heard me come in. She asked me what I was doing. I told her Clarissa was in the car and she needed to sleep. My mother helped me put her to bed."

"She wasn't asleep," Cam hisses. "She was dead."

"She was asleep," Allen says. "I gave her necklace to my mother. To keep safe until Clarissa wakes up."

R&D for a security tech startup. It's more interesting than it sounds.

"That was you," she says. "That night on the road. You got

the tracker from your job and put it on Blair's car. You were following us the whole time."

"I wasn't trying to hurt you," he said. "I only wanted to stay safe. All of this is your fault."

Safe. Cam almost laughs. *Safe.* This worthless little man.

She'd wanted vengeance, she'd wanted justice, she'd wanted fire raining down from the heavens. She'd wanted a story with an ending that made sense. Instead all she gets is this dollar-store asshole who killed a girl because he didn't like the word "no."

His pathetic white face, Cam thinks, her heart breaking, was the last thing Clarissa saw.

Clarissa, I'm sorry, Cam thinks. *I'm so, so sorry.*

Allen stands up again, the stairs creaking, and reaches into his pocket. Pulls out a gun so small it looks like a toy. "It's my mother's," he says. "I didn't want her to live alone without any kind of protection. It's a dangerous world out there."

"You're going to *shoot* me?" Cam says.

Allen holds the gun in front of him. His hands are shaking.

What a dumb way to die, Cam thinks, and the doorbell rings.

Allen stops, lowers the arm with the gun. The doorbell rings again. Someone is pounding on the front door so hard Cam can hear it in the basement.

"Allen Dawson!" a woman yells. "You prick! Open this god-damn door!"

"Who on earth can that be at this hour?" Allen says, turning.

"That's my mom, you asshole," Cam says.

Irene on a rampage is an absolute force of nature. She is, Blair thinks, almost certainly capable of breaking down Allen Dawson's door with her bare hands.

But she doesn't have to. Allen Dawson opens the door mid-pound. He's wearing another button-down shirt, and he smells like someone has thrown up on him.

"Irene? What on earth is this about?" he asks. He sees Blair. "What are you doing here?" Irene kicks the door open wider and pushes past him.

"You can't—" he bleats helplessly, turning to follow her. Blair runs after them.

"Where is my child!" Irene shouts. "What have you done with my child!" There's a muffled yell from somewhere in the house.

"That is *my child*!" Irene bellows. *"Where is my child?"*

"What is this commotion!" Allen Dawson's mother exclaims, wheeling herself into the living room. "For goodness' sake!"

"That's it!" Blair says, pointing to the heavy turquoise pendant around her neck. "That's Clarissa's!"

"Oh, dear," Allen says.

That's when Blair sees the gun.

Brian Reloj sits at his desk, thinking.

Liechty isn't in the office yet.

He shouldn't leave the station without telling anyone.

You have to believe me. You have to.

"Aw, hell," he says, and takes his gun out of his desk drawer.

Allen's gun wavers between Blair and Irene. "Allen, be reasonable. You can't shoot all of them," his mother says.

"I'll drive them somewhere. Out in the county. Somewhere no one will find them."

Blair does not much like this turn in the conversation. "People will know," she says. "I told the police. So did Cam."

I told one police officer who probably didn't believe me, she thinks, but she's certainly not going to tell Allen Dawson that.

Mrs. Dawson makes a tutting noise and shakes her head. "Allen," she says tiredly, "perhaps I shouldn't have asked you to come home after all. This whole business has been nothing but trouble. I told him to go to the police," she adds to Blair and Irene. "About that poor girl."

"No, you didn't," Allen says. "You told me you would take care of it. You said you'd help me, and you did."

"You need to learn to take responsibility for your actions, Allen," his mother says.

Bit late for that conversation, Kathleen, Blair thinks.

Next to Blair, Irene is watching the gun. It's still pointed at them.

And then the doorbell rings again.

"Who *now*?" Allen says.

"It's the police," Blair says eagerly, hoping she's right. "I told you the police were coming."

"Get the door," Allen says, gesturing with the gun. "Tell them to go away. Don't open the door all the way, so they can't see inside. If you don't do what I say, I'll shoot Irene."

Blair holds up her hands, walks backward slowly. She doesn't want to turn her back on him, but she has to in order to open the door.

"Blair?" Officer Reloj says in surprise. "Is Cam here?"

"Cam? Why would Cam be here?"

Officer Reloj's eyes narrow. "What are you up to now? Can I talk to Allen?"

"No need! I made a mistake. Everything's fine!" Blair says brightly, transmitting *everything is absolutely not fine* at him as hard as she can with her eyeballs.

"You girls harassing this poor man?"

"We're going hiking later," Blair says.

Officer Reloj pauses. "Hiking," he says.

"I have to go," Blair says. If Allen shoots Irene, Cam is going to kill her. Assuming Allen doesn't shoot her and Cam too. "Goodbye!" She closes the door in Officer Reloj's face.

"He's leaving," she reports.

"Sit down," Allen says.

His back is to the living-room window. Blair catches a flicker of movement behind him, stares resolutely at the table in front of her so Allen doesn't turn around to see what she just saw: Officer Reloj, looking in at them. At Allen, with the gun.

She sits. Irene sits. She grabs Irene's hand and squeezes it. Irene squeezes back.

"Allen, you can let us go," Irene says in a voice Blair's never heard her use before, the voice she must use on her patients: calm, reassuring, authoritative. "You haven't done anything to hurt us. We can walk out the door, and everything will be fine."

"Shut up!" Allen says.

He raises the hand with the gun—

—and Officer Reloj kicks in the door.

"Get down!" Irene yells, pushing Blair underneath the coffee table. Someone is screaming.

Allen's mom, Blair thinks. *Allen's mom is screaming.* Is this where she is going to die? She didn't get to say goodbye to Cam. Or her parents. Or James. She didn't tell James where she was going. But why would she? They broke up. *Why am I thinking about James right now?* she thinks.

Officer Reloj runs into the room with his gun drawn and Allen takes his own gun away from Irene's head long enough to point it at Officer Reloj. Allen's mother screams *"NO!"* louder than she was screaming before and there is a single loud *bang* and Officer Reloj's shoulder erupts in gore. He makes a terrible sound and stumbles forward, his gun clattering to the ground.

"Allen, we need to call an ambulance for the police officer," Irene says in that same extraordinary voice. "He's going to bleed out. Allen, put the gun down. We can talk about this."

The gun, Blair thinks. She is under the table where Irene told her to stay. Officer Reloj's gun is a foot from her hand. Allen isn't looking at her.

He's looking at Irene and at the blood and at Irene again and at Officer Reloj. Everywhere but her, under the table, like she's playing hide-and-seek.

Don't think, Blair thinks. She throws herself forward and the table edge clocks her in the spine but she has Officer Reloj's gun in her hand.

"Blair, don't!" he shouts—

—but she is back at Brad's range surrounded by silence and the gun in her hands and her breath is still the hurdles in a line in front of her clear each one like flying toes flexed breath even—

Blair levels Officer Reloj's gun and shoots Allen Dawson in the kneecap.

Allen Dawson screams, staggers forward, his leg collapsing underneath him.

"Cameron P. Muñoz!" Irene shouts. "I am coming to find you!"

After all that, the cavalry turns out to be almost anticlimactic. Irene directs Blair to call 911 and apply pressure to Officer Reloj's shoulder while she runs into the basement to find Cam. Blair holds Allen Dawson's gun in the other hand, but Allen Dawson isn't going anywhere. His mother has stopped screaming; she sits in her wheelchair in a corner of the living room, white-faced and silent. The ambulance and more police arrive in a whirl of wailing sirens and shouting and running back and forth, packing Cam onto a stretcher in the basement, Officer Reloj onto a stretcher in the living room.

"I can walk," he protests, embarrassed. "He just grazed me."

"I can't believe you left me in the basement!" Cam yells as the EMTs carry her carefully up the stairs. "Blair! Get my phone!"

"Miss, now is not the time," an EMT says.

"My *phone*!" Cam shouts, ignoring him. "Blair, it's in his pocket!"

Blair lunges forward and plucks Cam's phone out of Allen Dawson's pocket as the police are cuffing him to a stretcher of his own. It's smeared with his blood, but it's still powered on. She runs across the front lawn to where the EMTs are loading Cam into the ambulance with Officer Reloj.

"One second! Let me give it to her!" Blair pleads.

"I'm fine!" Cam yells. "I don't need to go to the hospital, I swear! Now *give me my phone*!"

"Good lord," another EMT says. "What are you gonna do, kid, take a selfie?"

But Blair, ignoring him, has already put the phone in Cam's hands, and Cam's swiping frantically. She yelps with glee and shows the screen to Blair.

"That moron," she says triumphantly. "He didn't notice when he took my phone. It was in his pocket set on record the whole time. The last episode is going to be *lit*."

OFFICER RELOJ STOPS by Cam's a few days after the madness dies down. The reporters have given up camping out in front of Cam's apartment, although Clarissa's name is still all over the headlines. That's been nonstop since the police found Clarissa's body underneath Allen Dawson's mother's driveway. Much to Cam's chagrin, they confiscated her phone with Allen's confession.

Blair has turned down a request to be profiled for, ironically enough, *People* magazine. *I'm not dead,* she wanted to say. *You know that, right?*

Irene makes coffee and they sit in the kitchen.

Irene, Blair, Sophie. *Cam's three musketeers,* Blair thinks, and smiles.

Kitten trundles in and yowls mournfully at the fridge. No one pays attention to him.

Officer Reloj takes off his hat and holds it in his lap, twisting the brim. His arm is in a sling and his shoulder is bandaged.

"I'll be fine," he says to Blair when she asks. "But Allen Dawson is going to need a new knee. That was one hell of a shot, miss."

"Thank you," Blair says.

"I thought you would want to know the state attorney is filing charges against Dan Friley," he says without preamble. "There's no statute of limitations anymore on sexual assault against a minor. After Ms. Barbour came forward, four other women did too. The prosecution thinks they can find more."

"Will he have to drop the lawsuit?" Cam asks.

"It'll be hard for him to prove libel when what you said is true," Reloj says. "The sheriff's been suspended. He'll probably face corruption charges. Maybe conspiracy to commit sexual assault. They're still building a case."

"Nothing bad happens to cops," Cam says.

"Maybe so," Officer Reloj says. "But I doubt he'll win the next election."

"And Dawson?"

"He confessed. Not on your phone," Reloj adds. "I mean, to us. He'll plead guilty in exchange for a reduced sentence. They're still working out the details."

"What about his mom?" Cam wants to know.

"She won't go to prison," Reloj says. "That was part of the deal."

"Sophie's a prison abolitionist," Cam says. "I mean, we both are. I think Irene is too. And Blair."

Blair nods.

"I don't know anything about that, miss," Officer Reloj says. "I'm just telling you what's going to happen with the legal proceedings."

"Most survivors of sexual assault don't get listened to by the police," Sophie says. "It's a mistake to think that legal proceedings can bring about adequate restitution when the system is built on a white supremacist capitalist framework forged in centuries of genocide and slavery."

"I'm sure that's right," Officer Reloj says uncomfortably.

"How are Clarissa's parents?" Irene asks, rescuing him.

Officer Reloj grimaces. "Her mom didn't handle the news so well."

"I can imagine," Blair says.

"The father seems to be taking it a bit better. I think he's known for a long time that she was—gone. Really gone. You know."

"Brad says he and Jenny are talking to the Campbells about putting together a show of Clarissa's work," Irene says. "They want to raise money for Dan Friley's accusers."

Cam stares at her. "*Brad* says? To whom?"

"To me. When I talked to him," Irene says serenely.

"When did you talk to Brad?"

"When he called to ask me out to dinner the other night," Irene says.

"You're going out to *dinner*? With *Brad*? Like on a *date*?" Cam shrieks.

"Cam," Sophie says.

"You know," Officer Reloj interrupts, "you're all lucky to be alive. I hope you think twice before you undertake any more investigative journalism."

"Promise," Blair says sweetly. "Mr. Park already gave us an A."

"He gave *you* an A," Cam says.

"Cam still has to write a thirty-page essay on journalistic ethics before she gets her final grade. Anyway, our work here is done."

Reloj shakes his head. "I'll believe it when I see it," he says. "I heard you girls are going on the *Tonight Show.*"

"We said no," Cam says.

"I only wanted to show the invitation to my ex-boyfriend," Blair says.

"Maybe this is my cue to leave," Officer Reloj says, backing away from the table. "No more podcasts, all right? Leave it to the professionals."

Blair and Cam turn to him.

"One more episode," they say in unison.

BROOKE

I've heard a lot of things from a lot of people since I decided it was time to talk about it. *You poor thing. How horrible. What an evil man.* I can see what some of them are thinking: that I'm ruined, that I was stupid. That my life will be forever defined by a single thing that happened to me when I was young. The girl who slept with her teacher, they say to each other behind their back. Of course, he was a predator—but still, what kind of girl is dumb enough to say yes, and mean it, to a question she never should have been asked? If what he did—what *we* did—was my fault, nothing like what happened to me could possibly ever happen to you.

Maybe you believe despising me will keep you and your daughters safe.

Good luck with that.

I was seventeen years old and I wanted to be brilliant. He told me I was special. He was lying, but that doesn't mean it wasn't true. I thought he was going to help me become an artist. He was good at what he did. Believe it or not, he was an incredible teacher. He looked at what I painted in a way no one else had. He saw what I was trying to do, and he told me how I could do it better. He told me I had a gift that could take me somewhere else if I was strong enough. He told me a lot of things, and I believed them all.

And then one day after school he put his arm around me and leaned in, and I understood.

I was never sure of myself again, after that.

I don't know what he said to Clarissa. I've talked to some of the other women, and he told all of us the same thing. I doubt it was any different with her. I asked myself—we asked ourselves—what was wrong with us. Why did he pick us out of all the girls he could have chosen? Why were we so easy to fool? I wanted a different kind of life than the one that was in front of me, but I didn't think I deserved a bigger horizon. I think that's what he saw in me: a hunger that was also a wound.

I don't believe in regret. But sometimes I wonder how much more quickly I'd have learned to live for myself if he'd just left me alone.

Clarissa died before she could tell her part of the story. People will put words in her mouth. People will put words in my mouth, and I'm still alive. But that's the thing. I *am* still alive. I'm here. I have my kids. I have my work. I started painting again. I bought a ticket to Paris. I'm taking Charles and the baby, but I'll leave them with a sitter when I go to visit the Louvre.

He was wrong. I can see it now. I am—was always—good.

BLAIR

The thing I learned about Clarissa is that she was just a person. She wasn't better or worse than anybody else. If Clarissa hadn't died, maybe she would've done something amazing with her life. Does that matter? Does that make it worse than if she had made the same mistakes as anyone, learned the same lessons, muddled along until she found a place that mostly made her happy? Do we have to be lovable to be loved? Why do girls have to be perfect for their absence to matter?

Clarissa wasn't perfect.

But people will make a girl who isn't there into anything they want.

I think about how a photo of yourself never looks the way you want the world to see you. That moment of disconnect, every time you see yourself through the camera's eye. I think about how that's all that's left of her. All those stories, all those pictures. But none of them were her. When we came up with *Missing Clarissa*, we thought it only had a double meaning. She's missing. People miss her. But to miss something also means to fail to reach it. A failure to catch. A failure to understand.

Maybe none of us see what anybody else looks like, even the people we love. All we can know is how they look to us.

This is the end of our part of Clarissa's story. We get to go out into the world and make our own.

I'll tell you a chapter in what will be mine: One day I'm going to go to New York City. I'll walk up and down the crowded streets. I'll eat a hot dog from a sidewalk cart. I'll stand under the lights of Times Square. I'll take pictures of tourists and roasted chestnuts and the subways going over the Manhattan Bridge. I'll go to the library with the stone lions outside it and look for the shelf where one day my books will be. I'll walk across the Brooklyn Bridge at sunset. I'll sit in a café and write down what I see.

And I'll go to the Metropolitan Museum of Art and look at every painting. Not for me, Clarissa. For you. I'll go each day until I'm done. However long it takes.

Clarissa, wherever you are, I know I won't see you.

But I'll imagine you there.

ACKNOWLEDGMENTS

Oreville does not exist, but it is a town situated in a real place and time. The Olympic Peninsula of Washington State is the settler-appropriated homeland of many different groups of Indigenous people, including the Hoh, Jamestown S'Klallam, Lower Elwha Klallam, Makah, Quileute, Quinault, Port Gamble S'Klallam, and Skokomish tribes, all of whom have cared for this land for thousands of years and continue to do so today.

Sophie is indebted to the abolitionist organizer, educator, and curator Mariame Kaba, whose book *We Do This 'Til We Free Us* is a beautiful introduction to prison abolition and justice organizing. The free online zine *Racial Capitalism and Prison Abolition* (https://bit.ly/3IEeQHz) is another great place to start. Sophie's analysis of the settler origins of Sasquatch comes thanks to Colin Dickey's *The Unidentified: Mythical Monsters, Alien Encounters, and Our Obsession with the Unexplained*. You can, in fact, learn the Klallam language online, as well as learn more about the sovereign nations of the Salish Sea—the resources collected by the North Olympic Library System at www.nols.org/land-acknowledgement will get you started. Mr. Park has certainly read "The End of Evil" (https://culture.org/the-end-of-evil), Sarah Marshall's exploration of the mythology of the mastermind serial killer.

As for me—I am grateful to Andrea Morrison, Sara Goodman, Greg Ferguson, and the wonderful team at Wednesday Books: Lauren Hougen, Eileen Rothschild, Vanessa Aguirre, Olga Grlic, Soleil Paz, Kelly Too, Eric Meyer, Lena Shekhter, Mary Moates, Rivka Holler, Brant Janeway, Tom Thompson, Elishia Merricks, Maria Snelling, Amber Cortes, and Britt Saghi. Particular thanks are due to Melanie Sanders, who has known where all the bodies are buried for some time now; to Emiko Goka-Dubose, for the Young Lourdes; and to Maik Lübke, who had no idea what he was getting into when he took up with a writer.

And to you! Dear Reader, without whom none of this would be possible.

Love,
Ripley

Turn the page for an excerpt from

THE OTHER LOLA

Available March 2024

THE
RETURN

LOLA was gone before she ever went missing. Mattie's always known this, marrow-deep. Lola and her haunted cat-green eyes. Lola and her cloud of black hair, dense as night. Lola, the most beautiful person Mattie's ever known: keeper of secrets, teller of stories, barrier between Mattie and the harsh unfeeling world.

That Lola was born with one foot out the door.

Even as a child, Mattie knew.

But what Mattie has still, will have forever, is the before time. Summer nights, the woods behind the house alive with coyotes singing down the moon. First a single yip, and then the chorus. The thrumming frogs in the neighbor's pond falling silent. Windows open to the piney dark.

And Lola, slipping through Mattie's bedroom door sometime before dawn silvers the edges of the mountains. Coming home in the thick wolf-hour dark from wherever it is she goes, smelling of cigarettes and vanilla and something sweetish and musky that Mattie will recognize years later as weed. Crawling into Mattie's bed, under the covers, curling herself snail-tight against Mattie's back, inhaling the hay-sweet warmth at the nape of Mattie's neck. Whispering *You know I'll never leave you behind here when I go, Mats* into Mattie's sparrow-boned shoulders.

Mattie will carry that promise a lifetime long. Lola's humid body, her hot, whiskey-scented breath. Her long arms flung out, her legs kicking restlessly as Mattie holds perfectly still so as not to disturb her.

Lola muttering in her sleep as the stars wink out one by one, the sky lightens, the sun climbs over the mountains to wheel its way through another day.

But no matter how hard Mattie fights to stay awake, to bind Lola to the real and breathing daylight world—in the harsh light of morning, Mattie wakes again alone, the night before as blurry and wondrous as a dream.

And then, five years ago: the morning Mattie woke and knew Lola was gone for good.

And now: The girl who came back yesterday, the girl who says she's Lola, is somebody else.

It's not possible.

But it's true.

Lola's mouth, but full of lies. Lola's laugh refracted through another throat. Her eyes are the same green, but they're layered with different secrets. Stories Lola never would have told.

Mattie knows where the girl detectives live, and Mattie is going to make them help.

Their addresses are online, pictures of their homes plastered across hateful troll-filled forums and comment-thronged web articles.

Pictures of the girls themselves: the tall one, all angles and elbows and disordered hair, head down and one bony arm thrown up as she tries to evade the cameras outside her apartment building. The pretty one, trying to hide her sweet face behind movie-star sunglasses, her bright gold hair stuffed under a hat.

They're teenagers. They should be safe, their lives lived behind closed doors. But after what they did last year, they're everywhere. There's nowhere they can hide.

Mattie finds their class schedules—pathetically easy, since they all go to the same school. And then Mattie keeps looking, building a case. Finds their parents' workplaces, the license plate number of the pretty one's car. That's easy. Anyone could do it.

But Mattie isn't anyone. Mattie is patient, and persistent, and spends a lot of time alone online.

Mattie can find things no one else could.

The pretty one's ex-boyfriend, on a basketball court in North Carolina.

The tall one's girlfriend, smiling in the autumn sun on a leaf-strewn college lawn.

The cemetery in New York where her father is buried.

The cemetery in Mexico where her grandparents are buried.

Nobody in this world can keep a secret, if the right person knows how to look.

In the old Lola's bedroom, the other Lola is singing. Mattie puts a few things in a backpack, pulls on warm clothes. Out the front door into the sheeting rain without a goodbye.

Mattie doesn't talk to *her*.

In the old Lola's bedroom, the new Lola hears Mattie leave. The new Lola watches Mattie trudging down the long driveway, head bent. A flash of unease crosses the new Lola's perfect face.

Mattie doesn't trust her.

Mattie has good reason not to trust her. She is a liar, and a thief, and a lot worse than that.

The new Lola has no plans to go anywhere, now that she's here.

In the old Lola's life.

With the old Lola's new credit card in her wallet.

The old Lola's mother in her pocket.

The old Lola's brother willing, at least for now, to believe her.

Mattie will have to be persuaded.

But that's a problem for tomorrow.

For today, the new Lola sits on the old Lola's bed. She pulls the old Lola's diary out of the old Lola's dresser drawer.

Five years that diary lay concealed, undiscovered by the old Lola's own family.

Five minutes the new Lola had stood in the old Lola's room. Looking at the pictures on her walls: gloom, gloom, and more gloom. The clothes on her hangers: black, black, and more black. The books on her shelves: *Kurt Cobain: Journals. The Unabridged Journals of Sylvia Plath. Anne Sexton: A Self-Portrait in Letters.*

This girl kept a diary; there's no doubt about that.

I'm here, thought the new Lola. *I'm her. Where did I hide it?*

Her eyes had landed on the heating vent, held to the wall with a single loose screw that came away with a twist of her hand.

That was all it took to give her the old Lola's memories.

As if it were her fate to come here, to be this girl.

No fate but what we make, the other Lola thinks.

It's hard to have much pity for that missing girl, who sat in this princess's jewel box of a room, in this palace of a house, and chose to wrap herself up in darkness. But the void the old Lola left is a blank place, a workshop, an open door.

And now?

It's easy enough to come back. To walk into this house and see where the old Lola failed. Where her edges didn't fit. To smooth herself into a shape that slots into the void the old Lola left, and then remake it. A gentler, more pliable version of the girl who left for good all those years ago. A light, gentle Lola whose mother will want to keep her, not hide her away in shame.

The new Lola has valuable skills. She can feign softness, hiding what's hard beneath. She can smile sweetly. She can ask for nothing in a way that makes other people want to give, and give, and give.

It's easier than you think to be a girl everyone wants to love.

All you have to do is lie.

The old Lola's mother is so overjoyed to have the daughter she always wanted that she asks no questions.

The old Lola's brother—he's not so convinced. There's something reserved about him, a thread she'll have to unspool to keep herself safe.

And Mattie will be a problem.

But the new Lola didn't get to where she is without taking a few risks.

Settling in, the new Lola opens to the first page of the old Lola's diary. Humming "Heart-Shaped Box" to herself, she begins to read.

Day 0: Friday

THE UNINVITED GUEST

DESPITE her singular accomplishments in the field of cold-case resolution, Cameron P. Muñoz, ex–teen podcaster extraordinaire, nationally recognized amateur sleuth, and locator of the most famous missing girl in Washington State, would herself admit she's not the most perceptive person in the world.

But even she knows that someone's following her home from school.

She refused a ride home from her best friend and fellow onetime investigator, Blair—a refusal she's already regretting, as the looming December clouds are threatening downpour.

And now she's got a stalker.

Again.

Great.

In the first months after Cam and Blair broke their small hometown's legendary missing-girl story, reporters clouded around them like a swarm of summer gnats. Cameramen set up camp in Blair's cul-de-sac. Journalists lurked in the bushes outside Cam's apartment.

Both of them had to change their phone numbers.

Both of them had to change their phone numbers again.

Because everybody was calling: journalists, pundits, talk-show hosts. People from the internet who wanted their story, wanted their methods, or wanted them dead. Cam learned quickly to stop googling her own name, out of sheer horror at what she found: page after page of threats and recriminations and theories and lies.

> you are o ugly how do you look at yourselves
>
> if u hate the cops so much dont bother calling them when i rape u
>
> shld both just die so i don't have to listen to them talk anymore wtf
>
> Obviously, these idiots should have considered the possibility that one of the I-5 corridor's many serial offenders is responsible for this heinous crime
>
> verbal diarea,worthless. why do u hate white people anyway racist bitchs

Et cetera, and much worse.

Like, a lot worse.

Cam-doesn't-think-about-it-ever worse.

The kind of worse that she filed in a black hole inside her head and left there.

But that was a year ago. Since then, thankfully, most of the world has moved on. There's always a dead-er white girl with a more spectacular demise and better hair. Cam hasn't had to run from a reporter in months.

She's out of practice, and she's no track star like Blair.

Whoever this is, she'll have to face them.

A block before the front door of her building, she stops short and turns around.

The person behind her freezes, staring at Cam like a stunned deer.

Whoever they are, they're no reporter. They look about ten years old. Skinny and furtive, dressed in a knitted grandpa cardigan with leather elbow patches darkened by damp and a pair of too-large men's trousers cut off above the ankles and a wool newsboy cap.

What the hell? Cam thinks.

"Cameron Muñoz," the urchin says.

"What," Cam says warily.

"I'm Mattie," the person says. "You have to help me find my sister."

Oh.

That explains it, then.

"Not on your life," Cam says, and turns back around.

The pitter-patter of feet behind her. Bony fingers grasping at her elbow. Cam jerks her arm away from Mattie's hand.

"*No,*" Cam says again.

"Please," Mattie says. "I'm not some rando. I'm a freshman at Oreville. I know all about you. Nobody else can help me. You found that girl Clarissa. You and Blair. You found her when the police didn't do anything. That's why I need your help."

That's when the rain starts, a downpour that cuts through fabric like an icy knife.

"*Please,*" Mattie begs.

Cam does recognize this urchin. Huge sad eyes in a pinched white face, scurrying past her in the halls of Oreville High.

Mattie is already wet through to the skin.

"I'll give you five minutes," Cam growls, stomping the rest of the way home down the watery sidewalk. Mattie freezes for a moment, as if unable to believe the plea really worked, and then runs after her.

Cam's mom, Irene, is still at work. Cam offers up a silent

prayer of thanks. Irene is a tolerant person under most circumstances, but Cam has no desire to explain a sopping child
dripping rainwater all over the kitchen floor.

"Your lips are turning blue," Cam says. "Stay here. I'll get
you dry clothes. If you touch anything, I'll kill you. And I know
how to hide a body where it will never be found."

This isn't at all true, but Mattie nods, teeth chattering.

Cam doesn't want to turn her back on this weirdo.

But she also doesn't want this weirdo to go into hypother-
mic shock in her apartment.

That will be hard to explain to Irene.

Cam gathers up a towel from a pile of what she's pretty sure
is clean laundry on the living room floor and a sweatshirt from
a pile of what she's pretty sure is clean laundry on her bedroom
floor. Her pants will be far too long for her mystery guest, so
she filches a pair of sweatpants from a pile of what she's pretty
sure is clean laundry on Irene's bedroom floor.

Mattie hasn't moved, standing stiffly in the kitchen and
shivering so violently Cam worries her odd visitor will fly apart
at the seams.

"Here," Cam says, handing over her bundle. "Bathroom is
down the hall. You want something warm to drink? Tea? Coffee?"

"C-c-coffee," Mattie says, and takes the clothes. "Can you
call Blair?"

"No," Cam says, and turns to the coffeepot.

Ten minutes later Mattie is sitting across from Cam at
Cam's kitchen table, engulfed by Cam's sweatshirt, skinny ankles sticking out from Irene's sweatpants, wet clothes tumbling
in Cam's dryer.

Mattie takes a sip of coffee.

Cam's interviewed enough people to see that now that Mattie's here in front of her, Mattie has no idea where to start.

But Cam's not about to lend a helping hand.

When the coffee is gone, Mattie leaves.

End of story.

Cam's middle-aged black cat, Kitten, wanders into the kitchen, lashing his tail and eyeing the refrigerator. He gives Mattie a long, suspicious look, then turns his accusing gaze to Cam as if demanding to know what she's thinking bringing a damp stranger into the sanctity of his demesne.

You and me both, buddy, Cam thinks.

"Start talking," she says.

"I want to talk to Blair too."

"You are in no position to make demands," Cam says.

"Please," says Mattie for a third time. The line of Mattie's mouth is resolute.

Small as her uninvited guest is, Cam realizes, it will not be as easy to get Mattie out of her house as she hoped. She is a warrior of the mind, not the body.

She glances at the window, gives herself the satisfaction of imagining hauling it open, dragging Mattie from the chair, and giving Mattie a good solid push.

His mind apparently made up about the visitor, Kitten takes a flying leap into Mattie's lap, settles in, and starts to purr.

"Traitor," Cam says, and texts Blair.

"All right," Blair says. "Start from the beginning."

She came when Cam texted. She always does. Though Cam's message made absolutely no sense.

And now that she's here, she's even more confused.

It is extremely Cam to collect a scrawny nonsense-spouting stranger off the street, and it is equally Cam to make Blair come over and help her deal with it.

Cam's always been there for Blair too, so at least it's an even exchange.

But Blair never asks Cam to do anything that out of the ordinary.

So maybe it isn't.

"Make it fast," Cam says. "I don't know when Irene is coming home, and I do not want to explain you to my mother."

"My sister is Lola Brosillard," Mattie says as if Cam and Blair should know who that is.

"Who?" Blair asks.

But, Cam thinks, the name is familiar. All that time she spent online, looking for Clarissa.

Lola Brosillard.

"Your sister ran away," Cam says, remembering. "Three years ago?"

"Five. And my sister *went missing*," Mattie says. "She didn't run away." Mattie looks down at the coffee cup. "Lola's six years older than me. She got in trouble a lot," Mattie says to the mug. "Sometimes she would disappear for two or three days. But she always came back. She promised me she'd always come back, and she did."

"What kind of trouble?" Blair asks.

Mattie grimaces. "Sometimes shoplifting. Dumb stuff, though, nothing big. A couple times she got caught drinking in public. I know what it sounds like. But she's a good person. She just doesn't like doing what other people think she should."

"And then she went missing?" Blair asks.

"One night the summer after her sophomore year Lola and my brother, Luke, had a party at our house. Our mom was out of town, and they were supposed to be watching me. I never minded when they did stuff like that, though. Lola would let me stay up late and watch scary movies. And she'd buy me ice cream." Mattie smiles at the memory. "After their friends left, Luke and Lola went to bed. I was already asleep. My brother had a dream that somebody was in the house, a stranger. Except it wasn't a dream. In the morning, Lola was gone. The glass in the patio door was shattered, like someone had tried to break in from outside. Ruth—our mom—got home right after Luke woke up, and she called the police. They came, but they didn't do much. Just took pictures of the door and wrote a report. Nothing was stolen, so I don't think they really cared."

"Your *sister* was gone," Cam says incredulously. "They didn't notice?"

Mattie shifts in the chair. "She ran away a few times before," Mattie says. "Ruth called the police the first time. They found her at her boyfriend's house. It wasn't a big deal, but Ruth kind of lost it. I was in the other room when the cops brought her home and Ruth wouldn't stop screaming at her. 'How could you do this to me, how could you embarrass your family, how will I show my face in town.' That kind of stuff. After that, she stopped calling the police when Lola left."

"But she called the police this time," Blair says. "Why?"

"The window was broken," Mattie says. "She probably needed the police report for the insurance company."

"She didn't tell them your sister was missing?" Blair asks in disbelief.

"I did," Mattie says. "Because of the window. And Luke's dream. It felt different than the other times. I knew she hadn't run away."

"Different how?" Blair asks.

Mattie frowns. "Just . . . different."

"Then what?" Cam asks.

"They didn't believe me," Mattie says simply. "The cops put it in their report, but I could tell. And Ruth yelled at me afterward for dragging our family business out where other people could see it, and Luke told Ruth to leave me alone, and then we never talked about it again. And Lola didn't come back. So I was right, but nobody cared."

Cam stares. "Your sister didn't come home and you didn't *talk* about it?"

"I called the police again a week later," Mattie says. "But they don't listen to little kids. Ruth wasn't worried about it. Luke was her favorite; he still is. Ruth and Lola fought all the time. I mean, *all* the time. About everything. Lola's clothes, Lola's friends, Lola's attitude. You know how when you're a teenager, you're supposed to be mortified by your parents? With them, it was the other way around. Ruth didn't want people to see her and Lola together in public. This one time, Lola dyed her hair red—like, fire-truck red—and Ruth just screamed at her when she saw it. 'You're making yourself ugly on purpose to humiliate me,' stuff like that."

"That sounds horrible," Blair says. "I would've run away from that too."

"But she didn't," Mattie says. "I'm telling you, that night was different. I know she didn't run away on her own, because she never came back. She *promised* me she would never leave me alone with Ruth."

"You think someone kidnapped her?" Cam asks.

"Why else would someone break into the house and not take anything? Why else wouldn't she come home?"

"Who would do that?" Cam asks.

"I don't know," Mattie says.

"What about the other people at the party?" Blair asks. "Did they see something?"

"Luke gave the police their names," Mattie says. "And the cops interviewed them. At least they did that much. Everybody left around two in the morning. When they went home, Lola was sitting on the patio looking at the stars."

"You saw the police report?" Blair asks.

"I interviewed them too," Mattie says. "After I called the police the second time, and realized they weren't going to help."

RIPLEY JONES is a person of interest.

Don't miss the sequel to Ripley
Jones's unforgettable YA thriller

MISSING CLARISSA

She was gone
before she
ever went
missing

THE OTHER
LOLA

RIPLEY
JONES

A Novel

"Ripley Jones writes like a switchblade:
quick, sharp, and straight to the jugular."

—Justina Ireland,
New York Times bestselling author of *Dread Nation*